PRAISE F

"Dea Poirier delivers a pitch-perfect procedural with a strong-willed and relatable lead in Claire Calderwood—a big-city cop who returns to her small hometown when a fresh homicide echoes the long-ago murder of her sister. Bolstered by a romance and atmospheric prose that turns setting into character, this debut hits all the right notes."

—Loreth Anne White, international bestselling author

"In Dea Poirier's exceptional debut, Claire Calderwood is a detective in Detroit who is relieved to have miles and years between herself and her hometown of Vinalhaven, Maine. This is an evocative debut with exquisite writing that indulges your senses and compels your investment in Calderwood's emotional journey as she races against time to solve a case that has haunted her for more than a decade. Calderwood is a worthy addition to the genre. Her spirit, like Poirier's voice, is tenacious and captivating, compelling the reader's investment in her journey, and Calderwood is determined to hold her own against her male counterparts."

—Sandra Ruttan, author of *Suspicious Circumstances*

"*Next Girl to Die* is a smart, fast-paced, and intensely well-written procedural thriller, and it takes place in one of the best settings I've had the pleasure of reading in a long time: a lonely island off the coast of Maine. The island has more secrets than residents, with each character more ominously suspicious than the last. Poirier is a diabolical plotter, and this tight debut is fraught with tension and mystery."

—Wendy Heard, author of *Hunting Annabelle*

BENEATH THE ASHES

OTHER TITLES BY DEA POIRIER

Next Girl to Die

BENEATH

THE

ASHES

DEA POIRIER

THOMAS & MERCER

Published by Thomas & Mercer, Seattle
www.apub.com

Amazon, the Amazon logo, and Thomas & Mercer are trademarks of Amazon.com, Inc., or its affiliates.

ISBN-13: 9781542092784
ISBN-10: 1542092787

Cover design by Caroline Teagle Johnson

Printed in the United States of America

BENEATH
THE
ASHES

CHAPTER 1

In my mind, the corpse is hers. It doesn't matter that it won't be, can't be her. From the moment I hear that the victim is suspected to be a teenage female, she's all I can see. The other victims—the ones from months ago—they should cross my mind too. They don't. That's par for the course, though. If nothing else, my sister, Rachel, has always haunted my thoughts. Maybe she always will. I thought once I found her killer, things would change. But they didn't. Sometimes, I still see her staring back at me in mirrors. Sometimes, I realize there are shadows so big they'll eclipse your entire life, all that you are.

Though she died fifteen years ago, I only found her killer a few months ago, after taking a job as homicide detective back in my hometown of Vinalhaven, when another girl was killed in a manner eerily similar to Rachel's. But finding my sister's killer didn't give me the closure everyone expected. I'm relieved he's off the streets, but the fifteen-year-old wound is still as fresh and raw as if it happened yesterday. Closure is a goddamned fairy tale, if you ask me.

Cold wind whips off the water, covering my face in a spray of fine mist. It's enough to pull me from the thoughts of her, my sister.

The call from Camden PD I got earlier today replays in my mind. *We've got a body here in a motel, rough shape. We need someone experienced to take a look at this.* Given all the recent media attention on my last murder case, and as they were without their own homicide detective, they called me in hopes that I could help. Camden, Maine, isn't exactly spitting distance from my hometown—well, home island, really—of Vinalhaven, Maine. The bay separates the island from the coastline on which Camden sits. It shouldn't be far, but with the ferry ride to contend with, it can take an hour and a half or more. I've been on the ferry for twenty minutes, churning my way across Pen Bay from the island to Camden. In Maine, when you have the misfortune of living on one of the islands, the ferries are your only ticket to the outside world, unless you have the money for a water taxi or the luxury of your own boat. This was the bane of my existence as a child and one of the many reasons I swore I'd never come back here.

The ferry horn bellows, and my jaw tenses at the sound so hard my teeth ache. From far away, I may love the call of the ferries, but while I'm aboard, it's so loud it echoes to the sinew of my soul. Around me, beyond the far-reaching grip of the black water, the world is still veiled in snow. Though we're reaching the end of February, winter still has Maine in its grasp. The streets are clear, a blessing, but the trees and houses are so heavy with snow that from a distance they almost look like gingerbread. A frigid wind kisses my cheeks. Though I'm sure my face is red, angry from the winter's assault, the weather tethers me somehow, makes me feel present. My thick coat is tight around me, but chill still sneaks in.

My phone dings with a notification. Snow is coming hard tonight. If you can't get out of Camden by 4, you may want to stay there tonight.

The mask I wear for the job cracks, and a smile teeters on my lips as I reply to Noah's text. Thank you. I'll let you know how it goes. Noah and I have been dating for four months. We met last year while I was working a case. Noah is a reporter, and he was hell bent on cracking open my sister's cold case and solving it. Though I hated him at first, he got under my skin in the best and worst ways. He still does—and I wouldn't have it any other way.

As soon as I clear away the text notification, I see the icon for my email. There are seven unread messages in my in-box. I tap on the icon and glance at the list. Two emails are promos, trying to get me to purchase shit I don't need, and five are interview requests to talk to the media about my sister. Since Noah's article came out a couple of months ago, I've been getting requests almost daily for interviews, exclusives, quotes. Though some of them have offered me a hefty payday, my assistance with Noah's story is as far as I'm willing to go to help the media. After all, they just want to profit off my pain. None of them give a fuck about me or Rachel. Pages over people, revenue over relationships—that's all they care about.

In the months since the story broke, Noah's been on podcasts, sat for interviews, you name it. He's stood in the spotlight and handled it like it's what he was born to do. And I hate to admit it, but he's damn good at it. Better yet, he's so good it's kept off a lot of the pressure for me to stand in that spotlight with him. I'm more of a behind-the-scenes kind of woman.

I shove my phone in my pocket, and the grin I held for Noah goes with it. I need my game face on while I'm on the scene. The town of Rockland grows out of the mist ahead of me. The ferry platform is the first thing I make out, followed by the huge warehouses that fill the streets near the bay, the arms of the dock stretching out into the dark waters, and then the peaks of the sloping roofs beyond. When I finally drive off the ferry, I turn onto Port Terminal Road and roll to a stop at a traffic light. My fingers drum against the wheel as I wait to turn onto Main Street.

I follow the directions on my GPS heading north—I haven't been up here much, and I'm not familiar enough to make my way without a little electronic help, but I remember the area. I drive through the small towns of Rockland and Rockport before reaching Camden. The motel, Millay Inn, is at the foot of Bald Mountain Preserve, far enough from the ocean that the prices drop. But so does the quality of the clientele.

Once I make it to Howe Hill Road, I shut off my GPS. A huddle of cop cars sits at the far end of the motel parking lot in front of a room with the door yawning open. The building itself is the kind of low-rise motel you'd see at a truck stop in the Midwest, though this one has a bit more curb appeal with its baby-blue paint and white trim. The kind of place that's kept up just enough to still be charming. Though it may be inexpensive, it's clear whoever owns this place is trying.

A low crop of evergreen trees, dusted in frost, surrounds the building and grows up the side of the mountain until the foliage and the rising expanse beyond both blur into a gentle slope of white. I grip the door handle harder than I need to and shove it open. A blast of cold air hits me in the face, and I pull on my coat before slamming the door. My driving up didn't make any of the officers glance my way, but the noise sure does. They eye me as I approach. I flash my badge out of habit. Beside the cars stands the CSI van, its doors wide open, displaying the gear inside, and I grumble under my breath. They can get out here this quickly for Camden? It always took them nearly five hours to get to Vinalhaven. As bitter as I'd like to be about it, I don't have time for that now. The sound of engines, like roaring snowmobiles in the distance, snares my attention.

As the growls of the engines fade, I turn my attention back to the other officers. "Sergeant Pelletier called and asked me to head over here from Vinalhaven," I explain as I approach. Their eyes all cut to me.

The guy to my left is squat with shaggy dark hair that's too long to be allowed on most forces. His eyes crawl up and down my body, like he's sizing me up. I grit my teeth, waiting for him to open his mouth, but the guy to my right speaks first.

"Detective Calderwood?" he asks, and I introduce myself.

"I'm Clint Wilkens," he explains. Clint extends his hand to shake mine.

Clint is about six inches taller than me, with broad shoulders. His skin is dark, umber, his hair shaved. When he smiles, dimples etch

4

themselves into his face on either side of his wide mouth. He's got on the typical police coat, a poufy hunter-green thing, with the police force patch over the heart.

"Nice to meet you. Where could I find the sergeant?" I ask, glancing toward the motel.

"I'll walk you," he says as he motions toward the room with the door open.

"What do we have?" I ask as we walk. This isn't the kind of situation where you default to the weather, so I skip past the small talk and niceties.

"Body of a woman, we're guessing between sixteen and twenty-one, found bound to the bed, no identification." We reach the door together, and I glance inside. There's no way more than a few people could fit inside at a time. I can make out the burnt-orange shade of the carpet, wood-paneled walls, and the corner of a floral comforter, but I can't quite see the body.

As I look around, I hope they've followed proper protocol to secure the scene. Finding a body in a motel isn't ideal as it is. There will be latent evidence *everywhere*—hair, fingerprints, likely even semen. The sergeant didn't give me any details, and I'm going to need information fast to be of help here. The first forty-eight hours of an investigation are the most crucial. I hate showing up to a crime scene this late. There's so much I've already missed out on. Now I'll have to play catch-up.

"No one has identified her yet?" I ask. I find it odd that in a town of this size no one has recognized her. This town has double the population of Vinalhaven, but it's still small enough that surely someone would know her. Was the body of someone from out of town dumped here?

He shakes his head. "Sarge, got Detective Claire Calderwood here for you," he says into the room.

As I stand, waiting for the sergeant to emerge, the tape woven around the posts outside the door flickers in the breeze. Markers have been placed on the floor, cataloging where evidence was found in the room.

Roxie, my old partner from Detroit, would have a field day with this. The sergeant glances toward us, then walks over. He's probably in his midforties, lean with wide-set brown eyes. His lips press together in a firm line, the sadness still clearly etched on his face. I have to look up to meet his gaze. He stands about eight inches taller than me.

"Sergeant, this is Detective Calderwood," Clint says, introducing us.

Sergeant Pelletier extends his hand, shaking my gloved one firmly. "Thanks for coming." His voice is gravelly, low, aged beyond his visible years.

"Of course," I say, because I feel the need to say *something*. "Can you catch me up?"

He doesn't start speaking right away. Instead, he waves some of the others from the room, making room for us, and I go in after him. "Housekeeping found her body this morning after dawn."

When I enter the room fully, I'm finally able to see the victim and recognize why exactly no one has been able to identify her. Plastic sheeting is looped and secured over the victim's head, obscuring it completely. The naked woman is tied to the bed, legs and hands bound to the head- and footboard with yellow, rough nylon ropes. It's not the kind of rope you'd typically see on a scene like this. This close to the water, I expect to see ratty old rope that's been on the deck of a ship for half a decade. Nylon is far more expensive than standard rope. On her left hand, a brace wraps around her wrist and loops her thumb. Did she break or sprain her wrist?

Flesh around the ropes has been rubbed raw, so raw, in fact, that the nylon is tinged red in places. Gray debris covers her torso, and it isn't until I step closer that I can make out what it is—cigarette butts and ashes. Her milky-white skin is feathered with bruises, some fresh, some in various stages of healing. The wounds stick out to me, and I can't help but wonder what this woman went through before all this. How much did she suffer? Was she held somewhere? My heart aches for her. This job is a constant reminder that so many people die in ways they don't deserve. As I look down at her, I consider who she might be, whose life will change forever when we discover her friends and family.

"What the hell happened to you?" I mutter.

"It appears that an ashtray that usually stands outside the room for patrons to use was brought inside and dumped over the body post-mortem. We were considering that this might be a sex act gone wrong until we figured out that part. It seems unlikely that the suspect would have dumped the ashes if that were the case. It seems more like they're covering up a crime."

I glance at him, sure that my skepticism is written all over my face. Sex act gone wrong? There's no way in hell that's what this is. Plastic sheeting over the head isn't a sex act. That's homicide. This killer knew what they were doing. They had a plan. And based on what I'm seeing here, I don't think it was their first time. This looks too methodical. A motel is already a compromised crime scene on its own. But this? This is something entirely different. I've seen perps leave evidence at scenes before, and it's usually so obvious that it sticks out—gum, a cigarette, a small trinket that holds a perfect fingerprint. The dumping of cigarette ashes reminds me of Gary Ridgway. In the eighties and nineties, the Green River Killer would strangle his victims and leave gum or ciga-rettes at the scene to mislead police. Is our killer a copycat? A fan? Or just trying to obscure DNA?

"Clint told me there's no information about the victim in the room. No purse, wallet, phone?"

"That's correct. We haven't been able to look at her face because of the plastic, and there's nothing in here to indicate who she was."

Whoever did this also robbed her, then. Based on what I'm seeing, there's nothing left of hers in the room. Not even her clothes. Did the killer take them to hide evidence or keep them as a trophy?

"When is the coroner going to take out the body?" I ask. Usually, by now the body would have been cleared out. And considering the coroner's van is right outside, I'm surprised they waited for me.

"As soon as you're done taking a look. I thought it'd be more helpful if you could see the scene as it is, rather than the pictures."

I step closer to the bed, and the toe of my boot hits something underneath. On instinct, I take off my leather gloves, grab the latex gloves I keep in my pocket, and slide them on. "Has anyone swept under the bed yet?" I ask.

"No, not yet. We were going to have CSI do that after the body was removed."

Carefully, I lift up the bed skirt, hoping we'll find something useful—maybe scissors he used to cut the plastic sheeting or the rope. But it's not scissors I find. Instead it's a brown shoulder bag. I grab the purse and bring it over to a table alongside the wall, hoping to find identification inside.

"Looks like her pocketbook," I say to the sergeant. Inside I find a gold wallet and extract it. "Melanie Thomlinson," I read off the ID inside.

His voice is low when he says, "She was a high school student from Camden."

The dark thoughts of Rachel, the memories of her murder, press into me from all sides. But I push back against them. I can't let the thoughts in. I won't. My mind flashes back to the victims in Vinalhaven next. All the girls who died. This hits too close to home.

"I'll get someone on notifying her next of kin and officially identify her," he says.

I place the ID back into her wallet. Though I've got gloves on, I don't want to touch anything in this room more than necessary. We're going to have to collect everything we can. My fear is that lingering DNA in this room will have compromised any evidence. The killer who did this thought this out, planned it. Was the ashtray a last-minute idea? Or did he pick this place because it was here?

"I need to interview her family as soon as possible," I say.

"We'll have them identify the body today. I'd prefer if you held off on an interview until tomorrow. They'll likely be too shaken up to be of much use. I'm sure you understand this'll come as a shock."

I don't like to wait. But this is his case, his team, his town. If he thinks it's best for me to wait, I will. "Every minute the clock keeps ticking on this, it's going to make it harder to find who did this," I say. I'll follow his orders, but he needs to be aware that time is of the essence. In small towns like these, homicides are rare. This could be the first one he's ever worked, and he may not understand the typical procedures. "Did the CSI team have any idea of timeline?" I ask.

"They're directing us to the ME. They don't want to make any guesses without her review. She'll have news for us today, initials anyway," he says as he scratches his chin.

"Do you mind if I go talk to her? Or do you have someone on your team that you'd rather go?" I want to do it myself, but I have to be careful of stepping on toes. I don't know the protocol for this station or how protective everyone is over their sandbox.

"No, I'd prefer it if you went." He glances toward the door.

A question occurs to me, something I need to clarify before moving further. "What role exactly would you like me to play in this, Sergeant?"

"I need you to take the lead. We don't have anyone who has handled a homicide before. We can do most of the local interviews, but the rest of the investigation, I'd like you to assist us with that. We've got no experience here. I'm going to have you work with one of our officers. If you have any questions about Camden, the victim, she can help."

"Who?" I ask. Though I worked closely with one officer in Vinalhaven, I haven't had a partner since I left Detroit. And having one wasn't something I'd considered.

"I'll grab her," Sergeant Pelletier says as he walks out the door. He's gone for a minute and returns with a woman I'd guess to be in her early twenties and close to my build, though where I'm blonde, she's got long dark hair, as well as large brown eyes. Her brow is furrowed when Pelletier brings her into the room. Obviously he didn't discuss any of this with her—the shock is clear on her face. She glances at the body, then focuses on me, like she's forcing herself not to accidentally look again. Her pale complexion manages to go whiter. To her credit, though, she doesn't flinch like I expect her to.

I extend my hand toward her. "I'm Detective Claire Calderwood."

"Officer Austin Harleson," she says as she takes my hand. Her grip is stronger than I imagined it would be.

"Good to meet you," I say to Austin, then glance back at Sergeant Pelletier. "If you don't need me for anything else, I'm going to look for the person working in the motel office last night." Someone had to have seen the victim before she entered this hotel room. I need to determine if our vic booked this room herself or if she was brought here by her killer.

"The coroner will be grabbing the body. Take Austin with you to do the questioning," he says as he motions toward the door.

I head out of the room, Austin trailing along after me. Once we're both outside, I turn to face her. "This your first homicide investigation?" I ask, though Sergeant Pelletier said as much. But I've got to break the ice with her somehow.

Her eyes are a bit wide, jaw slack, not quite deer in headlights, but definitely getting there. "Yes, I'm a beat cop. He's never brought me in for anything like this, not that we get a lot of murders or anything. But I didn't think he'd trust me with something like this," she says, glancing between the door and me as she speaks.

"Are you up for this?" I ask. Homicide isn't for everyone. In fact, there are quite a few officers I know who have never wanted to work homicide, and I don't want to force her if this isn't her cup of tea.

"Of course I am. I want to work the bigger cases; I've just never been given the chance. I won't screw this up. Just tell me what to do, and I'll do it." She pulls her shoulders back as she speaks, as if the action might make her a little taller.

There are plenty of hardheaded, stubborn cops already. We need more people like Austin. As long as she's willing to learn, I'm willing to show her the ropes.

I continue toward the office at the end of the row of rooms, Austin beside me. The rest of the rooms are quiet as we pass, the blinds open, revealing empty rooms. If there were patrons staying in the motel, they'd have heard or seen the cop cars outside, and I'm sure we'd have people gathering around to watch. Though I have to wonder if anyone staying here last night heard a struggle or fighting coming from the victim's room.

The office stands at the end of the line of rooms. An old, weathered bench sits out front. Faded decals of snowflakes are stuck to the inside of the door, as if they'll liven this place up. Through the dirty glass door, I can see someone behind a wooden counter, their eyes trained on me. I open the door, and it chimes as Austin and I enter. The guy in the office squints at me from his slumped position in a desk chair, his blue eyes crinkling along the sides. A fresh crop of reddish stubble ghosts his jaw. His skin is pale, translucent, showing the spiderweb of blue veins beneath.

"How can I help you?" he asks, glancing from me to Austin. His eyes linger on her, on her uniform, then down to her service pistol, which is exposed by her open coat. I'm thankful I dress in plain clothes. Wearing the uniform attracts way too much attention and makes people twitchy.

I introduce myself as I approach the large desk that sits in the middle of the room. Other than the desk, the room is rather bare. A calendar hangs on one wall, as well as a picture of a snowy mountain-side and a map of the preserve, and what looks to be a fake potted tree stands in the corner.

"I'm Brenden Glass," he says, looking between us again. "What do you need?"

Did he not see all the cop cars in the parking lot? He must know about the body. One of his housekeepers called us in. "We're here about the woman who was staying in room seventeen."

He glances toward the computer on his desk, clicks the mouse three times, and types something. "What do you need to know?" His eyes settle back on me.

"Could you tell me who paid for the room?"

"Melanie Thomlinson," he says after verifying the information on the computer.

She used her real name. That surprises me. Then again, in a town this small, it's not like anyone would buy her using a fake one. They likely knew her. "She reserved the room, then?"

"Yeah, she came in last night around ten and asked for one." Brenden leans back in his office chair. It squeals in response to the movement. I note the time so we can pass that information along to the ME to help her establish the timeline.

"You were working at the time?" I know most motels like this have small staffs, but that's a long shift.

"I was. Usually work until around eleven or so, sleep for a few hours in the back." He motions toward a door I hadn't noticed. "If anyone needs me, there's a bell outside that'll wake me up."

"Do you usually work long hours like that?"

"My family runs the place. I work up here whenever I can. It's a pretty easy gig. I like working the night shift."

I can understand that. I'm a bit of a night owl myself. "What time was her body found?" The call came into the Camden station around seven, but I want to be sure that not much time elapsed between when she was found and when the call was made.

"Probably around six thirty or so," he says.

"When Melanie came in, how did she seem?"

He cocks his head to the side. The look in his eyes tells me he has no idea what I'm asking.

Austin takes a step forward. "Did she seem scared? Did it seem like she didn't want to make the reservation?"

Good questions for a newbie. Maybe the sergeant knew what he was doing putting her on this case after all. Some people have the instincts for this job; some don't.

"She seemed normal to me. I didn't notice anything," Brenden says.

"Was there anyone with her?" I ask.

He stares off into the distance for a moment. "No one came in with her, but there was a man standing outside."

"Did you get a look at him?" Austin chimes in again.

"Not really. He just looked like an average guy. I couldn't see his face. He stayed too far from the windows."

"Could you get a guess on his weight? Height?" Austin asks.

"No," Brendan says. "I didn't get a look at him."

"Do you have surveillance around the building?" I ask, though I didn't notice any outside.

He shakes his head. "No, no real reason to. There's not much crime over here. Not usually, anyway."

"Were there any complaints about noise last night?" I ask. If there was a struggle, someone could have heard something—that could at least help us start to nail down a timeline of Melanie's death.

"No one made any complaints last night. Then again, we only had one other person staying here, and they were right next to the office."

"Why was Melanie staying so far from the office?" Austin asks.

"She requested a quiet room. Said she was a light sleeper."

Chances are, if Melanie thought her life was in danger, she wouldn't have requested a secluded room. Hell, she wouldn't have booked the room at all. This leads me to believe that her killer was someone she knew, someone she was comfortable with. But that's not out of the ordinary. Random killings are rare. Most of the time a victim knows their attacker.

"Has she ever booked a room here before?" I ask.

His attention turns back to the computer. "Let me modify the search," he says, clicking the mouse again as his brows furrow. "No, I don't see that she did."

"Is there anything else you can think of that stood out to you?" I ask Brendan.

"Not that I can think of."

I pull a card from my pocket and slide it onto his desk. "If you think of anything else, please give me a call."

"I will," he says.

I turn toward the door, and Austin follows me. The cold air hits me as soon as I step outside, but I still pause to jot down notes from the interview. I need to interview her friends, her family. We have to figure out who Melanie trusted.

Austin and I walk back to the gathering of police vehicles, and I explain our next move. We need to go to the ME's office to see Dr. White, who I worked with last year during my homicide investigation. "I want to pick Dr. White's brain as soon as she starts working on the autopsy. Are you okay to attend an autopsy?" I ask Austin. If she didn't have her sights set on homicide, this may be her first rodeo. She may have never even seen a body before today.

Her already pale face goes a few shades whiter, like that's the last thing she expected to do today. I know the feeling. But at least her first autopsy will be with a fresh body.

"I'll be fine," she manages.

I walk to my car, then unlock it, and she climbs in the passenger side. The coroner has about a thirty-minute head start on us. My hope is that once we get there, Dr. White will already have the body on the table. That is, if she doesn't have any other pressing cases today.

Austin sits in the passenger seat, her hands folded in her lap, shoulders tucked. Her eyes are focused on the road ahead. She looks every bit as uncomfortable as I feel.

"If you'd rather ride in your squad car—" I start.

"No, it's fine," she interrupts before I can finish. "Sorry."

I glance at her and throw the car into reverse. Her cheeks are painted scarlet, and it makes her look a few years younger, like she's barely twenty. I turn left out of the motel parking lot and head back toward Route 1. Heavy gray clouds roll across the sky above us, blocking out the afternoon light. It doesn't look like snow this time; instead it looks like the clouds might dump rain. I hope they don't. With the temperature as low as it is, we'll end up with a thick layer of ice on the roads.

"How long have you been working for Sergeant Pelletier?" I ask. I want an idea of how long she's been doing this, but if I ask her how long she's been out of the academy, I'll sound like a bitch.

"Almost three years," she says. "I've always wanted to be a cop, though."

I can't help but wonder how she's going to handle her first trip to the morgue. I still remember mine. The case is etched in my mind. I walked in to find a woman who had been beaten to death by her husband in a domestic abuse incident. During the investigation, we found out it'd been going on for years. It broke my heart, but nailing the bastard was so satisfying. "So how are you feeling about your first homicide?"

She shrugs. "I don't have a feeling on it yet. And it's my first murder but not my first body. I'm not going to get sick seeing the body."

I turn to appraise her. "You're going to have to explain that," I say when she doesn't elaborate.

"It's a long story," she says, brushing it off.

"Good thing we've got a long drive." There's no way she's getting out of this without giving me more details.

15

She's silent for a beat. Then she finally glances toward me. "You might as well hear it from me. God knows you'll end up hearing about it from someone in town. No one can keep a word to themselves about anything."

That doesn't surprise me in the least. Every station has its own drama. Usually it's someone dating someone they shouldn't. But the biggest distraction is always when someone in the station is getting attention no one else thinks they deserve. Nothing can kill morale faster than an officer getting a promotion that seems unwarranted to the rest of the force.

"My mother was an addict. It wasn't so bad when I was younger, but it seemed the older I got, the worse she ended up. When I was thirteen, I tried to get her cleaned up." She smiles sadly. "She was actually clean for six months. But we had a fight. I said some things I shouldn't have, stormed out. When I got home the next day after cooling off, she was in our trailer. She'd relapsed and used too much. And she died." She looks down at her hands laced together in her lap. "I tried to save her. I looked up how to do CPR. But it was too late."

"I'm sorry," I offer. It's awful that she had to live through that. My heart aches for her. No child should lose a parent that way. She's lucky that she's on a different path.

She shrugs. "It's why I'm here. I think that too many of the guys on the force just see cracked-out junkies who are too weak to face the real world. But I've seen it firsthand. My mom wasn't weak. Drugs got their claws in her, and they were too deep. That's not her fault, and I'm sick of the world looking at addicts like they're pieces of shit." She finally looks away from the window. Determination glimmers in them when she focuses on me again. "So what about you? What's your story?"

My fingers tighten on the wheel as I focus, and though my instinct is to keep up a wall, to give her as few details about myself as possible, it's nice to be around someone again who doesn't know my life story. It catches me off guard. I'm so used to people here just knowing my history. That's what growing up in a small town will do to you. It's hard to remember that once I get off the island, my life before and Rachel's memory all stay back in Vinalhaven, that the ripples of what happened there don't extend beyond Pen Bay. I'd wager since Austin hasn't recognized me, she hasn't seen me on the news. I take a deep breath and fill her in on the details about my years in Detroit and then my case last year. Because I know if I don't tell her, she'll just find out somewhere else.

"Jesus," she says, but thankfully it's not pity or concern I hear in her voice—it's disgust. "I'm glad you caught that piece of shit."

"Me too," I say and consider how many more girls might have died if I hadn't.

We pass through small cities on our way to Augusta. The clouds finally part, revealing a sliver of blue sky. Snow clings to the sides of the road, reflecting the rare afternoon sun, but it's so bright I have to squint against it. As we turn into the small parking lot of the medical examiner's office, there are more cars packed in than usual. I pull into a space, throw the car in park, and climb out of my Mustang, Austin following suit.

As soon as I turn toward the building, another car door flies open. I turn, the noise drawing my attention. A woman with a sleek bob and curves I would kill for straightens to her full height. She's got on an open black peacoat revealing black slacks and a gray blouse beneath. I eye her as she strides toward us.

"Detective Claire Calderwood," the woman says. I raise a brow as I survey her. Though she looks familiar, I can't place where I know her from.

"I'm Lillian Landry. I'm a journalist with the *Pen Bay Pilot*."

I press my lips together and cross my arms while I wait for the inevitable, her questions—but I can't decide yet if they'll be about the new body or Rachel. I try not to sneer, but I'm not sure I manage. Even after coming to terms with Noah's line of work, I still can't convince myself that journalists are looking out for anyone but themselves.

She opens her mouth to say something, but I hold my hand up, silencing her.

"I can't comment on an ongoing investigation."

Her head bobs as if that's the response she was expecting. "I know, figured as much. But how are things since you caught Rachel's killer? Have you really had enough time to process that before jumping back into another murder investigation?"

Enough time to process it? No amount of time will help me process my sister's murder. But I have nothing to say to her. This is what I feared when Noah wanted to publish his story, that it wouldn't be only everyone in my tiny hometown that knew about my life but the whole world. They may think they know my story now because of Noah, but all they have is a keyhole view into my life.

"My personal life does not interfere with my work," I say and stride toward the doors, leaving Lillian staring. Footsteps trail behind me. In the reflection of the glass doors leading to the ME's office, I see Austin shuffling a few steps behind.

I shove into the familiar waiting room. How many times was I here last year? Three? Four? It all gets lost beneath the other case details. The sterile waiting room greets us. It's so bright the walls practically glow. As always, the air is heavy with the scent of cleaner. I swear it coats my tongue. Though chairs line the room, as if they anticipate a crowd, I've never seen anyone other than the employees in here.

The receptionist smiles when she sees me, recognition clear on her face. Then she glances toward Austin, her smile faltering, flickering like a light bulb. "Hello, Detective. Here to see Dr. White?" she asks, though I don't know who else I'd be here to see.

"Yes, she should be expecting me," I say before introducing Austin.

"One moment. I'll tell her that you and your partner are here," she says, picking up the phone. She's only on the phone for a few seconds, but by the time she hangs up, a door far down the hall clicks closed.

Dr. White appears in the hall, her lab coat nearly blending in with the walls. She's in her midfifties, I'd guess, with a wide face and large gray eyes. Her blonde hair has been cropped a bit shorter than usual, the ends of it dusting the shoulders of her coat. It suits her, making her face look longer and her cheekbones sharper. She's about six inches taller than me, plus a couple more with her heels. "Claire, good to see you," she says in a way that would lead most people to believe we were old friends. I introduce her to Austin quickly.

"Sabrina, how are you doing?" I ask as we follow her down the hall to the morgue.

"You know, would be better if things quieted down a bit," she says, and a grimace darkens her face, deepening the lines that bracket her thin lips.

This certainly isn't a line of work where you cross your fingers for a busy day. Nerves gnaw at me as we follow her. Not only am I anxious to see what we can find out about the victim, but I'm also concerned about how Austin will handle this. She may have seen a body before, but this is different. She didn't even want to look at Melanie's body while it was at the motel, not that I blame her.

"That bad?" Concern is thick on my words, my usual mask slipping. I've been so consumed with wrapping up my last case that I haven't paid much attention to anything else.

She shakes her head and waves me into the morgue. Cold air slips into the hall, cloaking me before I enter. Mist escapes with each breath as I approach the metal table in the center of the room. Austin hangs behind us. Beneath a sheet, the form of a body is clear. My mind flashes to what Rachel must have looked like on a table like this. But as soon as the thought appears, I banish it. I can't make this about her. Her book should be closed, and I have to keep it that way.

Will I ever be able to put *this* behind me? Maybe it's better if I don't. I've always been afraid I'd become desensitized to homicide once I found her killer. How could I keep doing this if it all stopped feeling so personal? Detectives who have lost someone are more invested, because we know what's at stake; we know what it's like to be broken.

"Anywhere you'd like to start?" Dr. White asks, dragging me back from my thoughts. "I saved cutting the plastic away for your arrival. Sergeant Pelletier told me that you were en route."

"I know you won't have gotten far yet. But anything you know would be helpful. If you want to start with the plastic removal, that'd be fine with me."

She grabs a clipboard, sifts through a few pages, and pulls back the sheet, exposing the corpse from the belly button up. I glance back at Austin, who's still several paces behind me. I wave her over. She looks a little pale but thankfully hasn't gone green. Once I'm sure Austin is fine, I turn my attention back to the body. The plastic sheeting covering her face has debris clinging to it, ash mars the skin on her arms and chest, and there's black clinging beneath her fingernails.

"Do you know the source of the cigarette ashes?" Dr. White asks.

"There was a large cigarette receptacle outside the room. It appears it was brought into the room and dumped on the body," Austin chimes in.

She glances to Austin, then back to me. "I took swabs from the plastic sheeting and checked to see if we have any latent prints on it or the tape, but I couldn't find anything."

"Just cut it as carefully as you can; we'll take it for evidence and have the CSI team take another look," I say, though I doubt there will be anything for us to get from it. Dr. White is fastidious. If there were something to be found, I'm confident she would have found it.

"As I'm sure you noticed, there are signs of trauma all over her body in the various stages of healing: what appears to be a broken wrist, along with some severe bruising on her arm. Based on the ligature marks on her uninjured wrist and ankles, I assumed the bruising was from her being bound. However, the bruising on her right arm is far worse than the left, and it appears to be older. I have to wonder if she was in a car accident recently or something to that effect to cause these other injuries."

I take all the information in. I noticed the wounds and some of the bruises on her body but not the additional bruising on her right arm until now. I assumed the ashes had led to discoloration.

Dr. White grabs a pair of scissors and begins to cut at the nape of Melanie's neck, snipping upward toward her jaw. Tension in the room thickens around us, and I can hardly breathe as I wait for her to peel the sheeting away. As she strips away the plastic, I focus on Melanie's face. Her wide lips are bloody; red congeals in the cracks in them and paints her chin. Faint bruises darken her right eye and her neck. If the bruising is starting to show, it has to have been antemortem. Once the blood stops flowing in a body, bruises no longer form.

Melanie's blue eyes are open, staring up. Dr. White leans in for a closer look, peeling the eyelids back with a gloved finger.

"Petechiae are present, which as you know can be a sign of asphyxia," she says as she glances to me.

"Are you comfortable with what we have here to rule it as asphyxia as the COD?" I ask.

"I'm pretty sure that is what I will rule it. However, I do want to open her up first, just to be sure. We'll also run toxicology, but they're backed up on that about three to four weeks."

"Three to four weeks?" Toxicology always takes a while to get back, but in Detroit, where I worked before moving to Maine, we were usually able to get it in two.

She nods. "They're using all the resources with some cases up in Bangor. Someone is tainting drug supplies. It's all hands on deck with that case."

I shift gears. Toxicology isn't high priority on this case anyway. "Semen?" I ask, but I don't dare to get my hopes up.

"I don't have preliminaries yet. She hasn't been on the table long enough. I took swabs of the fluids; I should know tomorrow."

"Do you believe that she was raped?" I ask.

She flips through the chart, though I think she's ruminating on my question more than she is looking at the pages. "It appears she did have intercourse before death, but I can't be certain if it was rape. There's nothing that can prove it either way based on the evidence on the body."

I want to deflate, but I don't. We'll find out more as time goes on. It'll likely be a few days before we have the full autopsy, but I want to know exactly what trauma she suffered before her death. That information can help me determine who might have done this.

"Sergeant Pelletier said the family will be coming by to formally identify her later today, but I've made impressions of her teeth to search dental records if necessary, in the event that we need them," Dr. White says as she looks at her clipboard.

"Thank you."

Dr. White and I finish up going over her preliminaries, and I'm troubled by the amount of injuries on Melanie's body. I'll need to ask the family if there is a reason to suspect abuse or if there was an accident recently.

Austin tails me as we head out of the ME's office. Her feet scuff against the pavement as she walks. I glance to the side and slow my pace, waiting for her to catch up. On the surface, she appears to be unfazed by the ordeal, as if this morning she expected to be dragged into a homicide investigation.

We climb back into my Mustang, and I turn to her. "What can you tell me about the victim? Did you know her?"

"Well, in the same sense that everyone in a small town knows everyone else," she says. "She was a couple months short of graduating, didn't get into much trouble. Pretty average, really. I would never have expected anything like this to happen to her."

"Have you ever noticed bruising on her before? Signs of trauma that you could see?"

She shakes her head. "No. I also didn't know about the cast, though."

"Did she get into a car accident recently?"

"Nothing that was reported to the station."

That doesn't mean an accident didn't happen. I'll be sure to ask her parents about it. "Do any of the teens normally hang out in that motel?" I pull out of the parking spot and turn right out of the lot, my tires crunching on the snow.

"Not that I've ever seen. There's a golf club, the bowling alley, Walker Park, the boat club, or the quarries in the summer." She ticks the places off on her fingers as she talks.

It sounds pretty similar to Vinalhaven. I'm surprised anyone would visit this motel and risk the rest of the town finding out about it. Usually in towns like this, if you were meeting someone at a motel, everyone in the town would know about it within an hour.

"Did anyone report her missing?" I ask as we pass large wood-frame farmhouses on either side of the road. The two-lane road is lined with towering trees that are dusted with snow.

"You'll have to check with the sergeant. If she was, no one let me in on it."

I don't know how this girl could have been missing all night in that motel without anyone noticing, especially if she was still in high school. The gray clouds above us grow thicker as we approach the coast. Thick white flakes spiral from the sky, freckling the road. I slow, not wanting to risk skidding.

By the time we pull back into the station, the sky is darkening, and a curtain of white surrounds us. I wish I could interview Melanie's family today, but with the weather heading sideways and Sergeant Pelletier wanting me to wait, Austin and I agree to call it a day. I head toward the docks, hoping that I can get a ferry back to the island tonight. After a fifteen-minute wait, I pull onto the ramp.

I drive back toward my rental, snow billowing around me, and plan to spend my evening going over notes on the case so far.

CHAPTER 2

The morning light reflects off the fresh blanket of snow. I squint against it as I stare out the kitchen window. I didn't get far yesterday. After I finished at the ME's office, dropped off Austin, and got back to Vinalhaven, it was nearly seven p.m. I spent my evening digging through the little I could find in the file from Camden PD. Overnight another six inches of snow fell on the island.

I sit in the kitchen sipping a cup of coffee. In front of me, toast is piled on the plate, the thin Camden file beside it. Though I might be back in Vinalhaven, my mind is far off, in Camden, going over the interviews I'll need to conduct today.

"Morning," Noah says as he wraps his arms around my waist. His lips graze my neck, sending a shiver down my spine and pulling me from my thoughts. As he moves, his long hair tickles my cheek and neck. The feel of him against me puts a smile on my face. He's been staying in my rental almost every night. At this rate he may as well live here, which is what he'd prefer. He's made that clear several times. But I'm still on the fence. I can't deny that I've thought about asking him, though only casually. That's a big step, and I'm still unsure if I'm ready for it. Maybe it's because I've never lived with anyone else. Maybe it's because I'm not *there* yet. At the very least, while I'm not ready to share an address with Noah, I have been considering giving him a key to my place. Baby steps. That's the best I can do right now.

Back when I lived in Detroit, though I picked up guys occasionally, I never wanted anything serious. A few guys stuck around for a little while. But I didn't really want them there. My job has always consumed the majority of my focus, energy, and time, and it always will. And that's the way I want it. It's easier being detached. Getting involved makes my life more complicated.

I glance at my phone and see another three emails requesting interviews. I swipe them away, ignoring them like I always do.

"How'd it go yesterday?" he asks, giving me a quick kiss before pouring himself a cup of coffee. As per usual, he's got on a retro band T-shirt, a tattered Sex Pistols tour shirt he's probably had for ten years. His Chuck Taylors are worn, but the faded black matches the shirt well. He adds so much sugar to the cup—at least six heaping spoonfuls—it makes me cringe. With all the sugar he consumes, it's beyond me how he keeps up his muscled physique.

When I got in last night, Noah was in the middle of working on a story, and I didn't want to interrupt him. Since Noah's article came out, he's been busy with stories, calls. The article started off slow but gained so much traction online that it was featured on several true-crime podcasts and even mentioned in the *New York Times*. Thankfully most of the attention has been focused on him, and I've been able to stay out of the spotlight. That's the way I want to keep it.

"As good as it could have gone. It's early, lots of unanswered questions so far," I say. But I also explain my new partner, or whatever Austin is, and the circumstances around the death. I shouldn't let the case bother me, but it does. I try to shake the feeling, the memories of Rachel, the other dead girls from last year, but they keep creeping into my mind.

"A partner, how do you feel about that?" he asks.

"Right now, I'm concerned about how she'll handle all this. She's got no experience. I'm not sure if she can really help me or if she's just going to get in my way." And I don't know if Sergeant Pelletier is really doing this to show her the ropes or keep an eye on me.

He sips slowly, testing his cup. It's nice that he understands the procedure for cases. I don't have to fill him in on all the details. That's one thing I've never had, a guy who really got my job, got me. And Noah does. My whole life has been laid bare in front of him, all that I am, and he has stayed. Hell, he dug his heels in deeper when I tried to push him away. We shouldn't be the sum of everything that's happened to us, but I was forged by loss. It made me who I am. So without understanding what made me this way, Noah could never understand me.

"I'm going to interview her family today, maybe some of her friends if I can track them down," I explain. "Camden PD will be assisting with some of the interviews as well, but I'm going to tackle as many as I can myself."

"So you can go ask the important questions," he says with a smirk.

"Something like that," I say, not meaning to return the smile, but I just can't help it. My gaze shifts back to my coffee while my mind wanders. "Look, I don't know how late I'll be at the hospital, and the ferry stops running at nine—"

"I've actually got to go out of town for a few days," he says casually.

I raise an eyebrow at that. He hasn't mentioned anything about going out of town recently. "Where to?" I ask. Him being away would actually be great. It'd allow me to focus on my case without feeling like I'm ignoring him. Struggling to balance my work obligations with a relationship and the attention that it needs has always been a problem for me.

"Do you remember Josh and Tina?" he asks.

When Noah and I began dating, he told me about this part of his past. It's what drove him to investigate cold cases. Josh was Noah's childhood best friend, and Tina was Josh's mother. Tina was murdered when

Noah was in middle school, sending Josh into a downward spiral. They never found Tina's killer, and it's always haunted Noah. Though I know it's the one case he's never dared investigate. From what I remember about the details, her death was connected to several others, the bodies all dumped in the same area.

"Yes, I remember," I say.

"My brother Cameron works at the police station there. He told me they found another body. One they think is connected to the original murders."

"Oh, wow." If they find new evidence on this body, that could mean their team could finally solve this case. New evidence often reinvigorates cold cases. That'd be huge for him. I know what it'd mean to Noah to finally put that cold case to rest.

"So I'm finding a flight today. Going to go down there and dig into it."

"I really hope you're able to help them find who did this," I say. He needs it. I know he does. I've been there.

"You won't mind that I'll be gone for a few days?"

"I'm going to be up to my eyeballs in this case. I may not even notice that you're gone," I say with a laugh.

"Ah, that's exactly what a man wants to hear," he says, smirking.

I shake my head at Noah, trying not to smile. "I've got to get to the ferry. Have a safe flight," I say, giving him a quick kiss. I relish the feel of his lips against mine, and then I throw on my coat and head out into the cold.

CHAPTER 3

I pull off Washington Street into the parking lot of Camden PD at eight thirty a.m., just as snow begins to fall. I bundle up in my coat and head inside. The station is downtown, huddled between several restaurants and a consignment shop. The building is short, made of brick, with white accents around the roofline, doors, and windows. I pass through an open lobby that also doubles as a waiting room. An empty receptionist desk stands against the far wall. The station is a ghost town when I get inside. That is, except for Austin, who's already stationed at her desk, still clad in her uniform. If she's going to be out with me working this case, I've got to talk to her about wearing plain clothes.

"Morning," I say as I approach.

She offers me a smile. "We're all set to interview the parents. Sergeant Pelletier and some of the other guys spoke to them yesterday. They've officially identified her as well."

Interviewing the parents and other immediate family is my least favorite part of the job. Some family members can hold it together for the interview, while others are so weepy that I can't get any information out of them. But it's essential. The family has info I can't get anywhere else, info that could make or break the case.

"Do you know where to find them?" I ask.

"Yes, and they're expecting us around nine. We can grab some breakfast and then head over there."

I hardly touched my breakfast this morning—I find it difficult to eat when a case starts ramping up. My mind is too lost to the details. Austin and I walk out of the station together and climb into my Mustang. Though I've seen a diner and a café driving through Camden, I'm not sure where to go. After I follow her directions, we pull up to a coffee shop.

Austin orders her breakfast while I grab a coffee. Once we've both got our orders, we head back to the car. Austin eats while I drive, and I soak in every drop of caffeine I can.

Melanie's family lives in a three-story colonial on the north side of Camden. The streets are lined with ancient, twisting oak trees and maple trees frosted with ice. Fresh snow still coats most of the sidewalk. I roll my car to a stop in front of the house, my tires crackling on the hard-packed snow. They haven't gotten around to plowing the side streets yet. I throw open my door, and Austin follows suit, trailing me toward the house. I glance at her before I knock.

"Any questions before we go in?"

She shakes her head. "We're meeting with Fran and Matthew Thomlinson."

I knock on the door, my blood surging like it always does before I question a victim's family. It's so hard to know which way this is going to go—if it'll be good, if it'll be bad, or if it'll rip my heart out. It must be easier to do this job if you haven't suffered a loss of your own.

A few moments after I knock, footsteps thud inside, and a woman cracks open the door, peering out at me. I can make out a blue eye spiderwebbed with red veins, pale skin, and long white-blonde hair. After the woman eyes me and Austin, she opens the door fully, revealing a navy-blue robe over sweatpants.

"Sergeant Pelletier told me you all were coming." Her voice is hoarse, husky. But I can't tell if that's the usual pitch or if it's from all the tears she's shed.

"Thank you for seeing us, Mrs. Thomlinson," I say.

She nods, sniffles, and opens the door wider before waving us inside. The interior of the house is well decorated. Family portraits adorn the front hall. The air smells heavily of cinnamon. Fran leads us into the living room, motioning for us to take a seat on a light floral sofa. She shifts closer to a table beside the sofa, flicking on a lamp beside us. The lamp doesn't do much to illuminate the dim room.

"Do you two need anything to drink?" she asks as she eyes us.

I shake my head and glance at Austin, who does the same. "No, we're okay."

She perches on a chair across from us, like she's poised to run.

"Will your husband be joining us?" I ask.

Briefly she presses her lips together, then says, "No, I'm afraid not."

"Mrs. Thomlinson—"

She holds her hand up. "Please, call me Fran."

"Fran, I'm so sorry about your daughter. I cannot imagine what you and your husband must be going through right now. Thank you for meeting with us. I know it's probably still a shock."

With a slight nod of her head, she sniffles and then wipes her nose on a ball of tissues. The tip of her nose is red, like it's not far off from being rubbed raw. "Thank you," she croaks.

"When was the last time that you saw your daughter?" I ask.

Her brows knit together as she tries to remember. "Friday, I saw her at dinner. Then she was going to go do some shopping."

"Friday the twenty-first?" I ask, and her head dips in response. "Did you know that she was going to the Millay Inn that evening?"

She shakes her head. "No, I have no idea why she would have gone there."

"Do you know if she had ever visited that hotel before?" Austin asks.

"Not that I know of."

I clear my throat. I need to put the next part of this delicately. "I don't know how much of the scene Sergeant Pelletier explained to you, but it appears that Melanie might have brought a man back to that motel room with her. Do you know who that might have been?"

Her eyes go wide, and she straightens in her seat, as if the question has upset her, as if she didn't expect this line of questioning at all. "Are you saying that she had sex with someone in that hotel room?" The pitch of her voice goes up several octaves.

"It appears that she could have," I explain. "We don't know for sure. We're trying to build an accurate picture of what happened during the events leading up to her death. If she had been there with someone, is there anyone who comes to mind that it could have been?"

She shakes her head, but then her eyes seem to lose focus for a beat before snapping back. "Melanie had a serious boyfriend for two years. His name is Cade Dowling." Her lips press together. "But I don't think she would have gone to the motel with him."

"Two years? That's a long time for an eighteen-year-old," I say. "Why wouldn't she have met him at the motel?"

"Yes, she was serious about him. But they broke up recently. I don't think that she wanted to get back together with him—but he really wanted to. He was hounding her. He tried proposing. He really didn't take the breakup well at all."

"Do you think that he would have been capable of hurting your daughter?" I ask.

"Love makes people do crazy things, things you don't expect. He had an intensity about him. I don't know if he would hurt her on purpose, but an accident. I could see that," she says, her eyes going glassy again. Fran sniffles, then wipes her nose on a tissue.

"So you don't think she would have willingly gone to a hotel with him?" Austin asks.

Fran purses her lips. "After how he acted during the breakup, I just don't see her being comfortable with it. She didn't even want him coming to the house."

"Was there anyone else who Melanie had trouble with? Anyone else who had been fixated on her?"

She shakes her head. "Just her ex. Since she got out of the hospital, he's been around here constantly trying to check up on her. I believe he also showed up there several times."

"Has he showed up here unannounced?"

She fiddles with the tissue in her hands. "Yes, a few times. My husband made him leave, though. Melanie didn't even want to come down to the living room while he was outside."

I make a note of that. "Was there any reason you didn't call the police about it?"

"It just seemed harmless at the time. I didn't think he'd hurt her. We just thought that he was fixated on her because the breakup was so recent and that he'd get over it eventually."

The boyfriend is definitely at the top of my list for people to check out, but I need to know if there was anyone else. Her mention of the hospital has caught my interest, especially since Dr. White said it looked like Melanie had been in an accident recently. "You referred to the hospital. What was she in the hospital for?"

"She had an ATV accident a few weeks ago. She and some of her girlfriends like to take their ATVs up through the woods. She bounced off the back of one and fractured her wrist; then one of the scrapes she got had a minor infection. She wasn't there for long the second time, just a couple days, but that really made Cade freak out."

I jot that down. That explains the brace on her wrist. I'll need to talk to the hospital to see if he came by or if anyone remembers anything about her stay that sticks out. "How long ago was she in the hospital?" I ask.

"About a week ago."

"The medical examiner pointed out that there were several large bruises on her body in various stages of healing. Were those all caused by the ATV accident?"

"As far as I know," she says, straightening.

"To your knowledge, was Cade ever violent with her?" Austin asks.

She shakes her head. "No, nothing like that."

"Did she ever have unexplained bruises while they were dating?" I try again. Though her daughter may not have communicated abuse, it's still a possibility.

"No."

"And you don't know of anyone else who may have been physical with her?" I ask carefully.

"No, never."

"Is there anything else that you can think of that sticks out to you? Anything you think might help with the investigation?"

My question hangs in the air between us; then she shakes her head. "Not that I can think of."

"Can you write down the information you have on Cade Dowling or any of her friends you think it'd be worth speaking to?" I ask and pass over my notepad to her.

She writes down the information for me. Austin and I say our goodbyes and head out of the Thomlinson home. We pull away from Melanie's house, and I zero in on the first name on the list of Melanie's friends, Chloe Garcia. Austin helps me navigate across town to a house set back away from the road, a recently plowed driveway cutting through the snowy yard toward a canary-yellow colonial. Maroon shutters flank each window, and dagger-sharp icicles hang from the roof.

"Anything I should know about Chloe?" I ask Austin as I park the car out front.

"She's popular, cliquish. Her mom owns an art gallery in the center of town."

When we reach the door, I ring the bell. Though the sun has come out, it's barely added a breath of warmth. After we've waited a few seconds, the front door opens, revealing a young woman in black leggings and an oversize red flannel shirt. Her black hair falls in waves over her shoulder. She cocks her head as she surveys us.

"Chloe?" I ask.

"Yeah." Her eyes narrow as she glances from me to Austin.

"Could we come in for a moment to speak with you about Melanie?"

She hesitates, her features a mask, but she waves us inside. The house looks like an extension of the art gallery Austin mentioned. Inside, the interior is stark, institutional gray walls mixed with exposed brick that must have been added during a renovation, since the exterior is wood siding. Unframed canvases line nearly every inch of wall space, adding splashes of color and life to the rooms. Chloe shows us into a living room filled with sleek Swedish furniture.

"Why are you asking about Melanie?" she asks while we take a seat on the couch. Chloe sits across from us on a circular ottoman.

"I'm sorry to be the one to tell you, but Melanie passed away," I say gently. I'm a bit surprised she hasn't heard. I imagined that news would have spread all over town by now.

Chloe sucks in a sharp breath and shoves several strands of hair behind her ear. "No, that can't be. I would have . . . no," she stammers.

"I'm sorry," I say again as she shoves up from the ottoman and begins to pace in front of the table.

"How?" she asks finally, whipping toward us, tears pooling in her eyes.

"The details are not being shared with anyone but the family for now," I say, which is true, but I also can't bear to tell the specifics to this girl. Some facts are too terrible. They won't help her get closure. They'll only bring about nightmares. There's another reason I won't share the particulars, though—we intend to keep some of them as holdback evidence so that we can rule out any false confessions. I give her a little time to compose herself as she sniffles and tears coat her cheeks.

"I know this is incredibly difficult," I say gently. "But in investigations like this, time is of the essence. Every minute can make a big difference in our chances of finding who did this to her."

"It was Cade," she snaps, her eyes locking on mine. Her body has gone rigid, fists clenched at her sides. "If someone did this to her, it was him."

"How can you be so sure about that?" Austin asks.

"He went psycho after she broke things off with him. He got way too serious too fast. He was saying that he wanted to marry her, that they were soul mates." She shakes her head and crosses her arms. "A few times, she told him that he needed to take it easy, and every time he ended up threatening to kill himself or something if she broke up with him."

That intensity level is a huge red flag. "Did he ever hurt her or threaten to?" I ask, wanting to phrase this question carefully.

"No, not that she ever told me."

"Do you ever remember seeing unexplained bruises on her?"

"Unexplained? No. She was always out hiking, on her ATV, stuff like that." She sniffles and wrinkles her nose, making her displeasure clear. "She fell sometimes while she was out. She ended up with bruises that way."

"Did you see any of these incidents occur?" I ask. Abuse can easily be covered up with stories about falls or accidents. And many times, domestic abuse can lead to homicide. I need to be sure that's not what we're looking at here.

"No, but I don't think she lied about it."

"Is there anything else about Cade that we should know?"

"He was basically stalking her," she says as she starts to pace again. "He'd show up at her house and just stand outside, waiting for her to come out. Then if she didn't, he'd call her cell phone over and over again."

I make notes of all of that. "Is it possible that she was seeing someone else?" I ask. If this ex-boyfriend was stalking her, I find it unlikely that she would have booked a hotel room to meet up with him. But she booked it to meet up with someone.

"She mentioned being interested in an older guy," she says, her words almost a question, as if the thought just occurred to her.

"Did she say a name? Where she met him?"

Chloe shakes her head. "No, she didn't give me any details. She said she wanted it to be a sure thing first. She was afraid she'd jinx it."

"Jinx it?"

"Yeah, like he was too good to be true or something."

I try to make sense of that. An older guy who was too good to be true. This was likely the man outside the motel. If she was dating someone new, I'll need to speak with her other friends to see if anyone saw her with this guy or knows who he might be.

I finish up with my questioning of Chloe, and then Austin and I interview several more friends of Melanie's. All of them share Chloe's concern about Cade, but none saw any signs of abuse. And though I hope to find out more about this older guy she was seeing, she didn't mention him to any of her other friends. With the information about her boyfriend fresh in my mind, I text Sergeant Pelletier with the information on Cade. He's my best lead to follow up with for now. I want to set up an interview with him as soon as possible. In the meantime, I need to get to that hospital to see what they know about Melanie's stay after she had her ATV accident.

CHAPTER 4

I maneuver the car out of the driveway after the last of our interviews with Melanie's friends and steer back toward Camden. We'll have to follow Route 1 south toward Rockport to the Pen Bay Medical Center. It's a twenty-minute drive in good weather, but with the snow gently falling around us, I know it'll be closer to a half hour.

It looks as though they've plucked out the forest to build the medical center. The large building seems entirely out of place here, and though it seems absurdly large for a city of this size, the Pen Bay Medical Center supports many of the local communities. Hospitals are few and far between out here. Most of the time, we just go to an urgent care facility since the hospitals are difficult to find. Once I turn in, we weave our way through the parking lot and head toward the administrative offices.

I grab my phone, glancing at the name of the head of security that Sergeant Pelletier sent me when I told him my next stop. The double doors glide open automatically as I approach, and I head toward the receptionist's desk. A woman with cropped red hair clicks away at a keyboard. I pull out my badge, ready to show her when she looks up.

"Yes?" she asks without taking her eyes off the screen.

I introduce myself and Austin. "We're here to see David Bowden. Sergeant Pelletier from Camden PD told me I could find him here."

Finally, she glances at my badge for half a second before grabbing the phone. "David, there are some cops here to see you." Her words are clipped.

"Thanks," I say, though she doesn't look back at me, just returns to typing.

David Bowden strolls down the hall like he owns the place. Well, I guess it's him, judging by the confidence—security guys always have it—and the belt he wears that's adorned with a handgun, pepper spray, and handcuffs.

"Officers," he says as he approaches. "Detective Calderwood? Sergeant Pelletier told me to expect you two." A low chuckle rolls from his thin lips. "But he didn't tell me to expect *you*." He eyes Austin. "And you are?"

"Officer Harleson," Austin says.

Though I try to remain stoic, I'm sure I grimace as his eyes crawl over me, at what's visible through my open coat. But considering his eyes are surveying every inch of me other than my face, I'm sure he wouldn't notice either way.

"Yes, I'm Detective Calderwood. Thank you for meeting with me, Mr. Bowden. Do you have an office where we can speak privately?" I ask, glancing toward the nurse I know is eavesdropping on us.

"Of course," he says in a tone that's much too like a purr. "Right this way."

The halls of the administrative building aren't quite as stark as the hospital proper, but they're still pretty close. We pass many offices, the occupants clicking away on their keyboards or having hushed phone conversations. At the end of the main hall, we turn left and reach a large office. David waves us in. The right wall of the room is covered in surveillance monitors. There have to be at least forty shots playing from different parts of the hospital. But about every thirty seconds the footage switches to another shot.

Those cameras will be an asset if anything happened with Melanie's boyfriend while she was here.

In front of David's meticulously clean desk, there are two chairs, and he signals for us to sit.

"What has Sergeant Pelletier told you?" I ask as I take a seat, Austin sitting next to me, looking at ease with the situation.

"He said that you'd be popping in because of a homicide investigation." He laces his fingers together on top of the desk. "And that's all I know."

I bring up a picture of the victim on my phone and show it to him. "This is Melanie Thomlinson. Her body was found in the Millay Inn yesterday," I explain. "Her parents informed me that she was a patient here a week ago, and I wanted to see if there was a record of who visited her while she was here."

After I give him her information, he turns to his computer and begins to type. "She was being treated for an infection," he says as he glances to me, then focuses on the screen again. "From what I understand, she was here around thirty-six hours."

"Did anything occur during her stay that stuck out to anyone on the staff?"

He reaches for his computer mouse and clicks a few times. "Not that I see noted."

"Would it be possible for us to get copies of the surveillance footage from the time she was a patient here?" I ask.

"Would you like me to send it to you or to the Camden PD?"

"Send it to Camden first," I say as I jot that down in my notebook. With all those cameras, I'll need help digging through the footage anyway.

"You can email it to me and copy the sergeant," Austin says as she passes a business card to David.

"Were there any other injuries reported while Melanie was here?" If there'd been any other signs of abuse, an attack, anything like that, it would point me in a very clear direction, especially with Melanie's mother's comments. The bruising that was evident could easily be explained away by her fall off the ATV.

"I don't have all the details. The information I do have is very limited. Privacy laws and all that. Her doctor could give you more details," he says, looking at the screen.

"Would I be able to get a copy of her records?"

"If her family signs off on it, yes."

"Could I speak with her doctor or maybe the nurses who interacted with her?"

He nods. "Everyone who stays here sees multiple nurses and doctors, but I can get her last attending doctor for you. Would that help?"

"Yes, that would be helpful."

David puts in several calls and leaves the office, and within ten minutes, he returns with a tall, slender man with dark hair. When I stand up to shake his hand, the gray at his temples becomes more obvious, though he looks too young to be going gray.

I extend my hand to introduce myself, then Austin.

"I'm Dr. Ian Munroe," he says with a kind smile. "You're here about Melanie Thomlinson?"

"I am," I say, unable to return his smile. "I'm sorry to inform you, but she passed away. We are investigating the circumstances around her death."

His eyes go wide, and Austin gets up, offering Dr. Munroe her seat in front of the desk. I'm not sure if it's the shock, but he takes the seat, sitting down a little harder than I think he intends to. I sit next to him. David continues to hover near the door, as if unsure whether he should stay or go, before finally sitting back at his desk. Dr. Munroe fidgets, his fingers twitching against the edge of the key card clipped to his pocket, which displays his grinning portrait on the hospital employee badge.

"Someone killed that poor girl? Really?" He scratches his jaw, and his fingernails grate loudly against the stubble dotted there. Dark circles hang beneath his eyes, shadowing them. I know doctors typically appear tired, but Dr. Munroe looks especially so. Like maybe he hasn't slept well in days, weeks—or longer. "That's awful," Dr. Munroe finally says.

"It is. But I was hoping I could ask you a few questions so I can try and sort this all out."

"Of course. I'll help however I can," he says as he leans forward in his chair, resting his elbows on his knees.

"How often would you say you interacted with Melanie?" I ask. Based on what David said about patients seeing many doctors, I need to know what context he really has here. If he's only seen Melanie a few times, that'll severely restrict the kind of questions I can ask.

"I saw her probably two or three times for the period she was here. It's hard to keep track. We see so many patients every day," he says as he leans back in the chair and crosses his legs.

That's not going to give me much to go on, but then again, her stay was rather brief. "Did Melanie ever seem uneasy while she was in your care? Did she mention being scared?"

"Not that I remember. I think I would if she said something along those lines."

"When Melanie checked into the hospital, did she have any wounds that would have been indicative of abuse?"

He shakes his head. "No, not at all. She seemed to be perfectly healthy other than the infection near her wrist. Granted, I didn't give her a physical. But what I could see of her arms didn't concern me. And her demeanor was not consistent with that of a typical abuse victim."

"Did you see anyone lingering near her room? Or entering her room when they didn't need to be there?"

He scratches his jaw again, the skin pinkening under his nails. "Not that I recall, but I didn't spend much time in her room. One of the nurses did mention a boy trying to see her several times."

I perk up at that. "Do you recall which nurse mentioned this?" I ask.

"Nurse Jordan, I believe."

I jot that down. "Have you ever treated Melanie before for other injuries?"

He shakes his head. "No, I'd never seen her before." His brows come together, as if he's contemplating something. "There was one odd thing about her stay, actually."

"Oh?"

"Her chart disappeared. It was stolen from outside her room. I tried to have David check the security footage, but none of the cameras around her room were working."

"Has this happened before?"

"No, that's why it struck me as odd."

I note that detail down. "I won't keep you any longer, Dr. Munroe. Thank you for answering my questions. If you think of anything else, please call me." I pass him my card. .

He takes it and slips it into his pocket. "I hope you find whoever did this."

"Don't worry—I will."

David leads Dr. Munroe out and tracks down Nurse Jordan. A short woman with cropped black hair peeks around the doorframe, interrupting the conversation I was having with Austin, but I wave her in. She's got pinched eyes and thin cherry-red lips. When she spots me, she offers a hard smile, but her eyes tell me she's not sure if she's in the right place.

"Take a seat, please," I say before introducing myself and Austin.

"Is everything all right?" she asks, glancing between the two of us as she folds her hands together in her lap.

I explain the situation to her as delicately as I can.

"That's terrible. I can't believe that," she says. I guess the news from Camden hasn't made it down to Rockport yet. Or maybe being shut up in the hospital keeps the news from reaching them.

"Dr. Munroe mentioned that you saw a boy trying to get in to see Melanie a few times?"

"Yes, his name was Cade. He tried to sign himself in to see her several times. He was very insistent." She drops her voice. "And annoying about trying to see her. Melanie made it clear that she didn't want to see him."

"Did she seem scared of him?"

"No, more frustrated, I would say. She wanted him to go away and to leave her alone." She sweeps her hair behind her right ear as she speaks.

"Munroe also mentioned that Melanie's chart went missing."

She twists her hands, then looks at them tangled in her lap. "It did. At first, I thought that someone left it in her room or moved it to the main desk. But we were never able to locate it."

"Dr. Munroe seemed to think it was stolen."

"It might have been."

"Would you say that charts typically go missing?"

"From time to time one will be misplaced, but we always find it again."

I make a note of that. "Did you see Cade near her room around the time that the chart went missing?" I'm not sure if Cade and the missing chart are connected or what he would gain from stealing it. But with his insistence, I have to wonder.

"No, I never let him past the front desk. Someone would have to buzz him back, and I don't believe anyone did. I made it clear that Melanie did not wish to see him." She looks down at her feet for a moment. "It also seems like she would have brought it up if he made it back to her room."

"Thank you. Is there anything else about her stay at the hospital that stuck out to you?"

She glances from the door to Austin and finally back to me. "No."

I pass her one of my cards and ask her to call me if she thinks of anything else. David shows in three more nurses who all spent some time with Melanie. After I've questioned all three, the biggest lead I have is still the ex-boyfriend.

As Austin and I walk out of the hospital, thick gray clouds roll across the sky, hanging so low some brush the tips of the towering pines all around us. I shoot a quick text to the station to get them started on the paperwork to request Melanie's hospital records. It takes about fifteen minutes to get back to the station from the medical center, and all the while Austin is tapping away at her phone beside me.

"What are your feelings on this?" she asks me as I turn into the parking lot.

I let myself ruminate as I throw the car into park. "I'm not sure yet if her death is connected to the hospital, to the boyfriend, or if someone else was already planning to kill her for some reason we haven't considered yet. It's very odd that her chart went missing. I'm not sure what the perp would have gotten from it, but hopefully once we get her records, we can find out. There's a slim chance this was a sex act gone wrong, though my gut tells me that's not the case. I need to know more about her life leading up to her death to get a better picture of this."

"Are there any other answers we can get from the autopsy?" she asks.

"I'm going to call Dr. White tonight to see how she's coming with it. Though I doubt there's anything that we don't already know."

Austin and I walk into the station. She heads through the bull pen to her desk to start reviewing the surveillance footage that the hospital sent over, while I walk straight to Sergeant Pelletier's office. I rap my knuckles on the door, and he waves me inside. There's a deep crease between his eyebrows as he looks up at me. "How'd your interviews go?" I can really appreciate that he's a no-bullshit guy.

I fill him in on the details I got—on Melanie's stay at the hospital, the accident, and the missing chart—and he lets me know that Officer Blake is getting the parents' permission on the hospital chart.

"There's an ex-boyfriend we're going to dig into tomorrow. Things went really bad when she broke up with him a couple months ago. You and Austin have surveillance footage from the hospital in your in-boxes, though I'm not sure how helpful it will be. Apparently, the cameras near Melanie's room weren't working."

"Austin will be able to look up his address for you."

"Thanks," I say before heading out of his office. On my way out of the station, I say a quick goodbye to Austin, promising to meet up with her in the morning before Cade's interview.

I glance at the time on my phone, realize it's nearly eight, and decide it's time to call it a night. After all the interviews, I'm bone tired as I drag myself into my car and hit a drive-through for dinner. Five minutes later, I pull into a small motel. My mind churns over the details of the day. The ex-boyfriend may be a good lead to follow up on. But whatever happened to Melanie doesn't say *ex* to me. It says something else entirely. She was targeted. That I know. And by someone she knew, but scorned lovers don't usually take this route. If they were on really bad terms, as her parents and friends say, would she have willingly booked a hotel with this boy?

I settle into my hotel room before calling Dr. White. Last year, while I was working with her on a serial case, she gave me her cell for emergencies. I usually try not to use someone's cell if I can avoid it. But with our unanswered questions on this case, I need to know what else the autopsy is telling her, if anything. The phone rings as I grip it between my ear and shoulder. With my hands free, I open my bag of slop for dinner, extracting a burger and a pouch of fries. I flatten the bag on the third ring and drop my fries atop it, then make a puddle of ketchup.

"Claire," Dr. White says, a little breathless. "What can I help you with?"

"I wanted to follow up with you about Melanie, see if we've gotten anywhere."

"I opened her up today. There are signs of strangulation on the body, damage to the vessels of the throat, as if she was choked and then released over and over again. There was also a partially healed fracture to her wrist, along with trauma to the vagina and rectum. It could be consistent with rough sex or rape. Though there are signs of previous scarring to the vagina, which leads me to believe that she may have engaged in rough sex in the past. No semen or other fluids were present, though."

I consider her words. Though DNA could help in this case, it won't help if we have nothing to match it to. If the perp wasn't in the database, it won't do us much good until we have a solid suspect. With all the additional DNA in the room because of the debris, we need to build a solid case without it. "Did you see any other signs of old trauma on the body?"

"The signs of trauma you already saw."

"Do you know yet how you're going to officially rule it?"

"I'm ruling her cause of death general asphyxia, pending toxicology."

"And you think that could still take three weeks?" I ask, then take a bite from a fry.

"I'll push it as much as I can, but more than likely three weeks will be it. We did find a hair stuck in the tape that secured the sheeting around her head. It didn't look similar to her own."

"Do you think we can get DNA from it?"

"Not likely. I've set it aside with the other forensic evidence and cataloged it. It did not have a follicle attached."

While a single strand of hair could help us, I know that with forensics, it may not necessarily be enough. If the hair was shed without a root or broken off, our chances of extracting DNA from it are incredibly low. And with the resources that I know are available to the Maine State Crime Lab, it may not even be possible for us to test it.

"What color is the hair?"

"Brown, but it's not dyed. It's a natural shade. Melanie's hair was dyed."

I make note of that. "Thank you, Sabrina."

I finish up my call with Dr. White and pop another french fry in my mouth. It may not be much to go on yet, but it's a start.

CHAPTER 5

The next morning, I pull into the station at nine thirty. Our plan is to swing by Cade's house at eleven, but I want to get as much of a jump on this as I can. There's a chorus of voices emanating from the bull pen as I walk through the front door. I recognize several of the officers, Zane Holt, Clint Wilkens, and Sasha Lakely, seated at desks as I walk through. I remember seeing them on the scene. The station is hot, unusually so. The scent of burning coffee is heavy in the air. I feel the eyes of everyone in the room on me as I stride to Austin's desk. She smiles when she sees me approach.

"Morning," she says. "We should get a copy of Melanie's medical records today. Her parents signed off on it last night."

"Great," I say. "You still up for helping me with the interview today?"

"Of course, if you want me. I've never done an interrogation before."

I expected that, though. In my past experience in different stations, I've never seen a beat cop in an interrogation room. But I need another officer present anyway, even though it's not technically an interrogation at this stage. If she's going to be in this case, she might as well be up to her eyeballs like me.

Austin pulls a folder from a stack and flops it open on the desk. "Yesterday while we were at the hospital, Clint and Zane interviewed a few more of Melanie's friends. I went through some of the interviews this morning. According to them, she'd been at the hospital a month ago for the initial injury to her wrist. And after she got out, she was increasingly absent from school. But she wouldn't tell anyone what was going on. They assumed it was the ex."

Though Chloe seemed to think that Melanie might have been seeing someone. I scan the notes about the previous trip to the hospital and her distance from her friends. So was it Cade or someone else who was keeping her away?

"We also got the visitors list from the hospital—Cade's on it and in the security footage. I've started going through it. Zane is working on it as well. But I don't think we'll find anything, since they already informed us none of the cameras near her room were working. So it's unlikely we'll see who stole her chart."

I take that all in. Though I know we've got to check out Cade, my mind keeps going back to the guy Chloe mentioned. "Were her phone records pulled up already?"

"No, why?"

"If she was meeting up with someone, chances are there'd be some record of it on her phone. Whether a text or social media. Was her phone found in her things at the motel?"

Austin glances at her computer, clicks a few times, and shakes her head. "It's not listed on the evidence log. I haven't seen any mention of her phone."

Phones go missing a lot in cases like this, so it doesn't surprise me. But I wish we had it. "We need an officer to get her devices that are remaining from her parents' home today; maybe the phone is there. We've got to search them," I say.

"I'll have Blake handle it."

I sit at my borrowed desk, waiting for the computer to spring to life as I jiggle the mouse. Once it finally responds, I open the web browser and navigate to a search engine, then type Cade's name. Several social media profiles pop up. I click through each, finding his name and an avatar of a kid in football gear, smiling from beneath a helmet. Though I can see his name, picture, and list of friends, the rest of his profile is locked down, with no public information that tells me anything about him.

Next, I type in Melanie's name. Several profiles appear. Her main page is filled with messages of condolences, notes about missing Melanie, and collages of pictures of her from birth all the way up until her death.

Seeing it laid out like this makes me feel the loss more intensely. It's easy to compartmentalize a life you can't see. I swallow back the sadness climbing my throat and scroll further. She didn't make many public posts—most are inspirational or cute animals, plus a few photos of her on her ATV. Not the kind of information that's going to help me with this.

I click on her friends list, though I'm not sure what I'm looking for. She's not listed as in a relationship, and I'm not seeing any new friendships with men.

When the well of social media runs dry, I walk back to Austin's desk and lean against it, catching her in the middle of eating her breakfast. While everyone else has pictures or knickknacks on their desk, she's got nothing. This may as well be a borrowed desk. "So what can you tell me about this ex-boyfriend? I tried to google him, finding him on social media, but all his accounts were private."

"He's the son of one of the firefighters. His mom is a first-grade teacher. He's got a bit of golden-boy syndrome because he plays football." She wipes her mouth with the back of her hand, brushing away some of the egg that's stuck there. "Don't get me wrong—he's good—but he's not good enough for that attitude of his."

Some of the comments from the interviews come back to me. Cade felt like he and Melanie were meant to be together, that she was his soul mate. He wanted to get really serious really fast. It started to scare her off. Some girls want serious commitment in high school, but it seems that she wasn't one of them. Cade's intense reaction makes me wonder what was really going on. Why he latched on to her so hard.

"Has Cade ever been in trouble?" I ask.

Austin shakes her head. "No, nothing serious."

While Austin finishes her breakfast, I head back to my borrowed desk to prepare my thoughts for the questioning. At nine, I tug on my coat, grab my things, and signal to Austin that it's time to go. Light snowfall dusts the cars in the parking lot and freckles the dark pavement, making the ground look like a fallen night sky. The clouds above us are thick and gray, giving the impression it's much later in the day than it is. We climb into my car, and Austin navigates for me. We drive through the city toward Cade's house.

I roll to a stop in front of a cape cod that's a shade of blue normally reserved for nurseries. I climb out first, and Austin hangs back, as if steadying herself for what's ahead. She pops the door open and joins me on the shoveled walk that leads to the front door. I ring the doorbell and wait, with Austin standing behind me.

The door cracks open, revealing a man who looks like a carbon copy of the boy I saw in the football uniform online. He's built wide, with chestnut-brown hair, pale milky skin, and green eyes. His brows crinkle with interest when he looks from me to Austin. Thick lines deepen on either side of his thin lips as he appraises us.

"Can I help you?" he asks.

"Mr. Dowling, we're here to speak to Cade. I'm sure you heard about Melanie's death?" Austin asks, stepping forward. Her approach isn't as gentle as it should be, but Cade's father and Austin clearly know each other. And when understanding, not anger, ripples over his face, I know she's said the right thing.

He nods, a slight sadness hanging on his features. "I did. It's so sad. Come on in," he says, waving us inside.

The foyer is sparse, filled only with a coatrack overflowing with coats, scarves, and hats. To our left, stairs lead upward; to our right, the hall opens into a living room filled with sports memorabilia. The walls are painted a dark blue, and signed jerseys hang on nearly every wall.

"I'll get Cade," he says as he shows us to the living room.

Austin and I both take a seat on the overstuffed couch. After a few minutes, Cade joins us in the living room. His green eyes narrow on us as he perches on a recliner across from us, a bottle of water clutched in his hands. Mr. Dowling walks in after Cade, standing near the door with his arms crossed.

"Mr. Dowling, Cade is a minor, so you have every right to be here while he's speaking with us if you like. However, I think he may be more forthcoming if you are not present. Please let me know how you'd like to proceed," I say, speaking with confidence as I lay out the options.

For a moment, he looks between Austin, Cade, and me; then he disappears up the stairs. I listen to the path he takes before I begin to speak again.

"Thanks for coming down," I say.

His eyes flit from me to Austin, then back to me. "Does she need to be here?" Distaste hangs on his words, but I'm not sure why. Does he know Austin, or does he just not want to face this many cops at once?

"Yes, she does," I say.

"Shame."

I brush off the comment. He's got answers I need. "So, Cade, you dated Melanie?" Though I know he did, starting with the preliminaries makes people more comfortable in the questioning. If someone is comfortable enough, they'll let information slip they might otherwise keep to themselves.

He inclines his head but doesn't speak. Instead, he cracks his bottle of water open, then takes a long, slow sip.

"For how long?"

"According to her or me?" he asks, a challenge to his words. As if he's daring me to ask more.

It strikes me that he doesn't seem at all upset that Melanie is dead. Sure, we all process things differently, but this is jarring. He's cheerful, bordering on flippant. It could be that he's in shock still, that the death doesn't feel quite real to him yet. After some of the friends saying that Cade thought Melanie was his soul mate, I have to say I expected blubbering, *something*.

"Why don't you explain both timelines to me?"

"According to me, one year. Her, probably six months," he says simply.

"Why the discrepancy?"

He laces his fingers together and rests them on top of his knees. "She tried to break up with me, but I didn't accept her breakup."

I glance at Austin, and she cocks an eyebrow, as if, like me, she's not sure that she heard him correctly. "You didn't accept her breakup?" Austin chimes in.

He smirks, like it's the most normal thing in the world. "When you love someone, *really* love them, you can't let them go. You have to hold on." A smile slithers across his thin lips. But his eyes remain cold, distant. The look chills my blood.

"So instead of letting her go when she wanted to break up, you held on?" I ask, wanting to be sure that I'm following his logic properly.

"I did. I had to prove to her that I loved her."

"There are comments from her friends and family saying that you stalked her," Austin says.

Cade runs a hand through his hair, a low laugh slipping from him, and his eyes settle on Austin. "I wouldn't call it stalking. I was just making myself available. And I'm sure if they really thought it was stalking, they would have called the police." He smirks again, as if he's too clever for his own good.

"Did you try to visit her while she was in the hospital?" I ask, though I know that he tried several times, based on the information that we received from Nurse Jordan.

His eyes flash as they snap back to me. "Of course I did. I worried about her. I *love* her."

It strikes me that he's talking about Melanie as if she's still alive. I sit back on the couch, considering how I want to play this. If I come at him too hard, he may shut down. For now, I don't want him to think that he's a suspect. I need him to keep talking; I can't afford to have him clam up on me.

"Is there anyone that Melanie ever mentioned to you who she was having problems with? Anyone you noticed giving her trouble?" I ask.

Austin eyes me, but I don't turn to look at her. If she had experience here, she'd know what I'm up to. I just hope she keeps her mouth shut.

"No, not that I know of," he says. And that answer isn't something I'd expect a guilty person to give. If he did this, he'd look for an opportunity to point fingers at someone else. *Anyone* else.

"Who do you think hurt her?" I ask.

He sits back in his chair and crosses his arms. "If you ask me, I think she killed herself."

Killed herself by strapping herself to a bed with plastic taped over her head and then dumping cigarette ashes all over her own body? Now that'd be a magic act. But then again, no one outside of law enforcement knows those details. We've held that information back. Only the killer would know.

"And why do you think she would have killed herself?"

"She's been depressed since we broke up. She seemed distant from everything, everyone."

Maybe she was depressed and distant because her ex-boyfriend wouldn't stop stalking her, I want to snap, but I don't.

"I've heard from several others that you may have been fixated on Melanie, possibly dangerously so," I say carefully. I don't want to provoke him, but I need his take on it.

"Fixated?" He laughs, but it's humorless. His eyes are too sharp. "We are in *love*."

I have to wonder if this "love" of his became dangerous. Especially if he thought she was dating someone else.

"One of Melanie's friends mentioned that she might have been dating someone else. Do you know anything about that?" I ask, watching him carefully for his reaction. His eyes narrow as he looks from me to Austin.

"There's no way she ever would have," he says, waving his hands through the air as if the gesture can wipe the words still lingering there away.

"Cade, where were you on the evening of February twenty-first?" I ask.

"At home," he says simply.

"Can anyone confirm that?"

"My family, my computer. I was playing video games with some friends. I was online until around two in the morning."

I make a note to have someone at the station check into the alibi. I finish up my questioning with Cade. After we leave the Dowling residence, Austin and I update Sergeant Pelletier on the interview and have Zane confirm Cade's alibi, which ends up checking out. I spend the rest of the day noting what I found out from the interview with Cade and combing over other interviews before finally heading back to a hotel for the night.

As I slide under the comforter in the hotel bed, I shoot Noah a text to check in on him, but there's no response. I sit up. My gut aches as I look at the picture I have saved for his contact in my phone. I'm surprised to find that I miss him, that I wish he were lying in bed next to me. Though I want to leave him to his research, I find my finger hovering over the call button. It rings three times, and just as I'm about to give up, thinking it'll go to voice mail, he answers.

"Hey," he says, a little breathless, like he ran for the phone.

"What are you up to?" I ask, falling back onto the hotel bed.

"You caught me getting out of the shower," he says with a low laugh.

In my mind's eye, I can't help but imagine that: his muscled core glistening with droplets of water, a damp towel tied around his waist.

"How's everything there?" I ask.

"They're ninety percent certain this new body is connected to the others. Though she was dumped a mile from the previous victims, at the edge of the woods. They found a ligature still tied around her neck. All the other victims had been strangled with a similar rope. The date of death, anticipated age of the victim—they all seem to match."

"Oh, wow." When bodies like this pop up relating to cold cases, they can spark new interest, lead a fresh generation of detectives toward solving them. "Do they have any DNA yet on the vic?"

"They've run it through their internal database, no hits. The next step is to run it against familial DNA databases online. They're hoping they can find someone related to her."

"I hope they do," I say, and I mean it. Not just for her sake and the family but for Noah. I know how much this case means to him, how personal it all is. "How are you holding up?"

"Being back here is bringing up memories, but I feel like with this new evidence, maybe now they really stand a chance at solving it."

"Or maybe the story you're writing will add the attention it needs," I offer. As much as I love to hate journalists, I do have to admit that a lot of investigative reporting and interest in cold cases are what drives them to be solved. Otherwise they'd just get lost among the new cases that pile up every day. It's not that police departments don't want to solve them; it's about resources. If there's enough pressure from the outside, cities will give us more resources for these old cases.

He lets out a low laugh. "Maybe."

"You need to use your spotlight. Mention the story in some of your interviews. The brighter that spotlight gets, the bigger a shadow you'll cast. Use it to your advantage," I say. I know what he's capable of, and I know he can get attention on this if he wants.

"I'll consider that. How's your case coming?" he asks, obviously ready to change the subject.

I give him a Cliff's Notes version of events so far.

"I bet the boyfriend did it," he says quickly.

"He seems borderline sociopathic and obsessive, but the scene didn't scream intensity to me. I would think that given his obsessive nature with the victim, we would have seen a very different method of killing." The act was deliberate, sexual. But typically, in those scenarios where a lover is angry and intense feelings are involved, I'd expect to see a shooting, more physical trauma, or two parties being *punished*. This didn't say *punished* to me. It seemed like the killer wanted to humiliate and control the victim, which can line up with a scorned lover some-times, but I'm still not convinced that Melanie would have willingly gone to a hotel with Cade. The fact that the killer chose to suffocate the victim also shows they didn't want to kill her with their own hands. They didn't want to feel the life leave the body. It says *control but detach-ment*, wanting to punish but without seeing the victim and without being seen. "Maybe our killer is acting out punishing someone else through these victims. I've seen that before."

"I'd still keep an eye on him."

Noah and I spend a few more minutes catching up, until sleep drags me down. We say good night, and I drift off to sleep, wishing that he were next to me.

CHAPTER 6

It's been four days since Melanie's body was found, three days since Noah went to Tennessee. Though I've been through all the interviews several times, as well as her medical records, the most important evidence I've seen so far is piled in front of me. I've got the texts from Melanie's phone printed out, thanks to the Camden PD tech guy. He was able to comb through her devices after we got them from her parents. We were in luck—she had left her phone at home. However, that fact does strike me as odd. Did she forget it? Or was there another reason she left it behind?

I've sorted all the messages: the ones from known numbers, her everyday messages with friends and family, and then a few exchanges with two different burner phone numbers. The first number has messaged Melanie infrequently over the course of a few months, with messages that give a time and what look like coordinates. The messages go back months, but the most recent was February 18. At first, I thought they might have been messages from Cade, but his contact info is saved in her phone, and I can't see why he'd send her coordinates.

On my computer, I type in the coordinates, and they bring up several locations in Bald Mountain Preserve, Camden Hills State Park, and Meadow Mountain Preserve. Places all easily accessible. Is this her mystery man texting her places for rendezvous? Or is this something entirely different?

The texts from the other burner phone number lead me to believe she was seeing someone. Someone she must have been keeping secret, because there's no mention of dating anyone new in her texts to her friends. The messages start a week after she left the hospital the first time, for her wrist, around January 26.

203-555-2983: Sunday, January 26, 9:48 a.m.—When can I see you again

Melanie: Sunday, January 26, 9:49 a.m.—Who is this?

203-555-2983: Sunday, January 26, 9:49 a.m.—Do you give out your number that much?

Melanie: Sunday, January 26, 10:01 a.m.—Oh, lol, no

203-555-2983: Sunday, January 26, 10:04 a.m.—Tonight?

Melanie: Sunday, January 26, 10:05 a.m.—Can't maybe tomorrow

203-555-2983: Monday, January 27, 11:07 a.m.—Now?

Melanie: Monday, January 27, 11:38 a.m.—I'm at school can't

203-555-2983: Monday, January 27, 11:39 a.m.—After?

Melanie: Monday, January 27, 2:15 p.m.—You're persistent

203-555-2983: Monday, January 27, 2:16 p.m.—You're beautiful

Melanie: Monday, January 27, 2:20 p.m.—lol

Melanie: Monday, January 27, 2:21 p.m.—okay, tonight

The texts go on like that, but it seems they met up a couple of times. There's a mention of meeting up, then an outgoing call. But no confirmation via text. One of these messages occurred the night Melanie died, though there's no mention of the motel. There's no way to track whoever has this burner phone. And based on the research I've done, the area code of the phone is of no significance at all. Burner numbers from any area code can be assigned to any phone.

My phone vibrates on the table, and I scoop it up, hoping it's Noah. But my brows furrow when it's a Maine number on the screen, not his.

"Detective Calderwood," I say automatically.

"Hi, Detective, it's Brenden. You gave me your card."

It takes me a moment to place the name; then I remember the person I interviewed at the motel the first day, the son of the owners. "Yes, how can I help you?"

"One of our housekeepers just informed me that while cleaning up, they found . . ." He pauses, and my heart creeps into my throat, adrenaline burning my veins.

I straighten on the bed, hoping that they've found some evidence that could help with this case.

"We've discovered another woman's body," he says, his words shaky. I can imagine him trembling.

I swallow hard. At first, I think I've heard him wrong. But in the space of a breath, my instincts take over. "Keep everyone out of that room. I'll be there as soon as possible." By the time I hang up the phone, I've already got on one of my shoes and am scanning the room for my coat. As I pull on the other shoe, I call Sergeant Pelletier and inform him of the body. He offers to coordinate with CSI and the ME. My next call is to Austin. I tell her to meet me at that motel as soon as she can.

I climb into my Mustang, knowing time is of the essence. Not only do I need to get there to secure the scene, but I have to know what happened—if the circumstances are the same. Is this going to be like the last time? My mind races as I turn out of the hotel and floor it toward the Millay Inn. Snow sifts softly from the gray clouds above me, peppering the black asphalt. The trees huddling on the sides of the road are thick with snow and ice, their limbs so heavy they look frosted. When I climb out of my Mustang fifteen minutes later, the parking lot is nearly empty, and I can only hope that everyone has kept out of my crime scene.

My feet are unsteady on the ice as I head toward the office. A sharp wind blows, rustling the trees around the parking lot. As the frost-laden branches shift in the breeze, they crackle, icicles snapping and crumbling to the ground. Inside the office, I find Brenden sitting

61

wide eyed behind the desk. His hair puffs out awkwardly, like he's been tugging on it. He's paler than usual, making the dark bags beneath his eyes stand out.

"What room is the decedent in?" I ask.

"Room thirteen," he says, shoving a key across the desk toward me.

"Stay here. I need to ask you some questions after I secure the room."

He nods but says nothing. Back at my car, I grab tape, some plastic gloves, and markers. I'll need to cordon this place off as best as I can. It doesn't help that a cleaning crew already entered the room; they could have brought in trace evidence and contaminated part of the scene. My heart hammers as I head toward room 13. I snap the gloves on before I unlock the door.

The scene before me makes my heart lurch. A young woman's body is bound naked to the bed, her arms tied to the headboard, her legs to the footboard, limbs splayed wide. Over her head a plastic bag is taped with silver duct tape. Her pale flesh is feathered with gray across the torso, and I'm so distracted by the rest of the scene that it takes me a minute to process it—more ashes. This one has been left with the cigarettes, ashes, and debris on her again, though this time there aren't as many ashes. None of the victim's belongings are anywhere obvious in the room. But I step carefully toward the bed, checking to see if a purse was placed beneath it again. Sure enough, I find it. I look over her ID. The picture shows a young woman, age nineteen. Her coloring is startlingly similar to the first victim's.

I try to process it all. It's technically too early to rule this a serial killer, since by definition a serial killer requires at least three victims with a cooling-off period between them. However, based on how similar this homicide is to the last, it's screaming *serial* to me. If the killer is this careful and has such a fully developed MO, I'm sure our perp has done this before. The crunch of tires out in the parking lot catches my attention. I walk from the room and block off the scene with the tape.

Sergeant Pelletier is first to arrive. He climbs from his car, his square jaw set, his mouth a grim line.

"CSI will be here in an hour. They're leaving Augusta now," he says. He crosses his arms as he glances into the room but doesn't enter. Instead he keeps his distance, hovering just outside. "Looks the same."

"It's identical to the first scene, sir. This is methodical, laid out the same way. Body types of both victims are also similar," I say as I take it all in.

He glances into the room again.

"Can you handle this? I need to go speak to the motel manager again. I've got some questions for him."

"I'll make sure everything is secure," he says.

As I walk toward the motel office, Austin pulls up in her Fiat. She scans the lot, and then her eyes settle on me. She stalks over, her cheeks flushed from the cold. Her long hair is pulled back in a tight bun, and she's not wearing her beat cop uniform. Instead she's got on a button-up and jeans.

"What's the scene like?" she asks as she motions in the direction of Sergeant Pelletier.

"Same as the last one, identical. I'm thinking we might have a serial on our hands," I say, my voice low. There's not anyone out here to hear me, but I can't be too careful. As we approach the office, a van pulls into the lot. At first sight, I think the CSI team has arrived quickly, but then I see the logo on the side. The news.

"Fuck," I breathe. "How did they get here so fast?"

"Sergeant Pelletier had to use the radio to get people out here. I'm sure they've got scanners."

"Goddamn ambulance chasers," I say as I yank open the office door.

Brenden is exactly where I left him. It looks like he's been frozen with shock, his eyes still wide, staring. I step toward his desk. He's got a couple of chairs in the office. I grab one and motion for Austin to do the same.

"What can you tell me about the woman who was in room thirteen?" I ask.

He glances at his computer, clicks several times, then looks back to me. "Her name is Asha Weber."

"Did she check in alone?" I ask.

"No one else came in with her," he says.

"What time did she book the room?"

He looks at the screen to verify before speaking. "Nine fifty-seven p.m.," he says.

"So you didn't see anyone lingering outside like last time?" I ask. You would think after the first death here they'd pay more attention. Then again, I'm sure they didn't think it would happen again.

He shakes his head. "No. Since it happened, I've been watching everyone, trying to look out for anything suspicious. I thought she was alone." Tears well in his eyes, and I think he's seconds from breaking down. "I didn't want this to happen again. I'm sorry. I should have"—he throws his hands up—"I don't know, noticed something."

"This isn't your fault," Austin says. "It's okay. You didn't do this."

His shoulders shake as tears brim in his eyes. He avoids my gaze. I halt the questioning to allow him to compose himself. Once he's caught his breath and calmed down a bit, I continue.

"Did she seem to be in distress, scared? Did you get any sense from her at all?"

"She seemed happy. She smiled at me. I didn't think she was scared. She didn't give me any reason to believe there was anything wrong."

Again, this leads me to think that the victim knew her killer. Most women this age would not bring a complete stranger to a motel and be comfortable with it—especially so soon after another woman was killed at this very establishment. In a town this small, word has gotten around. Asha must have heard about what happened to Melanie. Though Melanie didn't tell anyone her plans, I hope that Asha spilled to someone where she was going and who she was meeting.

"Did she have a car here?" I ask. There are no cars in the parking lot, and there weren't when Melanie was found either.

"She did arrive in a car. I don't know if she was driving it. I saw it pass the office and park further down."

"Could you give me an idea of make, model, color?"

"It was dark. I couldn't really see. But I think it was a sedan, a larger-size sedan."

I note that down. There are lots of sedans around here, so that isn't going to help much.

"Is there anything else that you can think of that might be of help?" I ask.

He shakes his head. "No, I just—I need this to stop. I can't have people dying at my motel. Everyone will stop coming here."

We do need to start having an officer do nightly patrols around here. I don't want to stake out a cop full-time. We don't have the resources. But if I have someone drive by a few times a night, they can keep an eye out for sedans.

"If you see any more women that age check in here alone, you call me. Got it?" I say.

"I will."

As I head back out to my car, Austin beside me, I notice that the parking lot is now infested with news vans, as if they've multiplied since I've been inside. There's no way I can make it to my vehicle without passing them. Instead of avoiding it, I stride forward, head held high. When I'm halfway to my car, a man heads toward me and shoves a mic in my face. He's got a huge meaty brow that shadows his eyes, making them look like black pools. When he looks at me, I get the feeling he's trying to smile, but his face is too Botoxed to pull it off.

"Bruce Beckette with the Channel Seven news. What can you tell me about the scene? Is it true that the second body in less than a week was found here at the Millay Inn?"

"I cannot comment on an ongoing investigation," I say.

"So there is an investigation?"

The woman from the ME's office, Lillian Landry from the *Pen Bay Pilot*, strolls forward, standing level with Bruce. She's got on a pencil skirt and a black peacoat; the outfit is stylish but far too cold for this weather. Not a single hair is out of place in her sleek dark bob.

"Is Noah Washington helping you work this case?" she asks when I don't answer Bruce.

Austin steps in front of me, putting herself between me and the mic. She does it so swiftly it's like she's taking a bullet for me. "We can't tell you anything about what's going on here. But if you reach out to Kelsey Tucker, she's the press officer for Camden PD. We won't be taking any questions." Her voice is steady as she says this. To be honest, I'd thought Austin would shy away from attention from the media, but she's facing it head-on. I'm impressed.

Two other reporters approach us, mics in hand, but we're able to duck into my car before they get a chance to come within five feet of us.

———

Four hours later, after the body is picked up, I'm stationed at a spare desk in Camden, making a list of interviews I'll need to conduct for the new victim. I've had a preliminary conversation with the ME, and she's ruling this death asphyxia as well. This time there was no obvious trauma on the body outside of the wounds sustained during death. The phone on my desk rings, startling me. I grab the receiver, and Sergeant Pelletier barks in my ear, "I need you in my office."

I walk over, noting that he easily could have just called for me, since my desk is all of fifteen feet or so away. When I pop my head in, he's hunched over his keyboard, eyes focused on something I can't make out from here. I rap my knuckles gently on the door.

"Sir," I say.

He looks up at me, his dark eyes worn. Sergeant Pelletier has never struck me as the lively type, but right now, he seems even more muted than usual.

"The family has been notified, and they'd like to speak with you today to do the interview. Her father, James, wants to get it over with so they can move on with planning her funeral." There's an edge to his voice, like he doesn't think this is a good idea.

If he'll let me jump into this right away, I'm going to. "I'll grab Austin and head over there now."

"Just please go easy on them," he adds. "This is a small community. If we don't treat people right, it'll get out, and it'll come back on us."

Frustration needles me. I don't know why he'd think I wouldn't handle this with sensitivity. I may have a hard edge in the office, but I know how to talk to families, victims. But I don't say anything. Instead I just give him a tight-lipped smile and turn back to my desk. I grab my bag and coat and signal to Austin that we're going. The moment her eyes meet mine, she pops up from the desk and follows me out through the bull pen.

I shove the front door open, a blast of cold air greeting me as I step outside. The frigid wind howls as it whips around the building, and from farther down the street, the call of gulls fills the air. We climb into my Mustang, and I type the Webers' address into my GPS.

"Where are we headed?" Austin asks.

"We're going to interview the Webers. The dad wants to talk to us today," I explain.

She raises a brow as I back out of my parking space, gravel crackling beneath my tires. I turn onto Main Street, going left as I follow the directions of the robotic voice on my phone.

"They want to talk to us already?" she asks.

"Apparently so."

"Doesn't that seem . . . odd to you?"

"It does." It's not often that I have a family of a victim wanting to get their questioning over with or, in this circumstance, calling to rush it along. Most of the time I have to chase down family members, talk them into having the first interview. Usually they're angry, hysterical, shocked, and sometimes paralyzed—all things I expect. But no matter what their actual emotions are, they're usually far too busy coping with their grief to call us over.

I turn down a street lined with wood-frame houses, smoke spiraling from chimneys toward the gray sky. Towering oak trees stand in most of the yards, looming next to the large houses. I pull to a stop in front of a cape cod–style house that's daisy yellow with black trim. It reminds me of a bumblebee.

I climb out of the car and slam the door. Austin and I glance at the house before approaching. My whole body feels rigid with tension. Questions build in the back of my mind, and I can't get the idea that this is a serial case out of my thoughts. I need to figure out what connected these girls, and fast, before this killer finds another victim. I ring the doorbell and appraise the engraving on the door. Light floral relief is etched into the wood, which has been painted black. Floors creak behind the door before it opens. A woman leans against the edge of the door. Her eyes are raw, red, as they scrutinize me.

"Y'all the cops?" she says, glancing between us.

"Yes," I say and then introduce myself and my partner.

"I'm Yvette. James is in the kitchen." She sweeps her long brown hair over one shoulder before waving us inside. I climb up the steps into the house, realizing that I'm actually a few inches taller than Yvette, something that doesn't happen to me often. She's got on a long, billowy dress that shifts around her as she walks. She reminds me of a younger Stevie Nicks.

We follow her through a living room that's packed to the gills with antique wood furniture, a plush sofa and chairs, and a china cabinet filled with small glass figurines. The dining room isn't as well decorated as the living room. It's got a buffet on the wall alongside the simple rectangular table. A man with broad shoulders and a worn, haggard face is hunched in a chair close to the window. His shoulders are pulled so far forward it's like he's folding in on himself, as if the weight of his daughter's life is dragging him down.

"Thank you for meeting with us," I say. "I'm so sorry for your loss. I know that this is an incredibly difficult time, so if at any point you decide that you want to take a break or have us come back at another time, just let me know." I take Sergeant Pelletier's words into account while speaking. I know I don't have the best bedside manner usually, so I make an effort. This is his city, and I don't want to make any waves.

James looks up at me, his eyes sharp, an intensity behind them, as if those blue eyes are veiling a simmering rage that he's barely holding on to. I can't tell if the anger is aimed at me or if it's a side effect of everything he's been through in the past twelve hours.

"Please, take a seat," Yvette says, motioning toward the table. "Do you all want anything to drink, or are you okay with coffee?"

"I'm fine with coffee, thank you," I say.

"Me too," says Austin as she takes a seat. I slide into the chair next to her, a few feet from James.

He rests his hands atop the table, his fingers woven into one another, both hands clenched together tightly. I can't help but notice how muscular his arms are. His hands are huge, with thick fingers.

I take my notepad from my pocket. "Do you mind if we dive right in?" I ask, still on edge about the look that he's giving me.

"Let's get on with it," he says.

"How old was she?"

"Nineteen."

They're in a fragile state after the shock of losing their daughter, so I want to ease them into the questioning.

"When was the last time that you both saw Asha?" I ask.

"Last night, I saw her around seven when we had dinner. Then she went up to her room. I thought she was going to do her schoolwork and then go to bed like she normally does," James says.

Yvette finally sits next to us, placing cups of coffee in front of Austin and me before taking up her own cup of tea. Steam slowly spirals from her mug, curling in the air in front of her. "I saw her around nine. She had gone into the bathroom while I was going down to get something to drink. I passed her in the hall."

"Did anything about her appearance stick out at you? Did she look like she was ready to go out?" I ask.

She shakes her head. "No, she was in her pajamas. She didn't have any makeup on. Nothing that I would have expected to mean that she was going out. She knew she shouldn't be going out anyway." She sniffles and stares down at her hands.

"Why exactly shouldn't she have been going out?"

"She just got out of the hospital." Her eyes are wide as she says this, as if we should have known.

Before I can ask or say anything else, James chimes in. "Asha had her tonsils out about six weeks ago. Then she had some complications and was in the hospital for a week. She got out about a week and a half ago. But she was told that she needed to be careful about exposure to germs because her immune system is"—he stops and clears his throat—"I mean, *was* still on the weaker side."

She was in the hospital as well? That's the strongest lead we have so far on both of these women.

"Do you remember what doctor was treating her?"

"Doctor Munroe, I think," Yvette says, the lines around her mouth deepening with her concentration.

An electric spark crackles up my spine. Both women saw Dr. Munroe? That's something I plan to look into. But I need to dig deeper to see if there are any other patterns or if this doctor is it.

"Was Asha dating anyone?" I ask.

Both James and Yvette say no at the same time.

"Did she ever sneak out before that you're aware of?" I ask.

Neither parent has a quick answer this time. Finally, Asha's father speaks as he rubs at the back of his neck. "She was never caught sneaking out, but yes, we suspected it before," James says.

"Why's that?" I ask.

"There were times that we heard something strange outside the house, and we thought that it might have been her sneaking back in. But we never caught her in the act," Yvette explains before she takes a slow sip of her tea. Steam rises from the cup when she sets it back down.

We finish up with Asha's parents, going over the school she attended, her extracurricular activities, and the names of her friends and a couple of girls she had trouble with at the coffee shop she worked at. We gather her cell phone and her other devices and then head out of the home. Asha's parents inform me that her best friend lives a few houses down. Before heading to the hospital, I want to speak to this friend.

We step out of the residence, and I survey the street until my eyes settle on the house Asha's parents described. Tessa Parsons lives three houses down in a dutch colonial. The siding is a salmon color, making the teal shutters stand out. The colors are bold, eccentric, which really makes me wonder about the occupants.

Metalwork flowers are stuck among the snow-covered flower beds. And I'm not sure if the Parsons family is being optimistic about the upcoming spring or if they've left them out all winter. I climb the front steps and press the doorbell. It takes a few minutes for anyone to answer. The door cracks open, and a woman in her forties with a wide face and large brown eyes appraises me, then Austin.

"Is everything okay?" she stammers.

"I was hoping we could speak with your daughter, Tessa. Is she home?"

The woman cocks her head, her shoulder-length blonde hair swishing. "What did Tessa do?"

"Nothing, ma'am. I'm not sure if you've heard, but her friend Asha passed away," I say as delicately as I can.

Her hand goes to her throat, her long bony fingers lingering there as her chestnut eyes take in my face. Her mouth drops open, and she stands there, her mouth gaping like a fish. Silence thickens around us before she finally says, "Oh my God. No, no one told us." She stays silent, her eyes unfocused, before finally she seems to snap back to reality. She ushers us inside. "What happened to her?"

We follow her through the foyer and into the living room. It's a mess. Laundry is in piles, strewed all over the furniture. We caught her in the middle of folding it. She clears away piles on the couch and indicates for us both to take a seat.

"We're still investigating what happened to Asha, and we were hoping your daughter could help with some of the questions we have."

"Could she be in trouble?" she asks, glancing toward the ceiling, where I imagine Tessa's room is.

Why does she keep thinking that Tessa is in trouble? I feel like if Tessa had been in trouble with the police before, Austin would have mentioned it before we arrived.

"No, ma'am, we just want to ask her some questions about Asha," Austin says from beside me, the first words she's spoken.

"I'll grab her."

When she disappears, Austin and I share a look. Low voices filter down from upstairs, but they're too quiet to make out what's being said. A few minutes later, Tessa strolls into the room, and I get an inkling of why her mother thinks that she's trouble. Tessa's got short black hair, accompanied with black lipstick, thick eyeliner, and an assortment of facial piercings. She's got on a Ramones T-shirt, the same shirt I've seen Noah wear on a few occasions. Tessa stands across from the couch, eyeing Austin and me with her arms crossed.

"Tessa, would you like to take a seat? I was hoping we could talk to you for a few minutes."

I glance to her mother, unsure whether she told Tessa what happened to her friend. But the woman gives me a little shake of her head. She slips into the kitchen, far enough that her daughter won't see her, but I'm sure she'll be lingering close enough to hear our conversation.

"Tess, my name is Tess."

"Sorry, Tess," I say, hoping we can get past her teenage angst for just a few minutes so I can find out more about Asha.

"Why are you here?" she asks, looking at Austin.

"We're here to talk to you about Asha. I don't know if you heard, but she passed away last night. I'm very sorry."

For a moment, she's completely silent. Her jaw is slack, as if she's grasping for words but they're escaping her. The shock in her eyes is palpable, and in a flash, it's replaced with pleading.

"She can't be," she says, and her jaw twitches, her eyes going glassy.

"I'm sorry, but she is." This is the part I wish I could skip. Breaking the news to someone that a person not only died but was murdered— it's enough to break my own heart sometimes. Because I know exactly how this feels. I know what it is to have a person ripped away from your life. There are words that can alter the paths of our lives, and I am well aware that every syllable I utter now could bring devastation. I want to give these people what it took me twenty years to get: closure.

"What happened?" Her voice cracks, and she clenches her fists at her sides. A single tear rolls down her cheek, and an echo of pain whispers through me—a memory of my own loss. Red creeps up her neck, turning her pale face splotchy.

"That's what we were hoping you could help us find out."

She's silent for so long I have to wonder if she's going to help. But then something on her face shifts. She stiffens, as if all the grief is leaching out of her, replaced with determination. "What do you want to know?"

"Did Asha tell you where she was headed last night?"

She shakes her head and crosses her arms. "No, where did she go?"

"It appears she met someone at the Millay Inn. Would you say that's out of character for her?"

Her eyes bulge, not hiding an ounce of her surprise. "Um, yeah. As far as I know, she's never been there. Why would she even go there?"

"That's what we're trying to figure out." I make note of her answer. "How long have you two been friends?"

"Since fifth grade. And we've dated on and off for a couple years."

I arch an eyebrow at that. Asha's parents didn't say anything to that effect. Did they not know?

"I'm gay. She's bi," she explains. "Right now, we've been *off* for six months. She's still my best friend, though." Her face crumples, and then she chokes out, "Was."

I give her a minute to compose herself, but Austin clears her throat before I can jump back in. "To your knowledge, was she seeing anyone else? Someone she might have been inclined to meet at that motel?" Austin asks, putting it as delicately as possible.

"If she was, she didn't tell me about it." Tessa sniffles.

"Would she normally tell you something like that?" Austin asks.

"She's never kept it from me before. We had no secrets. There was no jealousy if we weren't together. I wasn't going to trap her in a relationship with me if she wanted to see other people." Her chin lifts with the words, a confidence held in them that is far beyond her years.

"Did you know anything about Asha sneaking out of the house at night?"

"Yeah, she snuck out sometimes."

"And where would she go?"

"Usually over here. Sometimes we'd hit a concert or go smoke pot."

I'm surprised she's so forthcoming. Most teens wouldn't readily give this kind of information—not to the cops, anyway.

"Would it be unusual for her to sneak out and not take you or tell you?"

Her eyes dart to the window, and I get the impression she's going to lie or withhold something from me. It's the first time she's really looked away since she came down.

"I'm not sure. Maybe."

"Is there anything else you can think of that might be of help to us?"

She opens her mouth like she's going to say something, then clamps it shut before shaking her head. There's a gleam in her eyes, like there's more waiting to pour out of her. But something is holding her back. Is it loyalty to her friend? Or is she afraid that her mother might hear?

I slip her my card, hoping that if her mother isn't listening, she'll change her mind about bottling up whatever she's withholding. "If you think of anything else, please call me. Anything you tell me will be between us."

"I will," she says before we say our goodbyes.

After speaking to Tess, the only similarities I've been able to find between the two victims are their ages, their appearances, and the fact that they were both in the hospital. As we climb back into my Mustang, I call Sergeant Pelletier and give him an update before our next stop— Pen Bay Medical Center.

On the way, Austin and I talk through the details on the case we have so far, the similarities. Both victims died at the same motel within two weeks of being released from the hospital; both had the same doctor. That's a pretty clear sign to me what direction we should be heading. We pass through Camden proper, streets lined with colonial, Victorian, and cape cod–style homes. After a few miles, the pine trees give way to the medical center.

We reach the front desk, and I flash my badge and wait for the nurse to get David for me after I briefly tell her the reason for my visit. If this shit keeps up, it seems David and I are going to get real cozy. The idea makes my stomach turn. I'm sure he'd love that.

The loud clicking of stilettos on tile floor draws my attention. A tall, slender woman in a flowy blouse and a pencil skirt glides toward me on shoes I couldn't even fathom walking in. She looks familiar with her sleek brown hair and slight features. I scrutinize her, trying to discern where I know her from, but it doesn't come to me.

She offers me a thin smile as she approaches. "Detective Calderwood?"

I take a step toward her and nod.

"I'm Vera McConnel, the CEO of the hospital. Do you mind if we go have a chat in my office?" she asks, and my brows furrow. She doesn't offer her hand, and I take note of that. I'm not welcome here, not wanted. Her words tell me it's not so much a question, and my assumption is if I don't go with her, I won't be speaking with David anytime soon.

We weave through the stark white halls. It's quiet on this side of the building, only the sound of our shoes echoing after us. Finally, we reach Vera's austere office. The walls are institution gray, along with the desk. The only other color in the room is her black office chair and monitors. Most offices we passed were pretty well decorated, touches of personality, family, *something*. This room is as sterile as a surgical gallery. There isn't a single picture or knickknack. It rubs me the wrong way. A separation between work and personal life is one thing; this is another.

"Mrs. McConnel," I say as we follow her into the office. I take a seat, and Austin sits next to me. "We're investigating a death; the decedent was a patient at this hospital. I'm sure you heard that another previous patient, Melanie Thomlinson, was found dead a few days ago."

She grimaces, and her eyes darken. "Yeah, my *husband*, Aidan, the director of the hospital, told me about it." She puts an emphasis on the word *husband*, like it's a word she's not happy with. But I can't tell if it's just having a husband that bothers her or if it's the one she's got.

"How long have you been CEO here?" I ask, glancing again at the unadorned office.

"Three years, right after we moved here from Georgia," she explains. "My husband and I grew up there." She puts the same strange emphasis on the word *husband*.

I decide it's probably best to avoid asking more questions that might lead her to talk about her husband. "Why did you want to speak to me?" I ask, since she's not coming out with it.

"I want to make sure that the information about both of these girls being patients here stays out of the media. I don't need that kind of attention on my facility," she says as she leans back in the office chair, her hands folded on top of the desk.

Austin and I glance at each other. I'm so taken aback by what she's said that I need a long moment to process it.

"I want to be sure that I understand correctly—your concern isn't for your patients but keeping your facility out of the media in connection with these homicides?"

"I am concerned about our *current* patients. What happens to patients after they leave this facility, that's not my problem. It's tragic, really." She waves a hand through the air as if dismissing the notion. Her words don't hold even an ounce of feeling. "But it's not the fault of anyone here that they died. I can't have that negatively impact our brand."

Frustration ripples through me, and my fingernails cut half moons into my palms as I fight the desire to strangle her. How can she be so callous? "I can't promise that the connection between them and the hospital will stay out of the media. There were reporters all over the motel; someone could have followed us here. I wouldn't put it past them," I say, then straighten up in my seat. "Now can we discuss the patients?"

She inclines her head, as if graciously giving me leeway to continue.

"What can you tell me about Asha Weber?" I ask. If she's going to haul me into her office, she's going to answer some questions.

Her eyes tighten, and she stiffens in her chair. After a few moments, she turns her attention to her computer and begins to type. I wait for her to scroll and click several times, but as she remains silent, her mouth a thin line, my patience begins to run short.

When she doesn't speak, I ask, "How long was she here?" I assume maybe if I'm more specific in my questioning, I'll get an answer.

Her eyes narrow on the screen. "She was here a little over a week. I'm not sure what she was being treated for," she says, not bothering to look up any of the details for me. "But the last doctor she saw was Doctor Munroe."

That confirms it. Dr. Munroe really did see both patients before their deaths, then. "I'd like to speak to Dr. Munroe today," I say, pulling out my notepad to scribble down the very little I have so far.

"I don't think that's a good idea," she says, giving me an icy look.

I raise a brow at that. "You don't think it's a good idea for me to ask the doctor questions about the second patient who has died after leaving this hospital in under a week?" Is she aware of details and trying to cover them up?

She shifts in her seat. "No, I don't."

I open my mouth to argue that point. But she's made her stance pretty clear. If she won't allow me to see Dr. Munroe, I'll move on to other questioning.

"Have all of your staff had background checks performed?"

She crosses her arms. "That'd be a question for the HR department. But I expect no, not *all*."

"As long as patients are dying after leaving this hospital, that's where your concern should be," I say, my voice firm, frustration seeping into every word. How she could care about her bottom line and not the people being murdered outside is beyond me.

Vera leans back in her chair and swivels left to right, her elbows propped on the armrests, her fingers steepled against one another over her lap. "From where I'm sitting, it doesn't look to me like you have a real reason to be looking inside this hospital. Law enforcement traipsing all over this facility, drawing media attention that we don't need—it all reflects poorly on us. These two girls both being patients at this hospital means less than nothing. Do you have any idea how many patients walk through our doors that are not murdered? It's the only piece of evidence you have, so you're grasping at straws, aren't you?"

I pinch the bridge of my nose as frustration roars inside me. She can't be serious. I've heard that CEOs are ruthless, but this is something else.

"You realize this could be construed as obstruction of justice, correct?"

She lets out a low, humorless laugh. "Do I need to get the hospital lawyer in here?" Her hand twitches toward the phone, and I know my bluff isn't going to work. I'd need actual evidence of some wrongdoing to pursue obstruction charges against her. At best, she's being a nuisance; at worst, I could seek a court order to force her to comply with the investigation. Doing so would bring plenty of unwanted attention to this hospital—though it would also cost me time. Time I don't have. Before I threaten her with that course of action, I want to try again.

"It may not be a coincidence that those victims were patients at this hospital. You could have a budding serial killer in this building. I'm not going to drop this investigation because it might look bad for your hospital. I need to talk to the nurses that treated her, and then Dr. Munroe. Either you can point me in the right direction, or I may be forced to inform the media that patients here are dying and the hospital is not cooperating with the investigation."

Her face hardens into a mask. "You wouldn't."

"Try me." The words roll out of me, a dare.

She glares at me, assessing. Austin shifts next to me, crossing her legs and bracing herself. But just as I'm starting to think Vera won't take the bait, she grabs her phone and starts to dial.

CHAPTER 7

Though we know that Dr. Munroe saw both victims right before their deaths, it's not him that I have my sights on yet. No, I want to talk to the nurses who work with him. Despite her reluctance to help, Vera's given up her office and started to track down witnesses for me. I've spoken to three nurses, none of whom know or saw anything useful. Though they all seemed nervous to answer my questions, all they've told me is that Dr. Munroe can be a little too flirty with some patients. But they wouldn't expand on this for me and then stated that they have no real concerns. I get the distinct impression they're not telling me everything. The main thing that stands out to me is that no one can remember seeing Dr. Munroe during the windows we believe both victims were killed in. Now that I've questioned the junior nurses, Vera's sending up Nurse Jordan, since she worked with Dr. Munroe a few nights ago.

Nurse Jordan peeks her head in, her cropped black hair slightly wavy today. She offers me a tight smile that doesn't show any of her teeth behind her bright-red lips. While I question this nurse, I send Austin to try to track down David. We'll need the security footage for Asha's stay. Though we've gone through all the footage from Melanie's hospitalization, we didn't find anything from near her room indicating who might have stolen her chart or if anyone managed to visit her that we weren't aware of.

"Nurse Jordan, thank you for meeting with me again," I say.

"Of course," she says as she glances around the room.

"Take a seat?" I motion to the chair beside me that Vera brought in for us. She sits down but doesn't speak, her eyes flashing between me and Austin, as if she's not sure who to address.

"This is my partner, Officer Harleson," I say, hoping to ease the cloud of tension that's formed in the room.

Her body is so stiff in the chair that she looks incredibly uncomfortable. Her eyes crawl over the room, as if it's the first time she's been in here.

"Is it all right if I ask you a few questions about Dr. Munroe and two patients who were treated here?"

"Yeah, I'll answer as best as I can," she says, trying to sweep a strand of hair behind her ear, but it's too short for that.

"What can you tell me about Asha Weber?" I ask as I pull my notepad from my back pocket.

"She came in a little less than two weeks ago for complications from a tonsillectomy. She was here about a week."

"In your opinion, did she need to stay a week?" The nurses have had differing opinions so far, but since she's a more senior nurse, I'm interested in her view. I would assume that a weeklong stay would be for something more serious. Especially since I know insurance companies try to force patients out as quickly as possible.

"She would have been fine to leave after a few days," she says as she shakes her head. "But no, Dr. Munroe just had to keep her for more observation." Annoyance is thick on her words. She drags out the word *observation* for emphasis.

"Can you tell me more about that? Does he do that often?" I would think it'd be noticed by management if he was routinely having patients stay longer than needed. I can't imagine the headaches that would cause both from customer complaints and for billing. Staying at a hospital for a few extra days can cost thousands.

"Anytime he's got a cute little patient like that, he has them stay longer so he can flirt with them. He's always showing those girls way too much attention and practically ignoring all his other patients." She crosses her legs and glances at the floor like she has more to say but is afraid to come out with it.

That alarms me, especially since it seems these victims have gone with their killer willingly. I could see them trusting a doctor. "Have you ever seen him be inappropriate with these patients?" I ask.

"Like touching them?" She shrugs. "I think he touches them more than he needs to. But he says he needs to, that it's part of his job. He gives them *exams*"—she puts heavy emphasis on the word—"that they don't need."

"Could you be more specific?"

"Pelvic exams for conditions that should never require such a thing. He'd always come up with some excuse or another as to why it was necessary."

"So you've brought it up, then?"

She nods. "Brought it up with him and reported it. I told HR that I had concerns. Nothing was done. They don't take it seriously. There are so few doctors willing to work in hospitals like this; they'll never do anything about it."

"Is there anything else? I just want to be sure I have a complete picture that might keep something like this from happening again," I press. She's got more to tell me; I know it. "How old, typically, are these patients?"

"The ones he gives the exams, what I've seen anyway, they're all over eighteen," she clarifies.

I jot down a few more notes. "Have any of these patients ever made a complaint about his advances or the unneeded exams?"

"To me? No. Formal complaints, not that I'm aware of. But I wouldn't be involved in that," she says, uncrossing her legs before recrossing them.

"Did he ever make any advances toward you or any of the other nurses that you know of?"

She scoffs. "No. The other nurses, I've heard rumors, but I didn't know for sure. But he's never tried anything like that with me."

"Is there anything else you think would be helpful?"

"Just ask him about where he was when these girls disappeared. He has a nasty habit of disappearing."

"I'll be sure to do that."

After the nurse leaves, I speak to two others, but only one hints at the flirtation by Dr. Munroe. I'll need to speak to him again to see what I can get out of him. I grab a cup of coffee and ask Vera to track down Dr. Munroe for me. It's already getting so late in the day; I'm concerned that he may have taken off. I glance toward the window. The sun glows on the horizon, bathing the snowy landscape in orange. The tips of the evergreen trees burn red, like bloody spearheads.

I sip my coffee back inside the sterile office, and Vera pops her head in. "Dr. Munroe is heading up here. But I've got to go home. Take as long as you need, though. We need to get this wrapped up." She makes a little swirling motion with her hand, as if I wouldn't know what she meant.

"Thanks," I say. Her words ring hollow. Because I know she doesn't mean she wants this wrapped up for the sake of the patients. No, she wants this wrapped up for the sake of business. If people find out that patients at the medical center are dying suspiciously, that'll add a fog of fear around here that won't be lifted for decades.

"Detective Calderwood, good to see you again," Dr. Munroe says as he strides into the office. He's got a wide grin, displaying the dimples on either side of his mouth. His blue eyes match the scrubs he's got on.

That grin, his demeanor, could charm a cobra, but to me, it screams Bundy.

"Please, take a seat." I motion toward the chair across from me.

He chuckles. "I'm having flashbacks of being called into the principal's office," he says as he sits down.

"Get into trouble a lot as a kid?" I ask, and his smile falters almost imperceptibly, but it's back to full strength a beat later, like a flickering light bulb.

"Oh, you know," he says, shrugging off the question entirely.

I do know. I got into plenty of trouble after Rachel died. But something tells me my trouble and his are worlds apart.

"So I'm not sure if you heard—" I start.

"Yeah, it's awful," he says, interrupting me. But that's just fine. I'm more than happy to give him enough rope to hang himself. "I can't believe another poor girl died."

I sit silent, allowing him to continue. I want him to lay it all out for me. He goes on for a few minutes about how lovely they both were, special girls who didn't deserve anything like this. Then his eyes meet mine again.

"What do you think happened to them?" he asks, and I know the tactic. He's trying to shift the power in the room. If he's asking questions, he's in control.

"What do you mean?" I ask. I want him to be far more specific. I want to know what he knows.

"Have you figured out how they died?"

My blood turns to ice at the question. Because that's not a question someone would typically ask.

"What makes you think we don't know the cause of death?" He's not going to shift the power in this room, and he's not going to get information from me.

He's silent for a long moment, too long. "I just figured we would have heard something by now if you knew."

Wrong answer. This whole conversation with Dr. Munroe has rubbed me the wrong way. There's something in his eyes. A knowing.

"What can you tell me about Asha's treatment?"

He clears his throat and rests his right elbow on the armrest, then leans his whole body to that side as he crosses his legs. "Asha had a routine complication after a tonsillectomy. If you eat certain foods too soon after the procedure, it can make the back of the throat hemorrhage. That's what happened in her case. She presented in the ER with severe bleeding. We cauterized the wound, then held her for observation to ensure the wound didn't reopen. There were also concerns she was developing an infection. She had elevated white blood cell levels."

I glance at my notebook. "And you kept her for several days to observe her after the procedure, even though it was a routine complication?"

He nods.

"So that would be the typical recommended stay for most patients, then?"

"Every patient is different." He shifts in his seat, like this line of questioning is making him uncomfortable. "But for her, it made sense."

"And why is that?" Austin asks. Dr. Munroe looks at her, his face contorting, as if he hadn't realized she was there.

"She was afraid the wound would start bleeding again. She wanted to stay until she was sure it wouldn't reopen."

"And did you give her a pelvic exam while she was in your care?" Austin asks.

His carefully plastered-on smile cracks, and something dangerous plays behind his eyes. But as soon as I notice it, it's gone, and he's pulled the mask back on. "Of course not. There'd be no reason for that." He glances toward the door. "Look, I really need to get back."

"Just a couple more questions," I say, hoping that he won't leave quite yet. "Where were you between nine p.m. and eleven p.m. yesterday evening?" I ask.

His eyes go wide, and a low laugh slips out of him. There's a sharp edge to it. "Do you think I did this? Really?"

"Please just answer the question, Dr. Munroe."

"I was on rounds," he says flippantly and glances toward the door, like he's considering leaving again.

"And who can corroborate your whereabouts?" I ask.

"All the nurses on staff." He crosses his arms. The charisma has vanished as if sucked clean out of him.

"None of them saw you from nine p.m. to eleven p.m.," I say. I asked all of them. And Nurse Jordan specifically pointed out that Dr. Munroe has a habit of disappearing.

His jaw twitches. "I was napping in the staff room. It's a long shift."

"And the records will show that your badge was swiped to enter and exit the room?"

"I forgot my key card. A nurse let me in."

I clear my throat and straighten in my seat. "Okay, and who was that?"

His eyes narrow. I guess he hadn't thought that far ahead. "It doesn't matter where I was. It's none of your business."

"What kind of car do you drive?" I ask, glancing between him and my notes.

"Car?" he asks. He tilts his head slightly, the way you'd expect a confused dog to react.

"Yes, your car. What make and model is it?"

"A 2019 Honda Accord," he says, rubbing the back of his neck.

"What color?"

"Black."

Though that's a very common car, it matches the type Brenden thought he saw at the motel when Asha arrived. We know both girls rode with someone, as no cars were left at the motel. I lean forward in my chair a little. "Would you be willing to provide your DNA to rule yourself out?" This is the final nail in the coffin. This is what normally flips them.

He lets out a low sigh, but defeat on his face tells me that he knows he's got no other options. "Fine, whatever."

"They'll need you to stop by the station tomorrow by ten a.m. to provide a sample; otherwise I'll get a court order," I say. The court order is a bluff, for now.

"Fine. Can I go?" He pushes off the chair and strides out of the room before I say another word.

And I can't help but smile, because I know exactly where this is going.

Austin and I leave the hospital, both feeling like Dr. Munroe is our best lead on the case so far. If I can tie him to the motel, we might be able to get a warrant to search his place or vehicle. Especially since his car matches the one that Brenden saw at the scene.

While we were tucked away in the hospital questioning the staff, night seeped around us, and a fresh layer of snow fell. As we walk to my car, it's hard to believe that the bulk of the day has slipped past us. But I suppose that's how investigations like this go: time slips through your fingers like water when it really counts. We climb into my car, and the crisp air clouds in front of us as I start the engine.

When we reach Camden PD, I climb out of the car with Asha's devices in hand. I walk into the building, Austin trailing behind me. I throw open the front door, stroll through the bull pen, and turn right down the hall that leads to the office of Camden PD's tech guy, Kenneth. I drop off the tech to him, getting a promise that tomorrow we'll have a log of calls and texts. Back at my desk, I dig into my files, hoping that answers are on the horizon.

CHAPTER 8

Though I got myself a nonsmoking room, the yellowed walls and the stale scent of smoke tell me this place likely doesn't enforce the rules. That's what you get for fifty dollars a night, I suppose. I lean back on the bed, going over my notes for the twelfth time. Thankfully, I asked the woman at the front desk for a room away from the other patrons. It's not that I plan on making any noise, but hotel walls are paper thin. I've got to be careful with some of the calls I have to take.

I text Noah to see how he is before I hit the sack for the night. He's been quiet all day—since he started working this new story, really—which is unlike him. I want to deny that it's putting me on edge. I've never been one to be uneasy about a guy growing distant, but this silence stretching between us is making me wonder if he's okay—if we're okay. But I try to ignore it. He's probably just busy with his new assignment.

The sound of footsteps in the hall distracts me from my thoughts, and I pray that no one has booked one of the rooms beside mine. But when the footsteps stop directly outside my door, I sit up in bed and listen. Boards in the hall groan as someone shifts their weight on them. Time seems to slow as I wait to see if they'll move on. When they don't after a couple of minutes, I slip from bed. I creep closer to the door, listening. Low voices filter through. I debate what to do—pretend I'm not here or try to get them to move on? I decide to go for the latter.

"Can I help you?" I call through the door. The voices die, and somehow, this puts me more on edge. My pulse kicks up a notch as I slide closer, listening. It could be a simple mistake; that'd be the logical explanation.

When I'm inches from the door, I can hear whispers on the other side, though they're too hushed to decipher. I glance back at the night-stand toward my gun and decide to grab it. There's a chance I'm being paranoid, but I'd rather be prepared and paranoid than dead. The cold metal presses into my skin, but the weight of the weapon in my hand does little to bring relief. Outside the door, the floor creaks again, sending my stomach into my throat.

I edge closer, but when I get to the peephole, there's no one there. I open the door, glancing down the hall, left to right. But there's no indication that anyone has been there at all. I shut the door and lock it, but it takes a long time for relief to come. It was probably someone just passing through to get to their room. This is a small, quiet town, and it's not like anyone would try to seek me out here.

Once the adrenaline in my blood fades, I call Noah. In the quiet moments like this, my thoughts drift to him. It's not just that I've barely heard from him in days. I need to talk to him. Maybe it'll help me realize I'm being stupid. The phone rings four times, and I nearly hang up, expecting it to go to voice mail.

"Hey," he says finally, his voice breathy, like he ran to the phone again.

"I was afraid I wasn't going to reach you," I say, allowing the unguarded truth to roll out in a way I wouldn't with anyone else.

"Were you now?" The way he says it, I can practically see the cocky smirk on his face.

I ignore his comment. "How'd your day go? Getting settled in for the story?" I ask. I don't pry into his assignments, not even the one about my sister, not until well after we wrapped up the investigation, anyway.

"In a way. This one is going to take some patience . . ." His words trail off.

"Any idea how long you'll be there?"

"I don't know yet." He sighs. "This is something I've always wanted to do. I just don't know if I can do it. It's a bit close to home. You know?" There's an edge to his voice that makes me wish I could wrap my arms around him.

"Believe me—I know," I say, a heavy breath escaping with my words. "Take your time, though. Really. Give this all of you that it takes. I'll be here if you need me."

"Thanks. You're the best. You know that, right?"

"I try." I chuckle. "How are things going back there? How is it seeing your family?" Though I don't know much about Noah's family other than the fact that they don't get along, I'm sure he can't avoid them his entire trip. I've always wanted to know more about them, but every time I've asked, he's skirted the subject, not wanting to give me details about them or his past.

"I talked my brother into giving me the cold case files. He's technically not supposed to, but they clearly need the help on this. Thankfully, he's the only family I've seen so far. I've sworn him to secrecy that I'm even back here," he says, his voice filtering in and out with static on the line.

"Did you find anything in the files?"

"Six women other than Tina, Josh's mom, were killed. They were all strangled and dumped in the city within a six-block radius of one another. They think that all these women were sex workers, because of the location. But I know there's no way that Tina was involved in that. She had a good job."

"Ligature or manual strangulation?" I ask as my mind sifts through the details.

"Ligature," he says. "That's all I know so far. How's your case coming?"

"The strongest lead is the hospital. Both victims were there within two weeks of their deaths," I say as I pick at a stray thread on the comforter.

"Any suspects in the hospital?" he asks before I can add more.

"There's a doctor there who saw both victims, and he's being cagey about his alibi," I say, before filling him in on the rest of the questioning and then the strange text messages I found on Melanie's phone.

"Have you checked out the coordinates yet?"

"I haven't been able to. Tomorrow, though, that's what I'm going to do first thing."

"Did you at least look them up?" he asks, fabric rustling in the background, and I imagine him shifting on top of the bed in his hotel room.

I scoff at his question. "Of course I did, Noah." Annoyance bleeds into my voice. Does he think I'm an amateur?

"And?" Excitement lifts his words.

I rattle off each location, explaining to him what I found.

"Did the second victim have the same texts?"

"We don't know yet; I'll find out tomorrow. Until then, all I can do is guess at it. But if those coordinates are on both phones, that's a substantial lead. Either way, I'm scoping out the locations."

Noah yawns, and I can't help that it makes me do the same.

"Go get some sleep," I say.

"If you insist. Call me tomorrow if you find out anything." He pauses for a second. "Actually, call me even if you don't find out anything."

"I will," I promise.

"Good night," he says.

I parrot his words, though I consider saying more. I bite it back, because it's too soon for *I love yous*.

I hang up the phone. After it's on the charger, I slip into bed, and within seconds of my head hitting the pillow, I'm asleep.

———

A thunderous crack wakes me. My body moves on its own as I bolt awake, diving behind the side of the bed farthest from the door. The remnants of sleep cling to my mind, muddying my thoughts. It takes me several beats to remember where I am. *The hotel.* My heart pounds, and adrenaline burns in my blood. I try to sort out what's happening: the deafening crack, heavy footfalls on the floor, muffled voices. I reach automatically for the nightstand, trying to feel for my gun in the darkness.

Footsteps grow closer, and the bed creaks as a heavy weight climbs on top of it. I have to get out of here, to move. But my limbs are so weighted they may as well be chiseled from granite. Large hands wrap around my biceps, lifting me from the floor. The smell of sweat and cigarette smoke makes my nostrils flare. In the darkness, the wide form of a man takes shape in front of me. Automatically I thrash my legs, flailing toward the person who's grabbed me. My foot connects with a body, the impact hitting with a hollow thud.

"Jesus fucking Christ," a man spits, and though I can't see him in the darkness, I'd bet he's doubled over. More hands grab at me in the dark, and though I try to kick out again, I hit nothing but air.

"Get your fucking hands off me," I growl.

"The kitten's got claws," a man says behind me before throwing me hard against the wall. As soon as I hit it, the air is forced from my lungs, and his body cages me, pinning me against it. If this guy tries to rape me, I'll tear his balls off with my teeth.

"Calm down. I'm just here to deliver a message, and we'll be on our merry way," the man in front of me says, his voice low. His stinking breath hits my face as he talks. It smells sour, like he drank beer hours ago.

"Oh? And what message is that?" My words come out as a gasp, the adrenaline and exertion making it hard to catch my breath.

"Stop investigating those girls, their deaths. Rule them as suicides, and no one else will get hurt," he says.

I want to laugh at him, to scream at him to get out of my face, but I don't. If I can convince him that I'll do as he asks, I can get my gun and find out who really sent these assholes.

"Fine," I say, my voice far steadier than I expect it to be.

"Fine?"

I nod my head, though in the dark I'm sure they can't see it. "This isn't my town. I work for Vinalhaven. I was just doing someone a favor. If I'm stepping on someone else's toes, I'll take the first ferry back in the morning. I really don't need this to be my problem." The lie comes far too easily. I almost convince myself.

The man moves backward, his weight shifting away from my body. The moment I sense he's far enough, I dive toward the nightstand, flip on the lamp, and grab my gun. My eyes scream at the sudden light, but I force myself to turn around, facing my attackers. One has already made it to the door. He's hunched over, arm clutched around his middle, probably the guy I kicked. But the other guy, he's frozen near the window. Both are dressed in black, balaclavas covering their faces and hair.

As I swing the gun around to the guy near the window, I click the safety off and aim at him. He freezes, his hands in the air. God, it'd feel good to squeeze off a warning shot next to this motherfucker. But I don't. Through his mask I can make out his blue eyes and thin cracked lips. Circles of pale white flesh stand out beneath the mask. He's probably got six inches on me, and his build is slighter than I would have guessed from the force he used to press me against the wall. I glance to the guy near the door, just in time for him to slip out.

"God dammit," I mumble to myself. I train my gun back on the shitbag near the window. "Take off the mask," I say, motioning with the gun. I'm pissed the other guy got away, but it's still possible that we can track him down before he gets too far.

His hands tremble, still held toward the sky. And it takes him a long time to follow my instructions. I'm not sure if it's because of the fear or because he's afraid I'll recognize him.

"I mean it," I say and take a step closer for emphasis, not that it'd help my shot any. He doesn't know that, though. "There are a hundred other hotel rooms I can move to if I get blood in this one."

The man grabs the mask, yanking it off in one swift movement. He's got disheveled red hair, a thin, straight nose, and a wide jaw. I've never seen him before.

"Who sent you?"

He glances toward the door, like he's seconds from making a run for it.

"If you run, I'll fill your back with bullets before you even reach the door. I have good aim," I say, taking another step closer to him. I grab my cell phone and give it a voice command to call the station. If he tries to run for it, I want backup.

As soon as the dispatcher answers, I tell her to send other officers to the hotel and about the one on the run. This asshole is going to jail.

"Now, where were we?" I ask as I end the call with dispatch. "Oh yes, I was asking who sent you."

"I didn't get her name."

"Her?" I'd expect it'd be the killer. And of all things, I would not believe that a woman sexually assaulted that girl, killed her, and left her covered in ashes. That would follow no pattern I've ever heard of. Women usually kill men.

"I met her near the hospital."

"And what did she look like?" There's an edge to my voice, probably because I don't believe a goddamn word he's saying. I hold my gun steady, still trained on him as I speak.

"Long brown hair, hot. Probably a C cup."

Boobs? Really? I open my mouth to try to coax more out of him, but the echo of feet in the hall warns me our time has come to an end. Bodies flood in through the door, three officers with their weapons drawn. Zane leads the pack, followed by Clint and Sasha. Clint moves forward automatically and cuffs the guy within seconds. He and Sasha haul the perp out of the room, and I deflate a little as they go. I click my safety back on, then slide my gun back onto the nightstand.

"You all right, Claire?" Zane asks as he holsters his weapon and steps closer to me.

I nod and give him a rundown of what happened.

His eyes are narrowed on me as he absorbs my words. "Don't worry, we've got him now. I'll take him back to the station to see what else I can get out of him."

"Thank you," I say.

"Anytime. That's what we're here for. Good night."

"Night."

Once Zane and the others are gone, I let out a breath that's been pent up for too long. After our chat, I think it's a possibility Vera sent them. But trying to put me off the case is one thing. Sending men into my hotel room—that's quite another. I'm not convinced she'd risk that, but I sure as hell plan to watch my back. As the adrenaline burns away in my blood, I grab my things from the room and pack them up. I trade my hotel room with the bashed-up door for a new one. As laced with adrenaline as I am, I doubt I'll ever get back to sleep. But as I lie in bed, the darkness takes me, and I drift off.

CHAPTER 9

The station parking lot only has two cars in it when I pull in on Thursday morning. I'm sure Zane and Sergeant Pelletier will be sleeping late after dealing with my late-night "visitors." One of the cars I recognize as Austin's Fiat. The other I don't know, but I say a prayer to myself that it belongs to Kenneth. I need the data from Asha's phone. Snow spirals lazily from the sky as I open my car door and slip out into the cold.

I shake the snow out of my hair as I walk inside. The scent of coffee is thick in the air. I cross the lobby, then the bull pen. Austin sits at her desk, head swiveling to survey me as I stride in. I wave to her, shed my coat and gloves, and leave them at my desk.

"Morning," I say.

"I made coffee," she says, barely looking away from her monitor.

"Thanks. Did we get the texts from tech yet?" I ask, then realize I should just say Kenneth, as he's the extent of the tech team in this office.

"He didn't have them when I checked in half an hour ago. But he did say *soon*," she offers, glancing at me.

"Munroe is stopping by around ten to give his DNA. Please get it to the forensics team and tell them that there's a rush on it."

"I will," she says, picking up her phone.

I grab a cup of coffee and walk down the small hallway leading to his office. The door is cracked open when I approach, allowing the hum of all the computer equipment to spill out. I nudge the door open and peek inside. The room is filled to the brim with servers and monitors, all stacked atop long wooden tables along the walls. Several boxes are scattered on the floor, overflowing with wires and components.

"Morning," I say, hoping my appearance doesn't startle him. With the noise in here, I'm not sure he could hear my approach.

He looks over at me, his long hair half in his face. He raises a heavily tattooed arm, waving me in before sweeping the hair from his eyes. Kenneth is probably in his early to midtwenties and looks more biker than computer nerd.

"Detective," he says with a grin.

"Please tell me that you've got something for me."

"I do," he says, flourishing a stack of papers.

I stride forward, taking them. The pages are separated by phone number, then by the time they came in. The first few pages are correspondence from friends and family. Then there are other numbers that contacted Asha the day she died. The 203 number that I've seen before, the same burner number that texted Melanie before her death. My heart pounds with the realization.

"That burner number was saved in her phone as *Hottie Doc*," Kenneth says as he swivels his computer chair back and forth.

That points me back to the hospital, the place the evidence has been pointing to all along.

"Were there texts from the other burner number?" I ask as I start to flick through the pages. Just as he starts to say yes, I see them. Pages of incoming texts containing the same coordinates as Melanie's phone.

"And there's no chance we can find out who owns either burner number?" I ask. Right now, we don't have enough evidence to get a warrant on Dr. Munroe to see if he owns the burner phone. No one has mentioned seeing him with either victim after they were released from the hospital, and while his lack of an alibi is suspicious, we need real evidence for a warrant.

"The first one, no. It's all prepaid with cash on that carrier. The other, though, I've started looking into, because the number sending out the messages has an unusual format. They're being sent by an anonymous texting service, not from a single person or phone."

"What do you mean?" I ask.

"Imagine it like this. Know the spam emails that you get every day?"

I nod.

"It's the same kind of thing, but instead of building email lists and blasting it out into cyberspace with an email marketing platform, they're using a different format. Their lists are cell phone numbers, and instead of coupons, they're sending out those coordinates." When he starts to talk tech, he becomes really animated, his hands moving as he speaks.

So someone is sending out mass messages with these coordinates? Why? Is it so that people can meet up at specific times? That's all I can gather, since each text contains a time and place. "There's no way to track how they're texting this?"

He shakes his head. "The service they're using isn't based in the US. And they pride themselves on keeping no long-term personal data for their customers. That way they never have to worry about privacy laws."

"Thank you for this," I say.

He waves his hand, as if it's nothing. "I'm still going through her social media posts and emails. Along with the call log. If I find anything that seems useful, I'll tell you ASAP."

"I want to see any emails or messages she sent within forty-eight hours of her death," I say, then give him the date and time to look out for.

"Got it," he says before swiveling back to his computer.

I take the printouts and walk back to the bull pen. Austin turns, looking at me with her eyebrows raised. I hand over the pages with the coordinates and the texts from Hottie Doc. While she looks them over, I test a sip of my coffee.

"Those are the same coordinates, and the same burner numbers that were texting Melanie as well," I say.

"What's our next step?"

"Grab your coat. We're heading to the first coordinates so we can check these out."

Austin nods, picking up her gear as I do the same. It's going to be cold out, but we've got to figure out what these locations mean and why they were sent to Asha and Melanie. Once we've got our things together, I shoot Sergeant Pelletier an email to let him know where we'll be.

We walk out of the station together; the snowfall has picked up in the half an hour I was inside. I turn on my car, blasting the heat for Austin's sake, and back out of my space carefully. Austin helps me navigate through the city toward the first location, Camden Hills State Park.

"I'm not sure how much snow they'll have cleared on the roads up to the top," Austin says as I turn off Route 1 toward the park. "People come up here to ski this time of year, but sometimes they don't plow it until late. People aren't usually up here in the morning."

Her words make me consider again if it's time to give up my Mustang for a car built for Maine winters, but I banish the thought almost as soon as it appears in my mind. I don't plan on staying here. Why would I need to change vehicles if I don't stay?

Though the path up the mountain hasn't been plowed, the snow hasn't accumulated enough to make the drive difficult. Once we get to the top, I pull into the small parking lot next to a cabin that's tucked back into the trees. A sign stands out front, marking it as a ski shelter. I open up my GPS app on my phone and punch in the first set of coordinates.

"Ready?" I ask, glancing toward Austin.

She nods. "Let's find it," she says before popping her door open.

The wind hisses against me as I slam the car door. I hold up my phone carefully with my gloved hand and look at the directions on the screen. It shows that our destination is a ten-minute walk from our current location. Far off in the trees, the roar of an engine cuts through the silence. Snowmobiles, I'd guess. Austin and I walk toward the snow-dusted forest.

Our feet crunch on the snow as we weave through a part in the trees. There's no path to be seen beneath the snow. It's not like we can rely on trails to get us to these coordinates anyway. Cold bites our exposed flesh, making my cheeks sting as we walk. I glance down at the phone in my hand, surveying the GPS. As we grow closer, the trees huddled around us begin to spread before finally opening to a large clearing at least two hundred yards across. On each side, paths have been cut through the trees, carving a trail at least fifteen feet wide.

"This is the place," I say, looking around for anything significant, but the ground is covered in at least six inches of snow. Even if there had been evidence here of what occurred, it would be buried beneath snow now. I rack my brain, trying to determine what this place could have been used for. It wasn't the scene of the crime. We know the women weren't killed elsewhere and brought back to the motel, since they checked in themselves, and there was no debris or dirt on the bodies—outside of the cigarettes and ashes, that is.

An engine buzzes nearby, and I look toward the sound. Curving toward us from the expanse cut into the trees on our right, an ATV shoots from the gap, snow kicking up behind it. The rider skids to a stop twenty feet in front of Austin and me before two other ATVs fly in. They all stop in a row, surveying us.

I take out my badge and flash it to the group. Two women drop down first, pulling off helmets to reveal long brown hair. Another follows those two, though she's got short red hair sticking out beneath a ski cap.

"Officers," the redhead says as she approaches.

I pull up the pictures of Melanie and Asha on my phone.

"Can I help you?" the woman asks when I don't speak.

"You might be able to," I say, showing the pictures on my phone to the women. "Have you seen either of these women before?" I ask.

They glance at the images, brows coming together, before they look back up at me.

"Yeah, we've seen them out here a few times," the redhead says, shifting back and forth on her feet, like she's uncomfortable.

"When's the last time you saw them?" I ask.

"Asha, probably three months. But Melanie, every week before she hurt her wrist."

Asha came out here on an ATV? No one mentioned to me that it was one of her hobbies. That's another connection between these two girls. I take the folded paper from my jacket with the coordinates printed on them. "Do these mean anything to you?"

She takes the paper from me, surveying it. As she scrutinizes the page, she scratches the back of her neck, then wipes her nose on her wrist.

"Nah, no idea," she says, thrusting the paper back at me without making eye contact. It makes me feel like she's hiding something from me.

"How about you?" I ask as I show the other women. Their reactions are similar, but they say nothing about it.

"No, sorry," one of them mumbles.

"If you think of anything," I say before passing them each one of my cards.

Austin and I hike back through the forest, and by the time we reach my car again, my feet and hands prickle from the cold, like I'm half-frozen. We drive across Camden, defrosting until we pull up at the next preserve. The trek through the woods leads us to a setup that looks similar, the coordinates indicating a large clearing with no evidence. The third location, about thirty miles away, is the same. But as we walk back to my car, a man in the woods catches my attention.

"You all doing okay?" the man calls to us. He's tall, likely over six feet, in a thick black jacket with a patch over the heart. As he approaches, I make out the logo for a park ranger.

"Yes," I say before introducing myself and Austin.

"What can I help you with, Detective?" he asks.

I explain the situation and why we're out here. Along with the other locations that we've visited.

"A few times in the past couple years, out near that clearing, I've seen ATV tracks in the morning and evidence of a bonfire. I was thinking that teenagers were meeting out in the woods, partying."

That would make sense; maybe the texts are how they communicate around here that they're meeting up. Though it seems a bit high tech for planning a bonfire.

"When would you say is the last time you saw this?"

His brows furrow, and he crosses his arms. "I'd say at least four months ago, if not a little longer."

"Have you ever had any reports of anyone getting hurt at one of these parties?" I ask.

He shakes his head. "No, not that I'm aware of."

"If you come across any more evidence of parties out here, could you give me a call?" I ask as I pass him my information.

"Of course, Detective."

Austin and I walk back to my car as I try to piece it all together. Did Asha and Melanie see their killer at one of these parties? Did Asha really ride on an ATV as well, or was she just there for the parties? Is it an unrelated coincidence? It has to mean something that both women went to the same parties, visited the same hospital, received texts from the same numbers, then ended up dead at that motel. Too much of this lines up for me to exclude any of it.

My phone rings, and Sergeant Pelletier's name lights up on the screen. I grimace. I was hoping that Noah was going to call.

"Calderwood," I say.

"It's Pelletier. Are you still out checking those coordinates? We need you on scene." His voice is strained, on edge.

My stomach clenches as I unlock my car. Austin glances at me, her eyes scrutinizing me as if she can sense the tension that's filled the air.

I open my door with my phone clamped between my shoulder and cheek. "What happened?" I ask.

"We got a call about another body. It's just like the others," he explains.

"Where?" I ask as adrenaline kicks up my heart rate.

"The Carle Motel off Route 105. I got the call a few minutes ago from the owner. She's real shaken up."

"I bet," I say as I shove my key in the ignition.

"How soon can you be here?" he asks, ignoring the edge in my voice.

"Less than ten. I'll see you when I get there."

"I'll get CSI and the ME's office over here in the meantime."

After I hang up with Pelletier, Austin helps me navigate to the Carle. The motel looks similar to the first scene, a one-story building in the shape of an L, painted a peeling canary yellow, letting some of the maroon beneath speckle the walls. Several patrol cars sit in the lot, yellow tape set up around them, blocking off the scene. I pull up behind the team, and Sergeant Pelletier nods at me as soon as he sees me.

I walk toward him, yanking my coat on, Austin's feet scuffing on the pavement beside me. Circles hang beneath his brown eyes, making them seem darker than usual. Stubble sprouts on his chin. It looks to me to be three, maybe four days of growth. The case is wearing on him. It's clear on his face.

"What do we have?" I ask as we approach.

"Jessica Riley, eighteen, suffocated with a plastic bag over her head, bound naked to the bed. It's the same as the other scenes, cigarette butts and all. She's got a cast on her left ankle that looks pretty new."

To my left, at the mouth of the parking lot, three news vans pull in one after another like a funeral procession. "Fucking figures. They can't stay away," I say.

Sergeant Pelletier stares over my shoulder, eyeing the vans with an intensity I wouldn't expect. He edges closer to the motel room. "We found something in the parking lot, in some of the leaves over there." He points to a bunch of leaves about twenty feet from the door of the motel room. In his hands, he's got a plastic bag. I take a step closer, appraising the contents. Inside, there's a key card for the hospital, some kind of identification tag for an employee.

"Dr. Munroe?" I say as I read the name off the badge.

———

I've had a bad feeling about Dr. Munroe since we started this investigation. Though we've now got his DNA, it'll likely be days before the forensics team is able to process it. And it could still take them weeks to get through all the DNA found in the first two scenes. Unfortunately, because of all the ashes at the scenes, there's lots of DNA on the bodies. Finding this key card, though, that changes things. Now we've got the break that we need to really look at him for this. Though this evidence is circumstantial, it's still a step in the right direction. Now what we need is to find his DNA or fingerprints on one of the bodies, the only way to link him to these horrendous murders. Or find an eyewitness who can put him with one of the victims after they were released from the hospital.

Sergeant Pelletier strides toward the motel room, glancing back at me to be sure I'm following. The scene is hauntingly familiar. Several beat cops stand outside the door, looming like bouncers around a club entrance. We muscle our way inside. Markers stand on the floor, highlighting evidence for the photographer and the crime scene techs who will arrive from Augusta. They'll need to process the scene and take all the evidence back to the lab. But those of us here can at least get some things prepped for them.

After I have looked at the bound, naked victim on the bed and studied the similarities to the other two murders, Sergeant Pelletier and I step outside. Everything is identical to the others. It's official:

we have a serial killer on our hands. Though it was clear to me before, now it fits the technical definition, since there have been three deaths. I glance at Sergeant Pelletier once we've got some space between us and the other officers. Austin hovers behind us like she's unsure if she should be jumping in.

"Can you have one of the other officers handle notifying the family, and we'll start on interviewing the staff here?" I ask.

"We'll take care of it," he says, looking to the team of officers. I imagine he's deciding who he'll give the task to.

"I need someone to call the hospital as well to find out if Jessica has been a patient recently. I'm guessing she was, because of the cast, but we need to be sure. It is possible she got it at one of the urgent care clinics."

"It'll be done by the time you get finished with your interview."

I say my thanks and turn toward the motel office. Austin walks beside me, her eyes darting between me and the scene. Unease is clear in the hunch of her shoulders and the furrow of her brows. Her mouth is a grim line. Clearly, she's as troubled by this as the rest of us.

"How are we even going to stop this guy? How many more girls are going to die before we catch him?" she asks.

"I wish I knew. At least we're getting somewhere now. We have the key card. That points us in a pretty clear direction. If this victim was at the hospital, that will give us a good reason to bring the doctor in for questioning. If he gives us some information that would allow us to get a search warrant, it's possible we could find the burner phone that was texting Melanie. It's too circumstantial for an arrest yet. There has to be something in that room if he was in there." There's just so much DNA in those rooms, thanks to the cigarettes and the nature of hotel rooms.

She nods, though it clearly doesn't look like she has much confidence in our ability to find the murderer.

A woman strides across the parking lot toward us. I recognize her sleek bob and pantsuit immediately. She doesn't come with a camera crew like many of the other journalists currently clotting along the back end of the parking lot. Instead, she seems to be alone. As she approaches, she shoves a strand of hair behind her ear and clears her throat.

"Detective Calderwood, I was hoping that I could speak with you for a moment." Lillian's voice is high, and it cuts through the dull roar of noise in the parking lot.

"I can't comment—" I start.

She raises a hand. "Yes, I know. You can't comment on the investigation."

My eyes narrow automatically, and my hackles rise. If she's not here to ask me about the investigation, that means she's here to talk to me about Rachel. That's the last thing I need on my mind right now. I arm myself with several choice words for this woman if she pushes me to talk about my sister.

"I wanted to ask you how you felt about the passing of Theo Washington," she says.

The name isn't one I recognize. With the last name, I suspect Theo is related to Noah. Though I'm caught off guard, I manage to say, "I have no comment."

"You have no comment on the passing of Noah's father?" she asks.

I swallow hard. "No."

I'm taken aback. My mind reels. When did his father die? I know that he's not close to his father. Is that why he didn't call me about it yet? Is he so absorbed in his case that he doesn't even know? Or did he not tell me because he didn't want to burden me with this? There are too many possibilities; I can't pinpoint one that I think is the most likely. I stride forward, forcing myself to continue to the office and not dwell on what this woman just told me.

"Are you all right?" Austin asks as we approach the door.

I reach for it, my hand resting on the handle, but I turn to her before I pull it open. "I'll be fine. I need to focus on the case. My personal life has no involvement with this." I'll talk to Noah later, but for now, this has to take priority.

She offers me a weak nod, her gaze still scrutinizing me. Even if I did want to dig into my feelings now, I'm not about to take that leap with a coworker, with my partner. This relationship has to stay strictly professional. She doesn't need to know anything about what might be going on in my life.

The office of this motel isn't much different than the last one. The walls are covered in a faded floral wallpaper that's white and blue. The design reminds me of old china. Worn dark-blue carpet covers the floors. It's got trails etched in it from the thousands of feet that walked this path before me. A woman who appears to be in her late fifties sits behind the counter. Her hair is dyed a shade of red that should be an exotic spice, not a hair color. It falls straight to her shoulders. She's got her lips painted the same vibrant shade, which makes the rest of her pale face disappear in contrast to the bright features. When the door shuts behind Austin, the woman looks up at us, recognition flickering behind her eyes.

"Ah, the cops," she says.

"Yes, and you are?" I ask. I clench my fists at my sides, trying to build a wall around the roaring emotions inside me, though so far, it's doing no good.

"Tilda Hollingsworth," she says. Her voice is low and crackles like an old radio.

"Were you the one who called?" I ask as I approach.

"Yeah, that was me. I was here when the cleaning lady, Ingrid, found her." Her lips press together, and she grimaces. The unpleasant memory is etched into her features.

"Did you work here last night as well?" Austin chimes in.

"I did for a little while. Not the whole night. My granddaughter wasn't feeling well, so I cut out of here for a few hours," she explains as she glances between the two of us, as if she's not sure who she should be talking to.

"Austin, could you bring up a picture of Jessica, please?" I ask. It takes Austin a few seconds; then she shows me a photo of the vic from Facebook. It's a selfie showing her reclining in an office chair, her face lit by a blue glow.

I take Austin's phone and show it to Tilda. "Do you remember seeing this girl?"

She scrutinizes the image, her brows coming together to form a deep gash between them. "Yes, she checked in around eight," she says.

"Was she alone?" I ask.

"Yes, she came in here by herself to book the room. It stood out to me, because it's not often that we get a girl that age wanting to book a room, especially not by herself. There was a man standing outside; she looked back at him and smiled a few times as I was checking her in."

Excitement makes my mind buzz. Could we finally get a description of this man? "Could you describe him?"

"He was tall with dark hair." She concentrates, as if trying to sketch the picture of the man in her mind. "He, well. He looked normal. Average. Nothing about him really stood out."

I want to deflate. "Did she say anything about him?"

She shakes her head. "Just that she wanted a quiet room because tonight was going to be special." The woman offers a shrug, as if it's something she's heard a thousand times.

"Are there any cameras outside?" I ask.

"Yes, but it hasn't been working for a while."

"Did you see if she drove a car here or if she walked?"

"I did see a car pull into the parking lot before the girl walked in. It was a newer sedan. Dark blue or black. I think. I don't think she was driving it. She mentioned being glad she didn't have to drive in the snow."

"Did anything about her appearance stand out to you?"

"She seemed really happy. Excited, actually. Oh, I think she did mention his name."

My heart skips at that. "A name?"

"As she was leaving, she opened the door and said a name. Trystan, I think."

I jot that down. How many Trystans could there be in a town this size? I think back to our first trip to the hospital. Dr. Munroe mentioned his first name was Ian. Could she have mistaken Trystan for Ian? Or if Dr. Munroe wasn't here, why was his key card in the parking lot?

I finish up my questioning with the motel manager and slip her my card. Austin and I walk outside, and I turn to her.

"Do you know of any Trystans that live in town?"

She shakes her head. "No, not around here."

"Have Clint check in at the hospital to see if there are any Trystans on staff," I say. Because the medical center supports so many small communities, it's very likely that employees there work out of town and commute in. There are likely plenty of staff members that most of the Camden residents have never met.

She pulls her phone out of her pocket and taps on the screen as we walk. "He'll have something for us by the time we get back to the station."

We walk back toward the room. Sergeant Pelletier approaches me before we even get close.

"Her family has been notified, and David from the hospital verified that Jessica was a patient there," he informs me. "She got a cast two days ago. Dr. Munroe was her physician."

"So I need to head back to the hospital and figure out what Dr. Munroe was up to while these girls were dying and how his key card got here."

He nods. "Let's bag him," he says. "At the very least having his card will be enough for us to hold him for the weekend."

My heart pounds with excitement at the prospect of bringing in Munroe. We may not be able to hold him for long, but this'll keep the hospital safe for a few days. And who knows what he'll say once he realizes we have his ID card. After climbing into a Camden squad car, Sergeant Pelletier and I head to the rear of the hospital with David. He brings Dr. Munroe out back. We've at least got the decency to arrest him in the parking lot behind the building, instead of dragging him out of the hospital. Austin hangs back at my Mustang.

Before we're able to read him his rights, the back door flies open, and Vera barrels through the door. She's got on a dress that hugs her thighs with a cardigan pulled over the top, secured to her throat. Rage simmers behind her eyes, and her long red nails look like talons as she puts her hands on her hips. Her eyes narrow on me, and her brows pinch together in the center.

"What are you doing?" She snaps each word at me like they're separate sentences.

I take a step forward, ready to verbally put Vera in her place, but Sergeant Pelletier steps in before I can. He explains that we're bringing in Dr. Munroe for questioning.

"You can't do this," she seethes. "He didn't kill anyone." Her voice takes on a shrill quality, and I can tell that she's on the verge of shrieking at us.

"Actually, we can. You can continue to make a scene if you would like, but we're taking him out of here for now," I say, my words clipped.

Sergeant Pelletier nods at me, indicating for me to get Dr. Munroe in the car. He's positioned himself between me and Vera, which I realize is likely for the best. There's a predatory look on Vera's face that tells me she might be weighing her options, trying to determine if she should interfere. She starts berating Sergeant Pelletier, yelling that we can't take a doctor who's still on shift, as I slide into the car. I wait a few minutes for Vera to calm down, and then Sergeant Pelletier and I catch up before he heads to his squad car.

Austin and I drive back to the station, a few minutes behind Sergeant Pelletier. When we spoke at the hospital, he tried to give me an out and have his officers do the questioning—but this is as much my case as it is theirs, and I intend on being involved with it every step of the way.

The tires crunch as we turn into the parking lot. Sergeant Pelletier pulls Dr. Munroe out of the car in front of us. I drive in beside them, shut the car off, and follow them inside. This late the station is mostly abandoned. The scent of coffee hangs in the air, along with the tangy sweetness of doughnuts. As we walk back to the interrogation room, Sergeant Pelletier has already dropped off Dr. Munroe, and he waves me aside.

"I need to talk to you for a minute," he says.

"I'll grab us some coffee," Austin offers, obviously understanding that the sergeant wants to speak to me alone.

Once Austin is out of earshot, Sergeant Pelletier turns to face me fully. "Are you okay with Austin being in there for this? I don't want her to interfere with the questioning."

I appreciate his concern. But Austin has no problem with sitting back while I take the lead, which is exactly what I need. "I'd like her to sit in with me. It'll help teach her the questions to ask." That's the whole point of all this anyway, to get her trained up so that one day she could be a detective. If she doesn't sit in on questionings, she's not going to know how to conduct them. There's plenty of shit you can learn about from books, but interrogating a suspect, that's something you've got to sink your teeth into. There's so much to be learned from body language and tells, things you can only learn by doing, seeing.

He motions toward the interrogation room. "I'll be behind the glass if you need me. The DA is coming here to watch part of it as well." That strikes me as odd. It seems too early to involve the DA in this investigation. We'd barely have enough to hold him if he lawyered up right now and pushed the DNA test.

"Do we really want to have her come all the way out here before we know more?"

"She's seen a lot about the case in the media. They're really running with the story. It's everywhere. There's a lot of pressure to get this wrapped up."

"If there's that much pressure, can't they task someone with keeping an eye on these girls after they're being released?" My tone is harsher than it needs to be. But considering how Vera's acted so far, I feel like the hospital is complicit. If you ask me, it doesn't seem like they give a damn about stopping the murders. Hell, I'm sure if Vera could get away with it, she wouldn't help a damn bit. She barely helps as it is.

He nods. "We're trying to work with them to get a better system in place. But Mrs. McConnel is resistant. With hospital confidentiality, they see some problems with putting tails on patients who are released."

Frustration ripples through me, and I clench my fists against it. "I'm sure if they made it clear to the patients *why* officers needed to keep an eye on them, they would agree to have our assistance."

"Believe me, I know."

"They should be doing everything in their power to keep their patients safe."

He nods again. "That they should. But if he's our guy, we don't need to worry about it. We can put a stop to it now." He glances toward the interrogation room. "Get in there and see what you can find out."

Austin stands outside the door holding two mugs of coffee. I appraise them. One is a Patriots mug; the other has a picture of a squad of officers from a comedy TV show. "Which do you want?" she asks.

I reach toward the squad cup.

"It's clean, I promise. I wasn't sure how you take it, though."

"Black is fine, thanks," I say as I wrap my hand around the mug, the warmth bleeding into my palm through the ceramic. Though I normally take it with cream, the coffee in the station is watery enough without it. "You ready?" I motion toward the door.

Her eyes gleam. "I thought you two were going to lock me out of the questioning," she says, glancing toward Sergeant Pelletier's office.

"Nope. You're sitting in."

Footsteps behind us draw my attention before we can head into the interrogation room. I turn to find Clint standing behind me. He glances between Austin and me. "I called the hospital like you asked," he says, looking down at a legal pad in his hands.

"What'd you find out?" Austin asks.

"They don't have any employees currently named Trystan. They did have one a year or so ago, but he moved out of state. They're not sure where he went."

"Thank you, Clint."

"Let me know if you need anything else," he says before he turns.

"What do you make of the name?" Austin asks.

"I don't know if she was mistaken or if we have the wrong guy. But we've got to talk to Dr. Munroe to find out," I say. It's easy enough to mix up names. It's also possible Dr. Munroe could have used a fake name. I turn my attention back to the interrogation. There's only one way to find out what his level of involvement was.

I throw open the door, and Austin trails in after me. Dr. Munroe leans back in his chair, his hair slicked back from the slope of his forehead. Under any other circumstances, Dr. Munroe would be a gorgeous specimen of a man, but with that charm, his demeanor, he may as well have *sociopath* tattooed on his forehead. He glances up at me through his lashes and smiles, the kind of grin that has no place in an interrogation room. Like he doesn't have a care in the world.

Austin catches my eye as she takes a seat. She worries her bottom lip with her teeth. It tells me that she's not entirely comfortable with this. But she'll get used to it; she'll have to. I was nervous during my first interrogations too. I sit in the metal chair across from Dr. Munroe. When my gaze settles on him, he raises a brow at me in a gesture that almost looks like a challenge.

"So, Dr. Munroe, do you know why you're here?" I ask before taking a sip of my coffee.

"Please, call me Ian." He smiles. "And yes, I would imagine it's because you think I killed those girls."

It strikes me as odd that he would bring this up so willingly—especially so early in the conversation. "Yes, you see, I'm having some trouble with the details. So I was hoping you could help me fill in some of the blanks. You worked with all three patients. All died shortly after leaving your care. You were noted to have had two of the patients stay longer than needed given their conditions. And one nurse has informed me that you frequently gave female patients exams that they didn't need."

"To be fair, a nurse is not a doctor. What exams a patient does or does not need is really my call."

I note that he does not dispute any of the other facts. "Yes, that it is. But can you explain to me why a patient in the hospital for a tonsillectomy would need a pelvic exam?" The last time I asked him about the pelvic exams, he denied them. Now it seems like he's admitting they did happen.

His brows come together, and he cocks his head slightly. "I didn't give any of them a pelvic exam. Did you see that in their charts?"

It wasn't in the chart; that was information from Nurse Jordan. Though if he did give an exam that wasn't needed, I'm sure he wouldn't have listed it in the chart. "A nurse informed me."

He leans toward the table, his eyes leveling with mine. "You can't just take their word over mine. Some of them just don't like me."

"And why is that?" I ask. I've got the sense from Dr. Munroe that he likes to talk, and I'm going to exploit that for as long as I can.

"They're always making up complaints about me. It never makes any sense. They just don't like that I'm not from here. Mainers only trust Mainers."

He's not wrong there. Just like people from Vinalhaven don't trust mainlanders. Having a bunch of people at the hospital dislike him doesn't make him automatically guilty of murder.

"Dr. Munroe, did you see Melanie, Asha, or Jessica outside of the hospital after they were released?"

He leans back and crosses his arms, which is the first sign of combativeness he's shown. Before now, he's seemed relaxed, open. Crossing his arms, though, that shows me that we're going down a path that he doesn't want to follow.

"I could have seen them at a grocery store or something. We live in the same town, for Christ's sake. It's not like I sought them out. I see many of my patients after they're released."

"Where do you do your grocery shopping?" I ask.

He glances away, his shoulders tight, as if he didn't expect me to ask any follow-up questions, like I'd swallow a spoonful of his bullshit and agree that it was honey. "It depends on what I need."

Out of the corner of my eye, I can see Austin turn to look at me. It's clear from the expression on Munroe's face that he's noticed this too. He clears his throat. He finally uncrosses his arms and leans forward, muscular arms propped on the table. "Sometimes Hannaford Supermarket, Megunticook Market; usually Market Basket."

"I see. I'll take a look at those, then, to see if you might have run into any of the victims there," I bluff. I have no desire to look at grocery store security tapes. I'm sure that he or someone else coaxed these girls to a motel, and that had to be done at a location that wasn't the hospital, but I don't believe that it was a grocery store either. How many teenagers are really doing the grocery shopping alone? No, whoever is after these girls would want them away from their parents.

"Can you tell me where you were the evening of February twenty-first?" I ask.

"I was at work."

"And can anyone verify that?"

His mouth twitches. "I'm sure the nurses can verify that I was there and that my key card was swiped to enter the building at the start of my shift."

"What can corroborate that you were there the entire shift and did not leave the premises?"

"If I left the premises, I'd have to scan my card to come back."

"So you scan your card *every* time you leave and return to the hospital?" I ask.

His eyes tighten, his glare so sharp I'm sure it could cut paper. "No, not every time. Sometimes I walk in behind another doctor."

"I see. I could ask David for the security footage."

"The cameras on the back door aren't working. I usually use that door."

How convenient. Why has he been concerning himself about which security cameras are and are not working? "Again, are there any staff members who could give you an alibi for February twenty-fifth or twenty-sixth?"

For a long moment, he's silent, as if weighing his options. His lips press together, and I half expect him to start chewing them. "I don't think anyone could vouch for me during those times. I was sleeping." This old song and dance again?

We go around in circles, Dr. Munroe trying to tell me that someone let him in or that he followed someone into the building. No matter what I say, he's got an instant answer. But I can't help but notice the red creeping up from his collar, the sweat beaded on his forehead.

"Like I said," he says for what has to be the fifth time. "One of the nurses let me into the bunk room."

I ask, "And who was that, exactly?" I hold my pen against my notepad, as if dying to write down this mysterious person's name. But we both know he's lying. The air is thick with it. His fists clench on top of the table, his knuckles going white. No one saw him go in there, because he wasn't in there. His key card points to him being at the motel, so if he wasn't out murdering these girls, he's got to give more to go on. Right now, every sign is indicating he did this. But what I can't come up with is motive. Sure, this guy seems like a dick who hunts pussy like it's going out of style, but I'm sure *plenty* of women are more than happy to be his prey.

"I'm done talking. I want a lawyer," he says, crossing his arms.

I put my pen down and shove up from the seat, Austin rising as I do. When we leave the room, Sergeant Pelletier approaches the door. "I've got this," he says. "Take the night off. I'm going to get his lawyer in here and see what we can work out."

"I'd really like to help with that."

"No, really, go. Actually, take a long weekend. You and Austin have been working this all hours. I'll take it from here. I'll call you if we get anywhere with it. Maybe if we keep him locked up, he'll start to feel more like talking. If he does, I'll call you in."

If that's how he wants to play this, I've got to let him do it. Frustration ripples through me. I hate feeling like my case is being taken from me. But at the same time, I can't help the relief I feel that we might have our guy. I say my goodbyes to Austin before heading out of the station. With my stuff in hand, I walk to my Mustang and drive back down Route 1 toward Rockport. From there, I can take the ferry to Vinalhaven. Gray mist rolls in from the bay, crawling across the twisting road in front of me like blood seeping from a wound. My mind spirals back to what the reporter said to me, her words leaching into my mind as I drive. Noah's father is dead, and he didn't tell me. Is it true? I need to find out. And that's exactly what I intend to do.

After I pull onto the ferry, I climb onto the deck, letting the cold air envelop me. I retrieve my phone from my jacket as the boat begins to chug across the bay. My hands trembling, I open Google and tap on the bar. Carefully, I type in *Theo Washington Died* and hit enter with my thumb. The connection is spotty on the water; the wheel spins and spins as it tries to pull up the results. I hold my breath as the page starts to load, and there it is, page after page of news results.

> Theo Washington, Founder of Raynor Energies, Has Passed Away

> Former Owner of Raynor Energies Dead from Cancer

> Ding Dong, the Coal Baron Is Dead

I scroll through, my eyes poring over the results. I tap on the first one. My heart tightens in my chest, as if someone is gripping it hard. A war of emotions rages inside me.

> After a two-year fight with thyroid cancer, the founder of Raynor Energies, Theodore Isiah Washington, has succumbed to his illness surrounded by family. He is survived by his wife of 39 years, Celia Elizabeth (Grover) Washington, and his sons, Graham Washington, Noah Washington, Lucas Washington, and Cameron Washington.

I shoot him a text, knowing I can't call him yet because I've only got a bar of service.

> How are you doing?

The ferry is approaching the island, the small mass growing out of the cloud of mist. Vinalhaven is a tiny island in the middle of Penobscot Bay. It's got about twenty-four miles of land total, or at least that's what they proudly told us while I was in school. I was unfortunate enough to grow up on an island my ancestors founded, none of their descendants brave enough to leave the heap of land they were spawned on, just like the lobsters that sustain most of the economy now. The town is a cluster of old, sprawling homes atop the rocky island and thousands upon thousands of pine trees. It's beautiful in its own way, but I'm far too jaded by this place, the town that took my sister from me.

Fog parts ahead of us, displaying the outstretched arms of the marina. This time of year it's packed to the gills with boats. Many of the tourists who summer on the island leave the boats here all winter, where they bob along, covered just like the furniture in the houses the tourists also abandon. They're like flocks of moths, fluttering around whatever place is the warmest.

The ferry docks, and I climb back into my Mustang before pulling it off the boat. I turn right down Main Street, then follow it through the arteries of the island toward the small downtown, past the police department I worked for last year, the bakery, the post office, a few restaurants, a hotel, and several more small restaurants, and finally reach my rental. By the time I unlock the door, I've got a reply from Noah.

Everything's fine. How's your case?

Fine?

I unlock the door and shove inside, cold sweeping into the stale house with me. With my teeth, I peel off my gloves, and then I dial his number as confusion assaults me. Does he not know? The phone rings several times before he picks up.

"Hey, how are you doing?" he asks, his voice quiet, like he's trying not to be overheard.

"Fine, Noah," I say, and suddenly words fail me. What do I say? How do I say it? I've delivered this kind of news at least a hundred times before. But to Noah? I'm not prepared for this. Though he hasn't told me much about his past, I do know how strained things are between him and his family. What if he lost his last chance to put things right? Do I want to be the one to deliver that blow? I take a deep breath, and the words finally rise to my lips. "A reporter here told me that something happened to your dad," I manage, feeling very much like I need to tiptoe around this.

"Oh, that. Yeah," he says, as if I've told him it's going to rain tomorrow.

"Are you okay?" I ask, a bit taken aback. Clearly, he knew. It's obvious in his tone. If he knew, why didn't he tell me?

"Yeah. I've got to go to the funeral and wake tomorrow," he states matter-of-factly. Though I knew that his relationship with his father was tenuous at best, this is much more apathetic than I would have expected out of him.

"Do you want me to come?" I ask, before realizing I can't really do that. But if he needs me, I'll find a way to do it.

"No, it's fine," he says, brushing my offer aside.

"What happened?"

"He had stage-four cancer. I didn't know about it until the day before he died. My brother Lucas called me to say that he wanted to speak with me before . . ."

"Why didn't you tell me?" I manage after a long pause.

"Because I don't like getting into this family stuff. It doesn't matter."

His words sting. Maybe because I want him to share those things with me. Maybe because I'm frustrated that I never had the option to keep anything about my family to myself. My dark past was laid bare before him.

"It matters to me because it's part of you. It made you who you are," I say, trying my best to convey my feelings. Things like this have always been difficult for me. It's hard enough for me to open up to anyone, but the thought that I'm opening up while Noah is shutting me out—that's not something I can stand. He's gotten to see the good and bad, the painful parts of my past. He knows how I fell apart after Rachel died, how my family was splintered, how my mother and father became so distant they may as well be strangers.

"I don't want to get into this. My past is just that. My family is part of that past. It's something I've left behind me."

But he hasn't. He's there with them now. It's not part of his past if he's still living with it, carrying that burden. And I know he is. Anger rises inside me at his words.

"I sure wish that I had that option with my past. But you've gotten to see it all; you've gotten to dig into it, whether I liked it or not. That seems pretty one sided to me. Hell, you got to write a story about it and had a front-row ticket to my sister's murder investigation." My words come out harsher than I mean for them to, but I don't regret them.

"Then I don't know what to tell you, Claire," he snaps. "Take it or leave it."

He's never spoken to me like this before. It catches me off guard and puts me on the defensive. I can't help the next words when they rise to my lips. "You know what? I need some space from this until you figure things out."

"Hold on—are you breaking up with me?"

"I need space to think. If you're not going to share things with me, if you're going to choose what parts of your life I get access to, that doesn't work for me." Silence thickens on the line. I glance at my phone to see if the call dropped. "I guess I'll see you around, Noah," I say before ending the call.

I get up and pace the room for a minute, needing to do *something*. The phone feels heavy in my hand, and I know what I need is to talk this through with someone, even if only so I don't call him back. Plopping down on the bed, I search out Roxie's number on my phone. Roxie and I worked together at Detroit PD for several years before I moved back to Maine. It was so difficult to leave her behind when I came back here. Though I'd never wanted to leave Detroit in the first place, leaving Roxie, one of the best friends I've ever had, was almost enough to make me stay. But my hometown's need to solve a murder case and their desperate plea made up my mind for me.

I need get her take on this. She answers on the second ring.

"Hey, stranger," she says, the smile obvious in her tone. Just hearing her voice eases the tension in my shoulders. And for the first time in several hours, I feel like I can really breathe.

"Hey, how are things with Lila?" I ask.

She lets out a short, humorless laugh. "Over."

I turn over onto my stomach, propping myself up on my elbows. My heart aches for Roxie. I'd hoped that she and Lila would sort their differences out again. When they're together and things are good, they're *really* good. "Why didn't you call me?"

"I'm still processing it," she says. "I was going to call you soon. I just hate failing again."

"You didn't fail." Times like this, I wish I were still back in Detroit. I don't want Roxie hurting there all alone. If I were there, I'd take her out for drinks and get her so trashed she wouldn't even remember Lila's name.

"That's not how it feels right now. But I couldn't pretend that I wanted more with her. It just didn't feel right," she explains, her voice thick with exhaustion.

"I'm sorry," I say, because I don't know what else would help.

"Anyway, let's talk about you. I can't think about Lila right now."

"Are you sure? I'm here if you want to talk."

"I know. Come on. What's up?" she presses.

With Roxie I can cut past all the bullshit, the *how are you*s, the small talk. Roxie is a meat-and-potatoes kind of friend, no bullshit you don't want.

I word vomit it all out to her. Noah being so guarded about *everything*—sure, he made it clear he's not happy with his family, but he was there for one of the worst parts of my life. He's seen bits of me that no one else has ever seen, aspects I didn't think I *could* show anyone else. Sure, Roxie knows, but that's different. My past would never make her look at me differently. But it sure as hell would make most guys do a double take.

"So let me get this straight," she says once I finally come up for breath. "Someone died, and he didn't bother to tell you? Not even a text?"

"Not just someone," I clarify. "His *dad*. His dad died. I texted him this morning, and he said everything was fine. He's keeping things from me." The detective alarm bells are going off so loudly in my brain I'm sure Roxie can hear them. Because it's never just one thing. There are always more. What else is he hiding? What else will he hide? I pinch the bridge of my nose as my eyes sting. I will not cry over this, over him, but fuck, the betrayal is like a punch in the gut.

"Jesus Christ," she says.

"Am I crazy? I should be pissed, right?" This relationship shit is still so foreign to me. I'm on uneasy ground. I've never been in this deep before. With other guys I could cut the strings and not give a shit. But Noah? I don't want to do that. I don't know what's reasonable and what's irrational. It was so much easier when I didn't let myself get attached.

"You have every right to be pissed. After everything he knows about you, how is he lying to you about this?" she asks. Her words are clipped, like she's as angry as I am. It only makes me love her more.

"What do I do, Roxie?" I ask, allowing myself to fall back on the bed, the phone still clutched to my ear. More, I don't understand why he'd lie about it. If there's anyone in the world who would understand, it's me.

"Kick his ass," she growls. "No, I'll come there—we can do it together."

A laugh slips from my lips. I can imagine her doing it too.

"Really, though, you've got to ask yourself, 'Is it worth fixing?' And even if you fix it for now, can you trust him again after this?" she asks.

The words roll around in my brain, swirling with the anger. Do I trust him enough to fix it? Do I want to fix this? If I close my eyes and imagine my future, what do I see? Who do I see? The key in my pocket must weigh a thousand pounds.

But she's right. I know my answer.

Roxie and I talk around the Noah issue until I can't stand the way his name sounds on my lips anymore. The conversation shifts to her cases, then to mine. I tell her about the MO of the killer, and she offers to reach out to her contacts at the FBI to run it through the database. I've always felt like these kills couldn't be our perp's first; he likely has others. Maybe that data can help us find other victims far outside of this net.

We finish up the call, and though my heart is still heavy, I do feel better.

CHAPTER 10

My eyes sweep across the bedroom in my rental, and my stomach clenches. All I can see is Noah here. This place is filled with too many memories. His jacket is still slung over the back of one of my dining chairs. A sigh slips from my lips. I'm going to have to move. All I can imagine is how I'll see Noah in every corner of this house from now on. Just like how I used to see Rachel around every corner.

Roxie texted me this morning that she intends to come to Maine for the weekend. She's coming to visit family and wants to make sure I'm holding up all right with my break from Noah. I'm also hoping that while she's here we can go over some of the data she's found in the FBI database for the MO of my perp. Even though Dr. Munroe is in custody, we've still got a case to build.

I roll over in bed. The sheets are cold, and I wish they didn't have to be. My eyes prickle when I remember what it felt like to have Noah's body curve into mine. My phone rings, Noah's name flashing on the screen, but I reject the call. A few seconds later, a text message dings.

Noah: Claire, please

I consider blocking his number, but I'm not ready for that yet. While I feel what used to be *us* unraveling, I'm not ready for it to be completely gone. I'm dipping my toes into the water of life without Noah. But I can't jump in. Not yet. Instead, I delete the text, which is nearly as therapeutic. How am I supposed to be in his life if he'll only share pieces of it with me?

I drag out my laptop and settle it in the middle of my bed. Once it awakens, I navigate to the search engine. Though deep down I know I'm only going to cause myself more trouble and pain, I type in Noah's name. I scan through the recent results, but none are what I'm looking for. They're all about our most recent case in Vinalhaven. Instead, I alter it to add Noah's hometown. Though many of the recent articles remain, a few pages in, I find something else—a much older piece of news.

An article from the *Daily Times* appears on my screen.

> Theo and Celia Washington are pleased to announce the engagement of Noah Washington to Emma Abernathy. Emma, daughter of Judge Frances Abernathy and previous lieutenant governor Adeline Abernathy, is a graduate of the University of Tennessee.

I stop reading as my stomach sours. Bile climbs my throat. Five years ago, he was engaged to someone else. And of course, he never told me. It's one thing to not talk about family, but this? He should have told me. I snap the laptop closed, as if it'll banish the toxic thoughts in my mind. I settle down into bed, pulling the covers up around my chin.

A numbness washes over me, and though I expect tears to come again, they don't. Instead, sleep takes me.

My phone vibrates, and I glance at the screen to see Sergeant Pelletier's name.

"Hello," I say after I accept the call.

"Claire, I've got an update on the two men who broke into your hotel room."

The *two*. So they finally caught the second guy, then.

"Gary Ventura and Jarod Trevino are both being held for one count of breaking and entering, one count of assaulting an officer, and two counts of possessing stolen firearms," he says. The low hum of other voices filters through the background, like he's walking through the bull pen.

"Have they said anything about who hired them?" I ask as I open the fridge and grab myself a bottle of water.

"Gary flipped on Jarod and told us where to find him. But both men still assert that they don't know who hired them. The calls to them were untraceable."

I straighten at that, cracking the lid of my bottle off. "Burner cell phone?"

"Yes."

"Does the number match the ones from the texts to Asha's or Melanie's phones?"

"No, it was a different number," he says, sounding as crestfallen as I feel.

"Did you get Jessica's devices to see if they have the same texts?"

"We just got them from her parents. Kenneth is looking at them now. We should know something on Monday."

"Has Munroe said anything yet?" I ask. It's killing me that I can't be there for the questioning. I know this is *their* case, but I want to see it through. I want to nail the bastard who did this, not lose him to the DA.

"Not yet, but we did look up some history on Gary Ventura. He used to work at the hospital with Dr. Munroe."

All roads lead back to that damn hospital.

"I'll call you if we get anything else," he says and ends the call.

———

Saturday morning a knocking at my front door startles me. I jump, realizing that it must be Roxie. I open the door to find her standing on my porch, luggage on one side and a box filled with wine on the other.

Her dark, short hair is swept up into a fauxhawk, the sides shaved short. Roxie has high cheekbones, deep-set brown eyes, and a nose with a kink in the middle, where a perp broke it during an arrest. Down the left side of her face, a scar cuts through her brow and traces a silvery line across her sepia skin. During our time in Detroit, a lot of guys liked to ask Roxie where she was *from*. Roxie was *from* Detroit, but that's not what they meant. What they really meant was, *Who in your family isn't white?* Roxie never told them, but I came to learn that Roxie was mixed race, black and Cuban on her mother's side and a hodgepodge of ancestry on her father's side—eastern European, Baltic, Italian. Roxie inherited more of her mother's features but got her father's height. She's nearly a head taller than me.

I grab her, pulling her into a tight hug. "I don't deserve you," I say as I squeeze.

Her leather jacket crinkles as she hugs me back. "Oh, shut up," she says. She pushes me back and thrusts the box filled with bottles of wine into my arms. I carry the wine to the kitchen while she brings in her luggage.

"So do I need to be your alibi?" she asks, grinning.

I laugh and shake my head. "No, I didn't kill him—yet."

She winks. "Oh, I know. Of course you didn't."

After we're done putting the wine away, I plop down at the dining room table. Roxie sits across from me. There's another knock at the door, and my stomach leaps. But it can't be Noah. Then I realize I ordered some groceries to be delivered last night. I let Jayden in the front door, and he lugs in several bags, placing them on the counter. I pay him, and Roxie joins me in putting the groceries away.

"Did I do the right thing?" I ask, trying to hold the emotions at bay so they don't overwhelm me again.

"I can't tell you if you did or didn't. But I trust that you did what you needed to do," she says.

"Do you question breaking it off with Lila?" I ask.

She shrugs but not in a way that's really convincing. "Sometimes. Did he tell you why he lied?"

"No, I didn't give him the chance," I explain.

For a long moment, she's silent. "Look, I have to say this as your friend, at least once."

I lean against the counter, crossing my arms as I wait for her to speak.

"Are you sure that you aren't looking for reasons to push him away because you're scared? Because you don't want to lose someone else?"

The words feel like a physical blow, and I bristle. My first instinct is to be defensive, to brush her off. But I can't deny that she might have a point—though I'm not ready to admit it aloud. I've never let anyone in before Noah. I've never wanted to. So maybe it hurts that he doesn't trust me enough to let me in the same way I've done for him. I open my mouth and start to say something, but the words don't come.

"You don't have to answer me. I just want you to think about it. I'm always going to be on your side, but you need to take a step back on this one," she says and grabs one of the bottles of wine.

"It's not even noon," I say as I eye the bottle.

She shakes her head. "All drinking rules go out the window during relationship crises; everyone knows that. And we've got two on our hands."

There's no winning this argument, so I point her toward the drawer with the corkscrew. A bottle of wine and a pizza delivery later, I feel like I've purged most of the venom from my wound, leaving a hollowness in its wake. Tomorrow I'll go to the Vinalhaven station, try to distract myself with work.

"I'm thinking of moving out here," Roxie says, her eyes on the window. "I've got family in Vermont. I want to be close, but not too close, you know?" she explains.

Really? Roxie is thinking of moving to Maine? Though I would absolutely love for Roxie to live closer, this isn't something I'd expected. I nod, though I don't understand. If it hadn't been for Noah and this case, I'd likely have fled to another state by now. After Dr. Munroe is charged, that may be exactly what I do, but I raise my glass for now.

"Well, cheers to that. Whereabouts?"

She grins. "There's a detective job in Bangor I've got my eye on."

That'd put Roxie only a couple of hours away.

"I heard rumors they may have two jobs up there," she says as she leans in conspiratorially.

"Is that right?"

A wicked smile crosses her dark lips. "We could get the team back together."

I can't deny that I love the idea. But do they really have enough going on up there to need two homicide detectives? I take a sip of my wine, letting the idea marinate in my mind.

"I'll tell you what—I'll apply after Munroe is arraigned and I know he's not getting out."

She stretches her hand across the table to shake mine. And I can't help but laugh. "What, is my word not good anymore?"

"Oh, come on—just shake it." She winks at me.

I shake her hand and take a sip of my wine. "So would this desire to move have anything to do with Lila?" I ask, raising a brow at her.

She rolls her eyes but doesn't look back at me; instead she looks at the table. "Maybe, maybe not. I'm not going to lie—the distance helps."

A few years ago, after Roxie and I first worked together, she admitted to me that she's got a bad habit of fleeing the state after a breakup. Breakup sightseeing, she likes to call it. Before she joined the team in Detroit, she'd worked in DC. She'd gone back and forth from DC to

Detroit for years and also lived in Washington and New York for a while.

"If it helps, and if you're sure." I just don't want Roxie to do anything she'll regret. I think she's got a habit of running away whenever things get serious—or whenever she wants to make sure things don't get serious, to be more accurate. Though I'm not one to judge: I run away before anything even has the chance to get serious.

Roxie eyes her bag on the floor and strolls over to grab it. In a fluid motion she unzips it, then pulls her laptop from inside. I watch her as she opens it and props it on the table, turning it to face me.

"Are you resorting to work to avoid talking about Lila?" I ask with a smirk.

She shakes her head at me. "I just remembered you'd asked me to look at the database for that MO." For a minute, she types on the computer, and then she turns it toward me. The screen is filled with what looks like an old search engine. "One of my contacts at the FBI shares her log-in with me so I can cross-reference things if needed. This is their violent-crime database that stores MOs for killers spanning back to the fifties, maybe even before. I haven't looked into much of the historical stuff."

I scoot closer to her so I can get a better look at the screen. She's got *ligature strangulation* and *binding* populated in the search field.

"I already looked for cigarette ashes or other debris left at the scene. There have been very few of those, and none in the past thirty to forty years. None of the killings where the ashes were present lined up with any other factors of the MO—most involved a stabbing or blunt-force trauma," she says as she scrolls through the results.

On her screen I see there are multiple killings that don't seem to be linked to my case, and then a listing with five victims catches my eye. "What's that one?" I ask, pointing to the results.

She clicks on the listing, and I start to read. The page outlines five women killed in the Daytona Beach, Florida, area between 2005 and

2008. Each woman was found bound, strangled, and dumped naked in the woods. It was suspected that each woman had been sexually assaulted based on trauma to the bodies. While some of the items line up with our current murders, the MO is still vastly different. Dumping a victim in the woods shows that the killer doesn't want to be caught. Dumping them in a motel? That screams that they want the attention.

"Did that one say anything about the faces being covered with a bag or plastic?" I ask as Roxie begins to scroll.

"No, nothing like that. They were all strangled with rope."

Roxie clicks on several other listings, each with *binding* and *ligature strangulation* as the main keywords. Many are too old to likely be related to this killer, and some of the others vary far too much from the rest of the pattern.

We spend hours drinking wine and going through the database. Finally, we decide to call it a night, and she takes the couch. I crawl bleary eyed up the stairs toward my bedroom, my stomach so full of wine it practically sloshes. When I fall into bed, it envelops me. I close my eyes, thinking of Noah and what could have been, if only he hadn't lied.

CHAPTER 11

Sunday morning, my head aches like it was split open and sewn back together while I was sleeping. When I glance in the bathroom mirror, my blonde hair looks like a rat's nest, and dark circles hang beneath my eyes. There's a thick film on my tongue, coating it completely in what feels like slime. I pop some Tylenol, brush my teeth, and head downstairs, expecting to find Roxie asleep on the couch. Instead, she's cooking.

"Where the hell did you get bacon?" I say as I amble toward the coffeepot. I know I didn't have any in the fridge. "And you made coffee? Will you marry me?"

She laughs. "I walked down the street to that little market, grabbed a few things. And don't get used to it. I've got to eat and run."

I sip my coffee slow, the heat of it tickling my lips.

"Going back to Detroit already?"

"Not quite. Heading to Bangor for an interview; then I'm heading into Vermont for a few days to see my sister."

I was hoping she'd be here for a few days at the least, but I don't plan to voice my disappointment. It was good of her to come here at all. And though I'm still not settled on what I'll do about Noah, I at least know whichever direction it goes, I can get through it.

"I'll keep my fingers crossed for you," I say.

"Sit down. Breakfast is almost ready." She motions at the table with a spatula in her hand.

I grab a couple of plates first, set them on the counter, grab some silverware, and then retreat to the table with my coffee cup. Roxie dishes out bacon and eggs, then carries them over.

"Thank you for making breakfast. This is delicious," I say as the first bite of egg melts on my tongue.

"We'll have to do it more often if I get this job."

Roxie and I make small talk over breakfast, and afterward I see her out. When I'm halfway through doing the dishes, my phone rings. But I ignore it. Chances are it's Noah. But instead of vibrating with a voice mail a few seconds after the ringing stops, it begins to ring again. I dry my hands and grab the phone. Sergeant Pelletier's name flashes on the screen.

"Sergeant," I say as soon as the call connects.

"Claire, I need you to get to the station." His words are slightly muffled, like he's wedged the phone between his ear and his shoulder.

I wait for him to break the news. Did they have to let Dr. Munroe out? Was someone else found dead? When he doesn't explain, I ask, "What happened?"

"Mrs. McConnel from the hospital is here. She says that she needs to speak with you about Dr. Munroe. I tried to question her, but she says that she wants to speak with you specifically. How soon can you get here?"

"It'll likely be at least an hour because of the ferry, but I'll get there as soon as I can," I say, wondering what Vera has to tell me. It's seemed that she's been holding back information all this time, so what's she been keeping to herself? I climb into my Mustang, weave through Vinalhaven, and wait impatiently for the ferry to arrive.

When I pull up in front of the station nearly an hour and a half later, my palms are sweating, and my heart is pounding like I've just run a mile. Relief washes over me as I realize I can focus on the case again and hopefully shed my worries about Noah for a while. I climb out of my Mustang, hands trembling as I enter the station. My mind spins as I consider what waits for me. As I cross the threshold, my guts clench.

"Where is she?" I ask as soon as I'm within earshot.

Sergeant Pelletier is wearing a wrinkled button-up and jeans that look like he pulled them off the floor of his bedroom. Dark bags hang beneath his bloodshot eyes. He steps toward me, away from his office. "Mrs. McConnel is in the interrogation room, waiting."

I'm surprised that she was willing to wait this long to speak with me. What's changed that she wants to open up now? Is she just trying to get one of her doctors out of lockup, or does she really have something that she needs to share with us?

"Has she said anything?" I ask.

Sergeant Pelletier shakes his head. "No. She's asked about Dr. Munroe a few times, though."

When I open the door, Vera has her head bowed, staring at the metal table in the center of the room. Though I'd prefer for Austin to be involved in this, I can't call her in right now. Vera's got on a flowy white blouse with navy polka dots on it, along with navy slacks. Under the table I can make out her leather heels. I have to give it to her—she knows how to dress. She always looks incredibly polished, but I guess as a CEO those first impressions really matter. The business world is not kind to women. I walk in, slap a legal pad on the table, and take a seat in front of her.

"Good morning," I say and take a sip from my coffee.

Her sleek hair parts around her face when she looks up at me, and her eyes are shadowed, like she hasn't slept in days. Her eyes are dull, lips cracked. It's jarring against the rest of her polished exterior.

"I want to start off by saying I'm not a bad person," Vera says, eyes wide. "You're going to think that, though, no matter what I say. But I'm not, okay?"

I nod, unsure where she's going with this.

"Have you ever wanted something, thought that something would make you happy, and then when you got it, everything just turned to shit?"

My mind flashes to Noah. I want to shake my head to be rid of it, to cleanse myself of him, but instead I say, "Can you explain what you mean?"

She sighs. "I need to start over. I feel like I'm going to puke."

"We can take a break if you need to."

She shakes her head. "No, I just need to grow a pair and get this over with. Look." She stops to take a sip of her water. Her eyes dart all over the room, looking at everything but me. "Ian, Dr. Munroe, I mean, couldn't have done this. You need to let him go."

Is she saying he couldn't have done it because she did? She's too hard to get a read on. Her body language is all over the place.

"And why is that?" I ask when she doesn't explain.

"Because he was with me."

"He was with you on February twenty-first, February twenty-fifth, and again on February twenty-sixth?"

"Yes," she manages, her eyes glued to the table. Her arms rest on it, and she clicks her long red nails on the smooth metal surface.

"Why was he with you? How can you be sure he was there the whole time?"

"Because we're having an affair. It's been going on for six months. We were at the Carle Motel each of those nights. I know my husband would never be caught dead in that part of town." She winces. "Sorry for the expression. I wasn't thinking." Her normally pallid complexion is splotchy, and beads of sweat cling to her brow.

"Oh" is all I can manage to say. It's not often that something catches me off guard, but this sure does. "So you would testify to that fact in a court of law?" If they were there, that would explain how his hospital badge showed up in that parking lot.

"Might as well. I was planning on telling Aidan soon anyway. I've been lawyer shopping." Vera offers a slight shrug.

"I see. And is there anyone else that can corroborate that you two were together?" This obviously isn't the news I was hoping for. Now I'm back to square one. If she's telling me the truth. Love can make people do stupid things. I know that firsthand. So is she lying because she loves him, or is she telling me the truth?

She bites her lip. "If you really need proof, I can provide it."

"If you want us to cut him loose, I need to see the evidence."

She grabs her purse, opens it up, and leafs through some papers. After a few moments, she holds a few out to me. I look them over, finding receipts for rooms at the Carle Motel on the twenty-first, twenty-fifth, and twenty-sixth.

"These only list your name."

"If you call, they'll confirm that Dr. Munroe was with me and that we were together in that motel while all the deaths took place. That's where we normally go. If you need others, I have a few from several weeks ago. You'll understand I've thrown the others out by now." Though I expect her to look ashamed, she holds her chin up, defiant.

"Give me a moment," I say as I rise from the table. I walk out of the interrogation room to find the station mostly empty. Both Zane and Blake are at their desks, though. I approach Zane. He glances up, smiling. "Detective."

I hold out the receipts for him. "I need you to call and confirm an alibi for Dr. Munroe and Vera McConnel. They claim to have been staying at this hotel on February twenty-first, twenty-fifth, and twenty-sixth. Don't lead the questioning by asking if anyone was with Vera. But if they mention anyone, I need a description and to know if the hotel staff saw either party leave between nine p.m. and two a.m."

He nods. "Got it. Give me a few minutes."

"Just knock on the door when you have it. Thank you."

When I walk back to the interrogation room, Vera is sitting at the table with her hands laced together atop it, her manicured nails gleaming in the light. I take my seat again opposite her.

"Let's continue. Another officer is checking on the alibi. Is there anyone at the hospital you can think of that would want to make it look like Dr. Munroe did this?" I ask, just in case he didn't drop his key card. Someone could have planted it at the scene on purpose.

She gives a one-shouldered shrug. "Nearly everyone. He rubs a lot of the staff the wrong way. Sometimes I think I'm the only one who understands him."

As we wait for Zane, a thought occurs to me about the two men who broke into my hotel room. One of them worked at the hospital. I can't help but wonder if Vera ever had interactions with either of the men.

"Do you happen to know Gary Ventura and Jarod Trevino?"

She lowers her chin, and one of her manicured brows rises at my question. "I can't say that I do, no."

"Gary Ventura worked at your hospital previously. He broke into my hotel room recently. Would you know anything about that?"

Her mouth drops open, but words have escaped her. Finally, she says, "Of course I wouldn't know anything about that."

Vera and I continue to talk for a minute. Though I ask her if anything else suspicious has happened at the hospital, she rebuffs my questions. With each second that passes, she seems more edgy, like she's dying to get out of this room. Sweat beads on her forehead as she picks at her fingernails. Finally, there's a light knock at the door. I stand and open it to find Zane.

"Everything checked out," he says, handing me the papers back. "They brought up that there was a man with Vera. They recognized him as Dr. Munroe, and they'd be willing to say so in court if necessary."

I nod. "Thank you."

After we've finished her statement, Vera stalks out of the interrogation room. There's a hunch to her shoulders I haven't noticed before, as if she's so tired she can't bear to stand up straight any longer. As she disappears out of the station, I turn back to Sergeant Pelletier's office. He sits behind his desk, sipping from a coffee mug. When I approach the door, he looks up at me through the steam rising from his cup. He motions toward the chair in front of him, and I take a seat.

"What'd she have to say?" he asks. I'm surprised he didn't watch through the one-way mirror.

"We need to cut Munroe loose. She's his alibi. They're having an affair," I say.

"Jesus Christ," he mutters, his voice low and scratchy. "Do you believe her?"

"I don't know why she'd risk her career and her marriage to lie for him if she wasn't. She seems very focused on her job and that hospital. I'm sure if she could jettison one doctor to save the reputation of the hospital, she'd do it. She doesn't seem the type to stick her neck out for anyone. Zane checked out her alibi. The motel staff confirms that she was there with Munroe during the murders. No one saw either of them leave." If Munroe didn't do this, we're looking for someone else in the hospital. And maybe the director of the hospital will be of more help.

He nods, clearly agreeing with my assessment. "What's your next step?" he asks.

"I'm going to go to the hospital to speak to the director, Vera's husband, after I check on the text messages Kenneth is looking into."

"I'll take care of Munroe in the meantime."

I finish up with Sergeant Pelletier before walking back to Kenneth's office. When I peek in, I find Kenneth in front of his three monitors with his headphones on.

"Kenneth," I say, more loudly than I usually would to be sure that he can hear me over the noise.

He glances over his shoulder and then swivels his chair around to face me. "Detective, I've got some texts for you."

Anticipation needles my spine as I step closer. He holds out the papers. This time they're sorted differently: the burner 203 number is on top. I scan through the texts to the last one. Our perp actually mentioned the motel. All the other times there was a phone call, which I imagine was used to arrange everything. Now that it's written out, though, if we can find who owns this burner phone, we have some solid evidence.

"The name was saved under *T*," he says.

"Trystan it is, then," I muse as I survey the texts. Under the pages containing the texts from T, I find more of the messages containing coordinates. No new messages, though. It looks like the last one arrived two weeks ago. So there have been no new bonfires since then? If the killer isn't meeting them at the bonfires, why do all these girls have the same messages? I'm not sure if it's a coincidence or if there's another angle to this that I haven't considered.

"Thank you for these," I say finally.

"Anytime. I haven't found anything of interest on any of the social media profiles of the victims. And none have sent any emails or arranged meetings with anyone within twenty-four hours of their deaths, minus the ones from the 203 number."

"Let me know if anything else pops up."

"I will."

As soon as I finish with Kenneth, I go straight for Austin's desk. When she sees me walking over, she grabs her coat and starts to pull it on. A hint of a smile tugs at the corner of my mouth. Austin is already starting to read me. That's a good sign. Those are the instincts she needs to hone and build on if she wants to succeed in this line of work.

"Where are we headed?" she asks, her eyes gleaming, as if she can't wait for whatever is next. God, I miss having that kind of enthusiasm. Now I know if I keep digging, it's likely not answers I'm going to find but another horror and another question. Some investigations drag you down dark paths from which you're unsure if you can ever return, if you can ever be the same after they're done. I used to think I was making the world a better place, but now I'm not sure that's even possible.

"We're going back to the hospital," I say. "Munroe has an alibi." We stroll out of the station as I explain the conversation that I had with Vera. She's just as surprised by the revelations as I was.

"What are we going to do at the hospital?" she asks.

"We're going to talk to the director. He may know something. One of the guys who broke into my hotel room worked at that hospital. Every victim has been there before their death. There's something there, and we've got to find it."

I pull out of the station parking lot and turn right on Route 1, heading south toward the medical center. As we drive, the gray sky roils above us, threatening more storms, more snow. We've reached the final stretch of winter, when you can feel the coming spring in your gut. I'm not sure if it's my desire for the oppressive cold to stop or if the season is actually starting to shift. Around us the pine trees are tipped with ice, like metal points attached to spears. Beneath the trees there's a patchwork of ice, snow, and mud. I follow the curve of the road ahead, passing houses and small shops, until finally civilization is swallowed again by nature. When the trees give way again, it's the opening to the hospital. I turn in.

A long, winding driveway curves through the trees toward the building. As we get closer, I make out a half moon of vans collected in one of the far parking lots. News vans. Word must have broken that the victims thus far have been connected to the hospital. That's not a bit that we planned on releasing to the media. *Someone* talked. There aren't many people in the Camden office. But I'm going to have to speak to Sergeant Pelletier about fixing this leak.

"What are they doing here?" Austin asks when she notices them.

"I'm sure someone told them there was a story here," I say under my breath as I pull into a spot next to the administrative building.

"Vultures," she says as she throws her door open.

Halfway to the building, I hear Vera's shrill voice. "Get these goddamn cameras out of here!" she yells, her arms waving toward the camera crews. From the looks of it, none of them are recording right now. I close the distance between myself and the scene. Several members of the camera crew move toward me as I approach. A small woman in a red blazer steps in front of me with a microphone.

"Detective, what can you tell me about the rumors that several teens who have been found dead in Camden have connections to this hospital?"

"I cannot comment on an ongoing investigation. However, we want to urge the public if they have seen anything suspicious or know anything about the victims to please reach out to Camden PD with the information."

I push past the row of reporters toward Vera. "Vera, can I talk to you for a few minutes?" I ask, my volume well over that of her tirade, when I approach.

Her fists are clenched at her sides, jaw locked and eyes shuttered, as she swivels to face me. She must have encountered the mass of media on her way back into the hospital after she left the Camden Police Department. I'm surprised she managed to make it back to the hospital before I did. It must have taken longer to catch up with Sergeant Pelletier than I realized. I glance to my left, noticing Austin is trailing behind me a few feet, as if trying to stay out of this woman's warpath.

"Detective." Vera practically hisses the word, all her composure from this morning melted away. I stride toward the building, not waiting for her. I know she'll follow, if only to escape the cameras.

Her heels click after me. I wait for her just inside the door. Austin follows her, eyeing her carefully.

"You said—" Vera starts as soon as the door closes.

"I think your office would be a better location for this conversation," I say, glancing down the hall at the gathered group of nurses staring at us.

"This is *my* hospital. We'll have this conversation wherever I see fit," she says snidely. I half expect her to slam her foot into the ground for emphasis. She doesn't. Instead she glares.

"We can do that if you'd prefer," I say calmly.

Her eyes bore into me, a withering stare I'm sure is meant to unhinge me. I'm not sure what effect it has on those here, but this woman doesn't scare me. She's an inconvenience, a soulless bitch, but not frightening.

"As I was saying, you said you were going to help keep this quiet," she says a little too loudly.

The gathering crowd of gawkers thrums at the end of the hall. Though I don't turn to look at them, the heat of their gazes crawls across my skin, making the flesh there burn.

"I said no such thing. Nor did Sergeant Pelletier. If proper security measures had been put in place—"

She cuts me off, her hand flying up so quickly I take a step back, thinking she intends to hit me.

"Vera, please," a man says from the end of the hall as he strides toward us. His voice is familiar. I think this is Aidan, but I'm not certain. I spoke with Aidan last year while investigating a case back in Vinalhaven. The man has broad shoulders and short reddish-brown hair. And I'd guess he's in his late forties or early fifties. His features are striking, with sharp cheekbones and a square jaw. A heavy brow shadows his eyes, the fluorescent light above making the effect even more arresting.

"Don't you start with me, Aidan," she spits. Her eyes settle on me again, shuddering with rage. Her fists ball at her sides. "Get out of this hospital."

I place a hand on one of my hips and set my stance wide, hoping that my body language communicates that I don't plan to move. If she wants to throw me out, she can try it. But instead, she walks down the hall, like she's on a tear. Aidan doesn't follow; instead he glances at me and Austin.

Nurse Jordan heads down the hall in my direction, cowering out of the way when Vera sweeps past. Her bright-green scrubs are far too cheery. She's got her hair tucked away from her face. The nurse's eyes are wide, her cheeks flushed pink. I should be relieved that Vera is gone, but I'm more concerned about what she's going to do now.

"You both okay?" Jordan asks.

"Don't worry about us."

"She's been like that the past few months." She shakes her head. "Let me know if you need me to answer any more questions."

I thank her before turning my attention back to Aidan. "Do you have a few minutes?" I ask.

He nods. "Come on. We can go talk in my office."

To my surprise Aidan's office is on the other side of the hospital. I'd imagined that it'd be right next to Vera's. Aidan's space is the polar opposite of his wife's. His walls are painted a hunter green, and Red Sox memorabilia hang on the walls along with stuffed pheasant and ducks. Like most of the men in Maine, he's clearly a hunter. His desk looks ornate, with carved legs, curled edges, and wood a shade of brown that looks like rich chocolate. I can imagine easily that some historical documents have been signed on its surface. And behind the desk he has several pictures of him and Vera on their wedding day.

"Lovely pictures," I say, gesturing toward them.

He follows my gaze, and a shadow darkens his face. Sadness hangs on the edges of his smile. "Was the best day of my life. I never thought I could love anyone the way I love that woman." His accent is thick in his voice.

The words make my own recent heartbreak bubble to the surface. But I can't let it. I grit my teeth as emotion threatens to crush me. My stomach sours under the weight of the turmoil, and I suck in a sharp breath through my nose.

"Where are you from originally?" I ask to distract myself.

"Georgia, the Atlanta area. That's where Vera and I met."

"Oh yeah, that's right. She told me about that when I spoke with her the first time."

"She did? I'm surprised she talked about me."

"Why's that?" I ask. Shouldn't a wife talk about her husband? But I recall the scorn in her voice as she spoke of him. He must know about that. Does he also know about the affair? That knowledge burns in the back of my mind. And I want to tell him. Because I know what it's like to be lied to. I would want to know.

He speaks again, pulling me from my train of thought. "She barely even talks *to* me anymore. I'm surprised she had anything to say about me." He sighs and finally takes his eyes off the pictures to turn around. The leather chair behind his desk hisses as he takes a seat. I want to ask, but I can tell by his face that he's not done speaking yet. It's just taking him a while to get the words out. And I realize I can't tell him. It isn't my place. "For the past few months, she's been distant. She blows up at all the nurses." He shakes his head. "I just keep waiting for the divorce papers. I know they're coming."

"I'm very sorry," I say, because I have no idea what else would help. But I've heard just about enough of his marital problems. I need to circle back to the case; otherwise I'll say something I shouldn't. "So this all started before the first homicide, then?"

He nods. "Yes, a few months ago."

There are several questions I'm going to have to ask about his wife. Vera has given me a bad feeling since this all started. Do I think she did the killing? It's not likely, but something in my gut tells me to keep going.

"Would you characterize your wife as a violent person?" I ask.

He looks up from the desk, his eyes wide. "Well, I . . . I . . ." He seems lost, words escaping him. "I'm not sure I know the answer to that question anymore. With how she's acted lately, I can't say that I would put it past her."

"Has she ever tried to assault you?"

"She's thrown things at me. But hit me? No. Never enough to do any real damage."

"That can still be considered assault, Mr. McConnel," I clarify. So many people think that women aren't capable of abuse. But they are. Emotional and physical. "Have you ever feared for your life around her?"

He lets out a low chuckle and shakes his head. "No, nothing like that."

"Does your wife have access to firearms?"

His eyes go wide at my words. "Well, yes. Most people who live here have guns."

That fact I do know. It's very common in Maine. But if she has violent tendencies and she's been unstable, I would want him to take that into consideration.

"I would recommend that you give removing them from your home or securing them some thought." Silence thickens between us for a beat, and I consider what I've got to ask next carefully. "Has your wife made you aware of our investigation into the homicides of three former patients from this hospital?"

He shakes his head. "She didn't, no. But David told me about them." He motions toward the window. "It's also all over the news."

They may be going through a rough patch right now, but it still seems odd to me that she wouldn't mention the homicides to her husband, especially considering he's the director of the hospital.

I rise from the chair, Austin standing beside me. "Please think about securing your weapons."

He shakes his head. "I don't need to do that. I know the old Vera is in there somewhere. Detective, I just want my wife back."

"Well, for your sake, I hope you find her. Do you know of an employee by the name of Gary Ventura?" I ask.

His brows furrow, his face a mask. "I can't say that I know him."

"He was apparently a worker here at the hospital. He broke in to my hotel room, assaulted me, and ordered me to drop the homicide investigations and rule them suicides."

He sits up straighter in his chair, and his eyes go wide. "Are you okay?"

I nod. "I'm fine. But it really makes me wonder why an employee of this hospital would show up at my hotel and tell me to drop the investigation. Especially since all the victims have been patients here."

"So you think that whoever is killing these girls works here?"

"It's a very distinct possibility," I say. Though I would say it's more than that: it's not so much a possibility but a certainty at this point. "Your wife doesn't seem to have any interest in helping us resolve this situation. Her concern is for the reputation of the hospital, not for the possible loss of life. So I ask that you please keep an eye open. If any employees are leaving the building at odd hours, not using their key cards to enter the building, please have David monitor it. Also, if there's anyone on staff who's trying to get access to patients who shouldn't have it, that would be another red flag."

He opens up a drawer in his desk and takes out a legal pad. I watch him write down everything that I've said. "I'll speak to David right away so we can start keeping an eye on this. I'm sorry that my wife hasn't been more helpful with this. But I can assure you I'll do everything in my power to help," he says before standing up and offering his hand to me.

I take his hand. "Thank you."

"No, Detective, thank you for speaking with me and letting me know about all this. I had no idea."

Austin and I finish up with Aidan and head back to the station. Snow falls gently from the rolling gray clouds as we walk to my Mustang. After a short drive through the empty streets, we roll to a stop in the Camden PD parking lot. Once inside, Austin walks to her desk, and I continue to my borrowed station. I jiggle the mouse and wait for the screen to pop back to life. I type Vera's name into a search engine, then scroll through the pages of results about her.

This is Vera's first job as a hospital CEO. Before this, she had high-ranking management positions at several different hospitals throughout the South. Her last was a hospital in Atlanta. I try a few cursory searches to see if there were any murders near the hospital while she worked there. But there are too many results, too many murders around that time, and well after she left. It'd be impossible to tie her to any of these.

Next, I search for Dr. Munroe, but there's not a single blemish on his record. He's only worked at small hospitals, none of which had any suspicious deaths near them. But I keep digging. I have to.

CHAPTER 12

With an extra-large coffee clutched in my hand, I head inside Camden PD. When I open the door, the scent of doughnuts is heavy in the air, the tang and the sugar coating my mouth. I take a sip of my coffee, breathing in the aroma, hoping to drown it out. It only works for a few seconds.

It's Monday morning, and after Vera's stunt yesterday, Munroe is off the suspect list. The investigation has hit a roadblock. And I'm not sure where else to go. We've got no evidence from the scene that wasn't tainted by ashes and nothing on the victims that points us in any direction, and I don't even know where they're meeting up with this killer before going to a motel. Though I've been searching, reviewing the interviews Zane and Blake did with Jessica's family, I can't find anything solid that ties these victims together outside of the hospital.

Melanie and Jessica were both outdoorsy and liked to spend time in Bald Mountain Preserve on their ATVs. But thus far, Asha didn't seem to have that kind of lifestyle. These girls weren't friends that I can tell, not even on social media. They didn't spend time together at school. Their parents never saw them together. The only things binding them are death and time in that hospital. But there are too many people in that hospital who interacted with each of these girls. Two of the junior officers have been working to see if any current employees have a criminal record, but no one has been flagged.

Inside the station, I walk by a receptionist's desk and weave through the bull pen. I nod at Austin as I pass her desk, then Zane, Blake, Sasha, and Clint. My temporary station is at the far corner of the room, close to Sergeant Pelletier's office. As I set down my coffee and take off my jacket, his voice cuts across the pen.

"Calderwood, in here, please," he yells in a way that reminds me vaguely of a principal. I haven't done anything wrong, but for some reason, my stomach shifts with unease.

I stride toward his office, gripping my coffee tighter than I need to. Sergeant Pelletier is hunched behind his desk, a blue button-up clashing with a split pea–colored tie. It makes me wonder if he got dressed in a rush. His face is flushed, stained by a spiderweb of red; it even manages to color the fleshy little ball at the end of his nose. He's got a strange look on his face, one I haven't seen before. He glances down at the desk in front of him, where his breakfast is laid out.

"What's wrong?" I ask as I step inside and take a seat.

"Wrong?" he asks, then glances at his breakfast again. "They put too many jalapeños in my burrito. It's kicking me in the face like I'm eating a damn firecracker."

"Oh" is all I can manage to say.

"In about twenty minutes, Tegan Hartley is going to drop in to see you," he says as he glances at his watch.

I don't have any idea who that is. I haven't heard the name before. "And she is?"

"She claims to be a friend of Jessica and Asha," he explains.

"Where did you get her information from?" I ask. So far I haven't found any overlapping friends between Jessica and Asha. It just seems strange if she was a friend to both victims that no one mentioned her.

"She called into the station and said she wanted to speak to an officer working on the case in person."

"Why is she just calling now? Did she say anything else?" Sometimes at this stage in a case, especially when it gets this much media attention, people will start probing departments for answers. It concerns me that this girl is coming out of the woodwork now and that she didn't come to us earlier in the investigation. Is she just feeling us out? Or does she have legitimate information?

"Blake is the one that took the call. He didn't say that she said anything else or offered information about why she was calling now." He looks back at the legal pad on his desk, as if checking to be sure.

"If that's all, I'm going to catch up with Austin before we talk to Tegan."

He waves his hand in dismissal. "That's all."

I walk out of his office and cross the room to Austin's desk. She's sipping from a cup of tea when I walk up and glances at me over the rim. Both of her hands clutch the cup, as if she's afraid she'll drop it.

"Hey, Claire," she says as she puts the cup down.

After pulling up a chair, I plop down next to her desk. "What can you tell me about Tegan Hartley?"

"She's twenty or so, works as a mechanic in town. She got in trouble three or four times for truancy, but nothing serious." Austin glances over her shoulder to see who's taking note of our conversation. Then she lowers her voice to add, "She's known to get around town, if you know what I mean."

I try not to let my frustration rise with that sentiment. That's something that always annoyed the shit out of me in Vinalhaven. Guys can fuck anything that moves and suffer no ill reputation, but a woman loses her virginity to someone she doesn't intend on marrying—and bam, she might as well stamp *SLUT* on her forehead. It's ridiculous. Even worse is when there's talk that a woman was asking for a horrible fate just because she had a libido.

"She's a mechanic?" I ask, trying not to let my lingering frustrations touch my words.

"She works on motorcycles, snowmobiles, ATVs over at Midcoast Custom Repairs."

"She gets here in twenty. Do you want to sit in on the conversation? She wants to talk to us about Asha and Jessica. She apparently knew them both."

Her eyes go wide for just a moment. "She did? Why didn't anyone else mention that she knew them? I've never seen them together."

"That was my question. Maybe no one knew they were acquainted."

———

Twenty minutes later, my desk phone rings. It's the receptionist alerting me to Tegan's arrival. I walk to the front of the station and find her leaning against the desk, chatting up the receptionists like she belongs here. Tegan looks like she should work at a motorcycle shop. She's got on a worn leather biker jacket, with patches sewn into the crinkled hide. Beneath the jacket, a vintage band T-shirt peeks out. From the pyramid on it, my guess is Pink Floyd. She's got on tight skinny jeans tucked into buckled motorcycle boots that go up to midcalf.

Her hard features go along with the clothes: high cheekbones, a pronounced nose, and lips that remind me of Angelina Jolie. When she sees me, the left side of her mouth quirks up, and she sweeps her long black hair away from her face.

"Tegan?" I ask, though I know she must be.

She nods, and I introduce myself before bringing her through the bull pen. "The only place we have to talk is the room we usually use for interrogations. Is that okay?" I ask. The only other option would be for me to kick Sergeant Pelletier out of his office, and I'm not about to do that.

"Whatever works," she says in a voice much deeper than I'd expect out of a woman in her early twenties.

I show her into the room, and Austin joins us. Tegan sits at the table, the metal chair scraping against the concrete floor. The back of her head is reflected in the one-way mirror behind her.

"Would you like anything to drink?" I ask.

She shakes her head. "I'm all set."

I take a seat, Austin sitting beside me. "So, Tegan, what brings you in here today?"

"I've been out of town for a couple weeks, and when I got back yesterday, I saw the stories about Jessica and Asha." Her voice is husky, filled with emotion as she says it. There're no tears, but I can tell that she's trying to remain composed.

"And how did you know them?" I ask.

She leans in, her elbows propped on the table. "If I tell you something that's not technically legal, could I go to jail for it?" she asks, all the emotion shed completely.

"That depends," I say. There are too many factors. I can't guarantee her that whatever she says wouldn't implicate her in some crime.

"What if I didn't do anything illegal—I just knew about it?" she asks.

"Well, if you didn't commit the crime yourself, but you were aware, then you could technically be charged as an accessory. However, the chances of that are low, and coming in here to volunteer information that helps with an investigation would put you in a good light. Chances are the DA wouldn't want to go after you for anything if you helped us to solve these murders," I explain. I try to dance around it as best I can. I can't tell her that she won't get in trouble for whatever she's about to tell me. But if she helps me catch whoever is doing this, I'll go to bat for this girl. I'll do whatever I can to help keep her out of trouble.

She's quiet, chewing her bottom lip, clearly lost in contemplation. "I knew Asha and Jessica because of ATV," she says in a low voice.

"I'm going to need you to explain," I say when she doesn't continue.

"Over in Bald Mountain Preserve—or some of the other preserves if it's too packed—we have races. I haven't ever participated, but they pay me to show up and help with the ATVs if anyone needs a quick fix. It's an easy two hundred dollars, so I almost always go. Jessica and Asha both raced. There was another girl they did it with, but I didn't ever interact with her. But I got drinks and had dinner with Jessica and Asha a few times."

Is that what the text messages they were receiving were for? Not bonfires? "Do you know about these?" I ask as I show her a sheet of the coordinates from my files.

"Yeah, those are sent out so people know where and when the races are being held."

I make note of that and then circle back to something else she said. "That other girl you mentioned. Could that have been Melanie?"

"I think so. I thought it was Miranda or Melissa, something like that."

"In the interviews we've done for Jessica and Asha, no one in their families, none of their friends, mentioned you," I say. Though there're no outward signs that make me disbelieve Tegan, I need to be sure that the information she's providing is accurate.

"We were careful. Asha, Jessica, and the others who raced didn't really have anything in common outside racing. And a lot of the women are so competitive; they're just there to win, not to make friends. So I don't think they saw each other outside of those meet ups. Racing ATVs and betting on the results isn't legal. No one wants to get busted or have it shut down. It's one of the few things we can do and have it totally to ourselves, away from the tourists."

I don't plan on shutting down their races. That's not my fish to fry. But I do need to determine if our suspect ever came to the races. Though I know this all ties back to the hospital, there's overlap here. "Nothing we saw indicated that Asha was involved in ATV," I say. Though it was clear for Melanie and Jessica, how did Asha keep it a secret?

"In middle school Asha fell off her brother's ATV and got a really bad concussion. She'd loved them back then, but after her fall, her parents made her promise that she wouldn't get on them again. They thought it was too dangerous. Though they let her older brother keep riding. About six months ago, she came back to the scene; then she was gone for a while because she got sick."

"Do you remember anyone named Trystan coming to the races?"

She shakes her head. "No, I don't remember anyone with that name."

"Were there races going on the nights Melanie, Asha, or Jessica died?" I ask.

She shakes her head. "I think there was one a few days before Melanie died, on the seventeenth or eighteenth, but she couldn't race because of her wrist. There wasn't another before Asha's death; that was too close to the other one. We usually space them out by a few weeks. And for Jessica, I don't know. I was out of town."

"Did you see Melanie with anyone at the race? A man?"

"Not that I remember."

"Do you think it would have been out of the question or out of character for any of them to have met a guy at the races and gone home with him or to a hotel?"

She offers me a one-shouldered shrug. "I didn't know them that well. But I did see Asha leave with a guy a couple times."

"Do you know who this guy was?" I ask.

She shakes her head. "No, I'd never seen him before. But that's not all that surprising. There are a lot of people who come to the races that I don't know. There are spectators; then there are those who actually race. Some people come from other towns—it's not just Camden. Typically, I only deal with the racers. I don't have any interest in those who are there to place bets. I'm there to keep the engines running."

"Was there anyone there that stood out to you? Someone who was watching the girls there a little too closely?"

"Not that I remember."

"When and where do these races take place?" I ask.

"It depends. They switch them up so it's less likely that they'll ever get found out and shut down. They used to do the same thing up north, in Appleton and Union, but they got shut down in both. Usually they're on weekend nights. But when is variable."

"They race in the middle of the night? That doesn't seem safe."

"Most of the ATVs have lights on the front, and they all know the area well enough that it's fine. One girl, I think it was Melanie, got hurt recently and broke her wrist. Other than that, she was fine, though. No one's been seriously hurt," she explains.

I really want to add a *yet*, but I don't. "The next time you hear about a race, give me a call," I say as I fish out one of my business cards.

She glances at the business card but doesn't take it. "Are you going to shut it down?"

I shake my head. "No, I've got no intentions of shutting it down."

Carefully, as if the card might bite her, she scoops it up and slides it into her back pocket. "I've got to go. Need to get to work for my shift."

"Thank you for coming in," I say.

Austin walks Tegan out, and I head back to my desk to type up my notes from the interview. Just as I've got nearly all of them done, my cell phone buzzes in my pocket. I glance at the screen, but I don't recognize the number.

"Detective Calderwood," I say as soon as the call connects.

"Claire, this is Vera McConnel over at the medical center," she says in a smooth, even voice, as if her breakdown over the media yesterday never happened.

"Yes?" I say, unsure why exactly she's calling.

"I wanted to give you a heads-up that we will be terminating Trent Ibben today. He will no longer be allowed on hospital grounds." She says this in such a way it seems like she thinks we've spoken about Trent before. But I have no idea who this man is.

"And he is?" I ask when she doesn't explain.

"He is the head of our custodial-services team."

"And why is he being terminated?" I ask, making sure to use the same phrasing she did. I noticed she's careful not to say *fired*, and I'm sure there's a reason for that.

"He was caught taking pictures of patients. Explicit pictures," she says, her voice low, her words careful.

"Oh?" I ask.

"Yes, some underage patients. Girls in their mid- to late teens."

"Did he have pictures on his phone of Jessica, Melanie, or Asha?" I ask.

She clears her throat. "Yes, he did. I wanted to make you aware, as I am sure that you will need to question him about this. We have also alerted the authorities to the fact that he has images of underage girls on his phone. I spoke to Sergeant Pelletier a few minutes ago, but I wanted to give you a call as well. He was caught in the act of taking the pictures by David."

My stomach flip-flops and then creeps up my throat as the information sickens me. If he has pictures of those girls and she's seen them, that could be enough for us to get a warrant. "Vera, would you be willing to sign a statement saying why he is being terminated and that both you and David saw the pictures? That should help us get a warrant." With anyone else, I'd be sure that they'd give us this information without any problems. But with Vera, who the hell knows.

"Yes, we'll both sign the statement, and then I'll email it over to you."

"You may get a call from the judge to verify," I explain.

"That's fine. I'll put my cell phone number on there as well. I want to get this wrapped up as quickly as possible. The faster that man is in jail, the faster we can guarantee that he can't kill any more of our patients," she says.

It seems that she's softened her edge a bit on stopping these murders. And she seems incredibly certain that Trent did this. While it doesn't look good for him, I need more evidence and a motive. I know that the reasoning behind her sudden willingness to help has nothing to do with loss of life and everything to do with stockholders and how her hospital is being portrayed in the media. The reporters have started giving it the title of the hunting ground for the Pen Bay Strangler. Which is obviously not ideal if you're hoping patients will actually come to your hospital.

I walk straight to Sergeant Pelletier's office and rap gently on the open door. "Hey, you got a minute?" I ask. He waves me in, and I catch him up on the conversations I had with both Tegan and Vera. He confirms that he's spoken with Vera.

"Can we bring in Trent for this and get a warrant?" I ask.

"We can bring him in, but I want to talk to him before we put in for the warrant. The warrant may limit us, because right now, what we can charge him with is child pornography and voyeurism."

"I'll grab Austin and go pick him up," I say automatically.

"I already have someone on patrol out picking him up. Sit tight. They'll be back with him soon."

I head out of the station and sweep my coat on, needing a few minutes of fresh air before digging into the interrogation. When I get to my car, I check my messages. Two missed calls from Noah and several texts asking me to please call him. Roxie's words come back to my mind. Am I just looking for a reason to push him away? I can't even take the key I made for him out of my pocket. For now, my silence is the biggest step I can take on the path that will lead me further from Noah and hopefully toward answers. It's strange how our lives braided together, and now, I can feel the threads that made *us* unraveling. But is that what I really want? The two sides of me are pulling apart at the seams as they war over which direction I should go. Instead of talking to him, I text Roxie and wish her luck on her interview.

I watch a patrol car pull into the parking lot a few minutes later. Zane and Clint get out, then pull Trent from the back seat. As they walk toward the door, I slide out of my car and follow them inside. Once they have him settled in the interrogation room, Sergeant Pelletier tells me that he's ready for me.

"I've already put in a call to the DA. We can rush a warrant on his phone, DNA, and his house if he has no alibi, since we've got Vera's statement and his access to the victims."

"I'll get what I can out of him, but I'll ask about the alibis first."

As we weave through the station, there's a low drone of voices cut by telephones ringing. When I open the door to the interrogation room, I find Trent leaning back on his metal chair like he may as well be on a dock in Aruba.

Great, he's either an idiot or a sociopath. Austin appraises him for a long time, like she's not sure what to make of it either. Finally, she gives me a look that tells me she wants to dig in.

"Hello, Mr. Ibben, I'm Detective Calderwood," I say as I sit across from him, my blank notepad still on the table.

Trent is a wide man, shoulders broader than his chair. His torso has a square sort of shape. He's got a chiseled jaw, a slim, straight nose. He's attractive, the kind of guy I'm sure could use his looks to lure women. Nothing about him says *predator*.

His eyes sharpen with curiosity when he looks at me, but that quickly fades to disinterest.

"I heard that you were suspended from your position at the medical center. Is that correct?"

He says nothing and doesn't even look up from the table. All right, more direct it is.

"Did you work the night of the twenty-sixth?"

Silence.

"The night of the twenty-first or the twenty-fifth?"

Silence.

"Have you visited the Millay Inn or the Carle Motel?" I ask next, though I doubt he's going to tell me anything. There's no response.

"Did you ever visit Bald Mountain Preserve, Camden Hills State Park, or Meadow Mountain Preserve during ATV races?"

He glances up at me, his eyes going wide. He hadn't expected me to ask that. His eyes drop again, and he goes back to picking at his nails.

I fold my arms atop the table and lean in, as if conspiratorially. "Look. If you don't help me here, I can't help you."

But still, he says nothing.

I push up from the chair and stalk back into Pelletier's office. "He won't talk, won't confirm or deny anything."

"I'll see if I can get a warrant without it," he says and picks up the phone. "Keep pushing. See if you can get him to say anything." But I fill him in on the ATV races. Though I intend to be true to my word for Tegan—I have no plans to shut them down—Sergeant Pelletier needs to know.

I pull Austin to the side and have her call the hospital. I need to confirm that he wasn't in the building while the murders took place. If we can get that information, that will make it even more likely the warrant will be granted. While Austin makes the calls, I check back in on Trent to see if he seems any more willing to talk. His eyes track me as I walk into the room, and it reminds me of a tiger watching a human in the zoo. But he says nothing; his mouth doesn't even quirk like he has the desire to.

A rap at the door draws my attention, and I slip back outside. Austin stands in front of me, a sheet of paper clutched in her hands.

"I spoke to someone in the human resources department. They confirmed that he was not at the hospital on February twenty-first, twenty-fifth, or twenty-sixth during the times the murders likely would have taken place."

I give this information to Sergeant Pelletier—who is still working on securing a warrant—and back out of his office. Austin retreats to her desk, and I go back to the interrogation room.

An hour later, Trent is still silent on his side of the table. Pelletier knocks on the door. Trent mumbles something behind me as I exit the room. Sergeant Pelletier stands just outside, a smile lingering on thin lips.

"We got the warrant."

With Ibben placed in the back of one of the cruisers, we curve through Camden to a small house right off the water. Blake slides out of his patrol car, Ibben in the back staring out at us. We prefer not to break down the door if we don't have to, and Ibben offered us the keys willingly if he was allowed to sit outside while the search took place. The wood-frame house looks like it used to be a periwinkle blue, but now there's so much moss clinging to the sides it looks like it's five years from being reclaimed by nature.

Two officers get the door open, and I follow them inside. I expect the house to smell like death inside. It just smells like stale cigarette smoke. The interior of the house feels like I've stepped into some time warp. It's got brown shag carpet, yellow wallpaper, huge glass lamps with amber-colored shades. On the walls, though, hangs something more recent—framed posters of women in bikinis. The stark contrast would be humorous if the situation were different. I give the house a once-over, getting an idea of its layout.

"I'll take the bedroom," I say, heading toward the hallway that leads to the left.

The bedroom is in worse shape than the rest of the house. Piles of dirty clothes cover most of the floor, along with mismatched shoes. There are stacks of used plates on the nightstand. The stink of dust and sweat is so thick in the air I'm tempted to open a window. It's stifling in here, only making matters worse. I head for the dresser and look through the drawers first. In the room to my left, I hear another cop searching.

"Found a computer!" a man calls. If Trent had pictures on his phone, I can only imagine what's on the computer. Most phones these days automatically back up to a computer or to the cloud. If he deleted pictures on his phone, there may still be traces elsewhere.

At the bottom of one of his drawers, I find a silver necklace with a mermaid on it. I'm not sure if it's evidence or not. I roll the charm over my gloved fingers and drop it into a plastic bag resting on the top of the dresser.

In subsequent drawers I find other similar tokens: a key chain, a class ring, another necklace—this one a cross. My instinct tells me that they're trophies. But I don't dare say it aloud. We need to verify with the families to see if they recognize them. I bag them all, just in case.

Other than the trophies, there's nothing in here that stands out. I walk to the room to the left of the bedroom, where I heard the laptop was found. One officer now searches the rest of the office, while Maggie—a tech I've seen at the station a few times—clicks away on the computer.

"Find anything?" I ask.

She nods. "He has a link between his phone and laptop. Any picture taken on his phone is automatically backed up here and on the cloud."

My heart pounds, and excitement floods my veins. I chew the inside of my cheek. This could be it. We could nail this guy to the fucking wall with whatever is on this laptop.

"And?" I ask when she doesn't continue. I walk around so I can see the screen.

"I'm just a tech, so I'm not entirely sure what it is I'm looking for, but there are lots of pictures here," she says while clicking through folders.

My eyes lock on the screen, and a picture opens in a large window, a selfie. Then pictures of memes, porn, and a flash of a face, but it's gone so fast I nearly miss it. My breath catches, and the tension in the room expands, thickening like a cloud around me.

"Stop. Go back," I direct her.

She clicks twice; an image fills the screen. There's a picture of a woman with dark hair asleep in a hospital bed, her gown pulled to the side to expose her breast. This isn't a woman I recognize, not one of the victims I've seen. But she clearly didn't consent to this.

"Continue, please."

She starts clicking almost immediately. More pictures of the same woman, several focused on just her breast. Then there's more filler, a picture of all black—maybe the inside of a pocket—then a blurred figure, shoes, a squirrel, another meme, a different woman.

"Slow down, please," I say, trying to focus on the features. I have seen this woman before. Her slim nose, dark hair: that's Melanie. In these pictures he's not just exposing her breasts while she's asleep; he's taken a picture of her underwear, pulling it to the side to expose her completely.

"Sergeant," I yell, and after a few moments he strides into the room, his cell phone clutched to his ear.

"Let me call you back," he says, shoving the phone into his pocket. "What do we have?" His eyes flick from Maggie to me.

"Show him the last four pictures, please," I say as Sergeant Pelletier crowds around the desk with us and hunches over to see the screen.

She flips through the pictures again, slower this time.

"Look familiar?" I ask.

Sergeant Pelletier crosses his arms and stares at the scene. His mouth is a thin line, his expression unreadable. There must be emotions hiding behind his dark eyes, but he doesn't show any of them.

"I need the time stamps from these pictures so we can figure out how close they were to when the victims disappeared," he instructs Maggie. "Claire, come with me. The DA will want to charge him formally for the child pornography and voyeurism. Maybe that'll make him talk."

Even if the pictures were taken of the victims close to their deaths, unless we can prove that the images were taken *in* that motel room, it's not going to do us much good. It's still circumstantial evidence. While I drive back to the station, I have Austin call Jessica's, Asha's, and Melanie's parents to see if they can identify any of the jewelry that we've found in Trent's home. After texting pictures, we confirm one bracelet belonged to Asha, a necklace to Jessica, and a ring to Melanie. While it's great that the parents have identified them, they don't remember what jewelry their daughters were wearing the day of their deaths.

Once inside the station, we head to the bull pen. Sergeant Pelletier reads Trent his Miranda rights and leads him to a cell. While they process him, I go over what we've found and try to gather my thoughts for the questioning. Once they're done with him, they deposit him back in the interrogation room.

Austin and I take a few minutes to catch up. Though Trent didn't give us anything the first time we questioned him, maybe being faced with all this evidence, what we know, will grease his lips some. With the plastic bags of jewelry we found at his place laced between my fingers, I walk into the room.

Trent's jaw is set when Blake hauls him inside. His eyes are tight, fixed straight ahead on the table until he takes a seat. He glances at me, then Austin, as we sit across the table from him. I slap a folder down between us, then drop the evidence bags. Though he says nothing, I watch his gaze trace over the bags. His eyes narrow, and he licks his lips before looking back up, his jaw tense.

"Do you recognize these?" I ask, tapping the bag, the necklace inside shifting.

"You've got nothing on me. None of my DNA. Nothing." He practically hisses the words at me.

It catches me off guard. I expected silence. Denial. Something else. Starting at DNA is a very direct approach.

"And how are you so sure that we don't have your DNA?" Austin asks, her tone combative.

"Because *I* didn't kill them," he says and cocks his head. His eyes gleam as he speaks.

"But you know who did?" I arch an eyebrow.

"I'm not a snitch." He snaps the words at me and clenches his fists atop the table.

"You may not be a snitch, but this"—I jab at the plastic bags, my finger slamming into the surface—"and those pictures, that sure makes you look guilty. Vera informed us that several of those victims on your phone were underage. We've got you on child porn, along with several other charges I know will come down from the DA. But if you didn't kill these girls, you've got to give me more; otherwise, you're going to be charged with murder, Trent." I'm bluffing. We don't have enough to charge him with murder, but if he thinks we do, maybe that will grease his jaws. Either way this guy is going to jail, but if he's going to say that he didn't do this, I have to know who did.

There's a knock at the door. It pops open, and Sergeant Pelletier waves me out. Austin and I stride out of the room together. Behind the sergeant, a woman in a sleek black suit well fitted to her wide frame stands with her arms crossed.

"Claire, this is District Attorney Victoria Parker."

She raises her chin slightly but doesn't extend her hand.

"My office is going to take it from here," she says.

"Trent is saying that he didn't commit these murders," I say to Sergeant Pelletier. We're not ready for a DA to take this. The case hasn't been built enough. I might be able to bluff Trent into talking, but if they try to proceed with only what we have right now, it's too circumstantial for a murder charge. There's enough to hold him on the two other charges, though; that will at least get him off the streets for now. I don't expect Trent to be completely truthful, but it still remains to be proven that he killed these women—and that he did so alone.

She offers me a tight, patronizing smile, her eyes saying what she doesn't. *Of course that's what he's saying.* What she really says is, "My team is used to situations like this; don't you worry. The Maine State Police will be interrogating him after we get him in the system on his current charges."

"And what if he didn't commit the murders?" I ask, probably a bit more forcefully than I should to a DA.

"Could you give us a minute?" Sergeant Pelletier asks, glancing to the DA.

She waves her hand as if extending permission. We walk together to his office, and he shuts the door once we're inside. He doesn't walk to his desk; instead, he lingers near the window with his arms crossed. "Look, they need to take Trent to charge him, but unless he confesses, as you know, we can't charge him for the murders."

"Then they should let us question him more. We might be able to get it out of him," I argue. I hate when a DA swoops in and takes a suspect before I'm done with them.

"They have solid evidence of a crime that they can charge him with *now*. You can always go to the jail to interview him more if you need. That's just how it works. We don't have the resources to hold him long term here. They'll question Trent on their own. If they get anything, they'll pass it to us." Annoyance leaches into his words, but I can't tell if it's aimed at me or at the DA for intruding.

I grit my teeth in an effort to bite back my frustrations; otherwise I'll say something that I regret. I know that much at least.

"Have we turned over Trent's devices yet?" I ask, an idea formulating in my mind.

"No, not yet."

"Don't mention it to the DA, or stall if you have to. I need Kenneth to look at the phone before we let them take it," I say.

He nods, his lips curving slightly. It's the closest to a smile I've seen on his face. "I'll do what I can."

As I stride from his office, I avoid looking in the direction of the DA. I walk to Clint's desk, and he glances up at me, his dark eyes shadowed by his brow.

"I need the phone we got from Ibben," I say, low enough that I'm sure my voice doesn't carry over the dull roar in the room.

He grabs the phone from atop a stack of documents near his monitor. It slides around in the plastic bag as he hands it over. "I was just about to give it to Kenneth."

"I'll handle it, thank you," I say before grabbing the phone and weaving through the bull pen back to the tech's office. When I open the door, I find Maggie, the tech girl from Trent's house, sitting on the desk next to Kenneth. I caught her in the middle of rehashing the scene to him.

"Hi, Detective," he says when he looks up.

"Sorry," Maggie says before slipping off the desk and sneaking around me out of the room.

"I didn't mean to interrupt, but I was hoping you could look at this phone. We need it ASAP. The DA is going to take it."

He takes the phone as I hold it out. While being mindful of the plastic bag, he opens it up and plugs a cable into the phone.

"What's the priority on this?"

"The phone number, text messages in and out, saved contacts. I need to know if this is the burner phone that's been messaging our victims," I say. My heart pounds as I try to estimate how much time we'll have with this phone—it can't be more than twenty minutes. I say a silent prayer that we can get what we need in that time.

"Got it," he says, his attention snapping back to the computer. I watch as he opens several windows, his fingers flying over the keyboard.

My phone buzzes, and I glance at it, finding a text from Sergeant Pelletier. The DA is asking about the phone.

"How long are we looking at?" I ask Kenneth as sweat prickles my palms.

"I can clone the phone, all but the pictures, in ten minutes," he says, without taking his eyes off the screen.

"How much longer would the pictures take?" I know I can buy us ten minutes, but any more than that is pushing it.

"An hour, I'd guess, based on how many he has on here."

I text Sergeant Pelletier. I need ten minutes.

Within a few seconds my phone buzzes with a reply. I'll do what I can.

A progress bar appears on Kenneth's screen. I watch it carefully, anxiety needling beneath my skin. If nothing else, what's on this phone could help make or break a murder case against Trent. There's too much on the line for these files to go to the DA without us getting answers. I know I might get a slap on the wrist for not following procedures, but I'm on loan to Camden. Quite frankly, as long as I solve this case, I don't care what the DA tries to do to me.

My phone vibrates again with another message from Sergeant Pelletier. They've got Trent in a car, she needs the phone ASAP.

The progress bar is still only twenty-five percent complete. I glance at the screen; it's only been three minutes since his last text. How did they get him in the car so fast?

I need a few more minutes, I reply, and my fingers twitch against my leg as I watch the bar. Footsteps echo in the hall as it reaches the halfway point.

"Come on, come on," I mumble to myself, as if it'll do me any good. My heart pounds as the footsteps draw closer. The progress bar ticks up: fifty-five percent, sixty, sixty-five.

The door cracks open, and Sergeant Pelletier peeks in at both of us. "We've got to hand it over," he says.

The progress bar climbs, ticking higher, closer to one hundred. A clicking fills the hall, high heels ticking on the tile.

"She's coming," he says, as if I hadn't put it together myself.

Sweat beads on the back of my neck. Ninety percent. The footsteps are right outside the door. Our time is up. I take a step forward as it hits ninety-five.

"I need that phone," the DA says from the hall.

I scoop up the phone inside the bag, ready to yank the cable out the second it hits one hundred. It ticks higher, hovering at ninety-nine. Once it moves, I pull out the cable and hit the button on the side to dim the screen before I resecure the bag.

"Thank you," I say to Sergeant Pelletier as I pass it off to him. The moment he curls his fingers around it, the DA pops her head in the room.

"Got it," Sergeant Pelletier says as he passes it to her. She flashes us a shark's smile, then clicks her way back down the hall.

"We got it, right?" I ask as I turn back to Kenneth.

"We did," he says, just as the printer to his right begins to spit out pages. "So first"—he types something on the screen, and a window starts to fill with text—"it's not a burner phone."

I deflate. I'd really hoped that we had him nailed. But just because this phone isn't a burner doesn't mean that he doesn't have a second phone. We just may have not found it.

"But," he says as he flourishes the papers toward me, "he has texts from the burner number with the coordinates."

I snatch the papers and pore over them. Sure enough, he received all the texts that the rest of the victims did. Was he there too? Did he meet them at the hospital or at the ATV races? The threads are all there, but I can't see how they connect.

"Thank you, Kenneth. I owe you a beer," I say as I flip through the pages.

The buzzing of the servers fades as I walk down the hall toward the bull pen, glancing at the texts that Kenneth printed out for me. But something sticks out to me about them. There are only incoming messages, and very few at that. Either he was very fastidious cleaning out old texts, or there's something else—he had another phone. I weave through the desks toward Blake, Zane, and Clint.

"When we searched Trent's house, are we sure there wasn't another cell phone?"

Blake and Zane exchange a look. "I didn't see one," Zane says.

"Me neither," Blake adds.

"Did we search his car?"

Austin chimes in. "His car wasn't part of the warrant."

I'll have to ask Sergeant Pelletier about expanding the warrant, though I don't know if they'll do it at our request now or if it has to go through the DA.

"Austin, could you call the hospital to see if there was a cell phone left in Trent's locker?" I ask.

She nods. "I'll call them now."

While she does that, I ask Sergeant Pelletier about the warrant for the car and explain that we'll need to tell the judge that we're looking for another cell phone. If we want a warrant expanded, we need a good reason for it. Austin waves me over to her desk as I finish up with Sergeant Pelletier.

"Did you find anything out?" I ask as I approach.

"There was no phone in his locker, but the nurse did mention that they found a cell phone in their parking lot and it's in lost and found."

I swallow hard. That could be the phone we're looking for. He could have dropped it when he was being arrested.

"When was the phone found?" I ask.

"Earlier today," she says.

"We need to go take a look at that phone."

She grabs her coat. The sun is burning low on the horizon when we step outside. The cold lashes against us as we walk across the parking lot. Austin and I climb into my car and drive back to the hospital. We're silent the entire drive as we carve our way through Camden to the medical center. I park the car, and we cut through the parking lot toward the administrative building. A nurse sits behind a large desk just inside the doors as we enter. I explain the situation with the phone to her.

"I can grab it," she says.

"Actually, I'd prefer if we did. It could be evidence," I say, pulling latex gloves from my pocket.

The nurse shows us to the lost and found. I stow the phone away in an evidence bag. Though I try to turn it on inside the bag, it appears to be dead. I say a silent prayer that it's just out of battery and not damaged.

Upon returning to the station, I pass the phone off to Kenneth. He looks it over inside the bag.

"This is an older model. I'm going to have to pick up a cable for this. I don't have one on me," he says as he glances at the clock on his wall. It's nearly seven o'clock. "It's getting pretty late, but I may be able to find one tonight."

"So we're looking at tomorrow, then?" I ask.

He nods. "Best-case scenario. Worst case, I can't find a charger that fits this, and I have to order one."

"Thanks for working on this," I say.

"Anytime."

I catch Sergeant Pelletier up on where we are, say good night to Austin, and walk out of the station, but I stop dead in my tracks when I find Noah leaning against my car.

"What are you doing here?" I ask, though I know the answer. But I honestly can't think of anything else to say.

"Claire, we need to talk."

CHAPTER 13

Noah stands against my car, his arms crossed over his muscled chest. As usual, he's wearing a leather jacket half-open, revealing a Pixies T-shirt, and I don't know how he's not freezing in this weather. I bite back my frustration as Roxie's words come to my mind. Am I really angry with him? Or am I just looking for an excuse to push him away?

"Talk? So now you want to talk?" I ask, my words sharper than I mean for them to be.

"I can explain everything," he says hurriedly.

"Are you really going to explain everything? Or will there be more omissions? If you're not ready for this, if you don't want to open up, I'm not going to make you. This is your life, and if you don't want to share that with me, it hurts, but I understand." For a second, I stop and clench my fists. A sickness spreads in the pit of my stomach. I didn't want to do this with Noah today, especially not here. "I've been there, and I know what it's like to want to keep yourself hidden away from everyone else. That's fine. If you want to do that, I won't make you change."

He starts to open his mouth like he's going to interrupt me.

"I can't do this tonight, whichever way this is going to go." I'm bone tired, and my mind is still too much in the case for me to deal with this right now. My emotions are locked away like they need to be during an investigation. "Go back to your hotel. If you still want to talk in the morning, text me."

"Please, can we talk this through tonight?"

I hold my palms out to him, as if I'm surrendering. At my edges, I feel the fissures there, like I might break down. Maybe I'm a coward because I don't want to admit to him how much it hurt me that he doesn't seem as deep into our relationship as I am. He was ready to move in, for Christ's sake, but he's not willing to share his past with me? How can you share a future without that?

"I can't, Noah." My voice cracks as I force the words out.

He takes a step forward and pulls me into his arms. Though I want to pull back, to keep the distance firmly set between us, I fold into him. I rest my head against his chest, feeling his warmth, listening to the beat of his heart. I take a deep breath, relishing the smell of him that I missed so much. Finally, I force myself to step back.

"Let's talk tomorrow," I say. "Please, I need a night. I think you need it too."

He scratches the stubble that's collected on his cheeks, his fingernails grating against it like sandpaper. Though it doesn't look like he agrees, he nods.

"Did I completely fuck up?" he asks.

"Not completely, about sixty percent," I say.

The corners of his mouth tug up at that, and he sweeps his long brown hair away from his eyes. "Not a passing grade, then."

I walk around Noah and open my car door. He moves out of the way to let me pass.

"Where are you staying?" he asks.

I shake my head. "Go back to the island. I'll see you there in the morning." Getting up early and going to the island will keep my mind off what's on that burner phone until Kenneth makes it into the office

173

around ten. It's a distraction I'll need; otherwise the pending evidence might drive me crazy.

Though I start to turn, he stops me before I can step away, planting a soft kiss on my cheek. "Good night, Claire," he says, the warmth of his breath misting the air.

"Good night, Noah," I say as I climb into my car.

CHAPTER 14

As I push into my hotel room, the exhaustion I feel stretches all the way to my soul. The door snaps shut behind me, and I hope putting distance between him and myself will help. Seeing Noah here, after everything—it's the last thing I expected to happen today. My body can still feel the lingering warmth of his touch. My hand twitches, as if it'll open the door without my permission so I can cross the bay to be with him, but I clench my fist instead. I won't go back there tonight. If we're going to continue growing our relationship, I want to go into it with eyes open, and he needs to do the same. Because I won't keep doing this with secrets between us.

The key I planned to give Noah seems to weigh ten pounds in my pocket. How is it that just a few weeks ago I thought we were ready for that step, and now we're here? Tears spill down my face, growing icy on my hot cheeks. I dig my cell phone out of my pocket and dial Roxie's number. I can't fix my own life, so I'll call and talk to her about hers. The distraction will do me good.

"Hey," she says as soon as the call connects.

"How'd the interview go?" I ask.

She lets out a low laugh. "I killed it. If they don't hire me, they aren't in their right minds." I can hear the smile in her voice.

"How are things going there?" she asks as she chews.

I catch her up on the case, the arrest, and the burner phone, then tell her about finding Noah outside the station.

"He came back there to see you?" She sounds incredulous as a best friend should.

I shift on the bed, the springs protesting as I move. "Yeah, and my dumb ass still had the key I was going to give him in my pocket."

"You still had it in your pocket?"

I didn't tell her that I've moved it from pants pocket to pants pocket, keeping it with me no matter the outfit, since I had it made. That's not an easy task when so many pants lack pockets. Maybe it's just become something of a comfort now, the familiar weight I expect to be there.

"Yeah, I just keep forgetting to take it out," I lie. But I know she'll see through it. She always does.

"So you haven't changed your pants in like a week, then?" she challenges, calling me on my bullshit.

"I have," I say, a bit too defensively.

"You've taken the key out and put it in other pants, then." Her words aren't quite a question. She chews in the background as she waits for me to reply.

I sigh. "You're making it into more than it is," I say, now tempted to rush her off the phone.

"Claire, are you sure you want things to be over with him?"

The weight of the question hangs in the air. And I swear I can feel it all around me, pressing against me. But I don't know. Should I want it to be over? Because I know what he did was wrong. And if I let it slide, will he just do it again? After all this time of not opening up to me, is he really ready?

"Because I want you to be sure that you want it to be over, and you're not just calling it quits because you think you should or because it's easier to push him away."

"I don't know, Roxie," I say finally.

"I'll support whatever you want to do; you know that. But I don't want you to regret whatever you decide." I hear her take another bite of her food.

"I know," I say in a voice so small it doesn't sound like my own.

"Maybe you should at least hear him out?"

"Maybe," I say.

Roxie and I chat for a few more minutes about where she'll live if she gets this job. And she insists again that I apply for the other spot. I urge her off the phone to eat her dinner. I promise that I'll think about it. But really, there are too many things on my mind to consider it right now. I have a murder to solve and a relationship rockier than the shores of Pen Bay.

CHAPTER 15

I'm awake at dawn, as if the horizon shifting from inky black to a streaked purple was enough to pull me from sleep. I try to distract myself with coffee and breakfast, but I can't get Noah out of my head. I check my phone, and there's a text waiting from him that was sent at two a.m.

I miss you and I'm sorry.

Though the ferry back to the island won't start running for another couple of hours, I know that chances are there's at least one person in Rockport with a boat who would give me a ride. I know if I don't do this, if I don't talk to him, I'll regret it, and I'll just stew back at the office until Kenneth gets in.

I wind my way through the hotel and climb into my car. The seats are so cold it bleeds into my legs and back despite my layers of clothing. I turn on the car and drive down Route 1 toward Rockport. Once I arrive at the dock, I park my car. A low fog gathers over the water, spilling onto the pebbled beach. I walk over to several men standing near a few speedboats, hoping the fog won't be a deterrent. The water sloshes against the wood beneath me as I approach. After a few minutes of negotiation, I find someone to take me to the island for twenty bucks.

The sun burns on the horizon as I walk down the worn wood of the dock. My captain is a middle-aged man with a beard that stretches halfway down his rounded belly. He climbs into his boat, a four-seater that's rusting at the stern, and I jump in after him. I position myself at the back, pulling my coat up around my neck.

"You ready?" he asks, glancing back at me.

I nod, and he starts up the sputtering engine. Cold wind lashes at my face as the boat picks up speed. We skip across the waves until we're swallowed by the fog. He eases up on the engine, and finally the fog parts, and the island rises out of the bay. My stomach twists as we approach, the way it always does. This island doesn't have good memories for me. All I can see when I look at it is the place that took my sister from me, the place that stole the lives of other innocent girls.

The boat surges toward the docks, and as he pulls in, I pass him the twenty. "Do you need me to stay to give you a ride back?" he asks.

I shake my head. "Thank you, but no. The ferry will be running when I head back."

"Suit yourself," he says, tucking the money into his pocket.

I walk down the dock toward Main Street, past the police station I worked at last year. Noah's hotel is across the street from the station, which led to him getting in my way quite a bit last year during the early parts of my investigation. I stare at the Tidewater Motel, where Noah's been staying for the past couple of months. The building is long. On one end it's one story, and on the other end it rises up to two. Wood shingles line the sides, the brown making the white trim pop. When Noah first started staying here, I wondered how he could afford it, but from the googling I did on his family, it seems they could probably buy the whole hotel if they wanted. Maybe this whole goddamn island.

My mind is scattered, fragmented, as I approach. Though I want to harden my heart, to shut him out, my rage has simmered. And as much as I want to move on, I also want to know why he lied to me. I can't walk away from this without understanding why, and as upset as

I am about him keeping his past from me, maybe I got too far ahead of myself.

For a long time, I stare up at the stairs that run along the outside of the motel toward his room, debating whether or not I really want to do this. Finally I test putting one foot on a stair, then another, and another, until I'm looking right at the number on the front of the door. I take a deep breath and knock.

It takes Noah a minute to answer. His hair is disheveled, as if I got him out of bed. It hangs below his earlobes now. Thick stubble clings to his jaw, darkening his face. But I like the way it looks on him. His eyes brighten slightly when he sees me.

"Claire?" His voice is hesitant, like he's afraid I might be a dream.

"Can I come in?" I ask finally. He hasn't moved.

"Of course," he says, stepping aside to let me through.

The inside of the hotel room looks lived in, *really* lived in. Two pizza boxes are stacked on the counter in the small kitchen. Spiral notebooks and paperwork are scattered on nearly every surface, like Noah has his own situation room. I'd also say he hasn't let a housekeeper in here for a while. I look from the small table to the bed, unsure where I want to sit. Finally, I decide the table is likely the better place to have a conversation. I try not to glance at the papers and folders there, but I can't help it. They're clearly for a case, the victims from Tennessee, I'd guess. With this mess, it's hard to believe he's only been back here for twenty-four hours or so.

"Thirsty?" he asks as he moves toward the small fridge.

"No," I say. I could use a drink, but I'm not thirsty. I expect to feel something, but a numbness has settled over me. "Please, sit," I say when he lingers in the small kitchen in the back of the suite. I'd swear that he's scared of me. What happened to the Noah who stood by my car last night? That's the Noah I expected to find. Not this beaten-down version before me.

He sits across from me, setting two bottles of water on the table.

"I want you to explain," I say in a voice so calm I surprise myself.

"Explain?" he asks as he cracks his bottle of water open.

"I want you to explain why you're incapable of talking about your past. I know that Tina and Josh are difficult for you to talk about, but what about the other parts of your family and Emma?"

"Oh," he says. It's clear I've caught him off guard. He must have thought I came here to make certain I wanted nothing else to do with him. He swallows so hard I can see his Adam's apple bob from across the table.

"When I was a kid, I hated my family. I had a tough time. I didn't fit in with them. And nothing I did made the situation any better. I met Josh in elementary school. Much to my mother's disappointment, we became friends."

"Her disappointment?" I ask. Though I know the basics of Tina and Josh's story, he's never gone into detail about their shared history.

"Josh didn't come from a *good* family. They were on the poorer side. They lived in a small house they rented on the wrong side of town. My mom tried to keep us from seeing one another. She just wanted me to have friends that traveled in the same circles as us. But I didn't want that. I loved Josh and his mom, Tina. They made me feel like family. They accepted me. They loved me for who I was," he explains. He eyes the table as he speaks, then finally looks back to me.

"In 2000, Tina was killed. Her body dumped near a spot known for sex workers. Six other women were dumped there, the ones I'm looking into. But the police were never able to find out who did it, as you know. Josh and I both spiraled after Tina died. He went to live with his grandma. When I visited, we got shit faced together. It was too painful to be around him without drinking. Four years later, Josh tried to kill himself. I walked in and found him in his room; he'd taken a full bottle of sleeping pills." Emotion swims in his eyes, and he swallows hard, as if trying to push the memories back down.

I reach across the table and grab his hand. The pain etched on his face and in his words cracks my resolve. I know that pain. I've carried it with me for years. Shutting him out when he's struggling like this—I just can't do it. He offers me a sad smile before continuing.

"I thought that after they saved Josh, he might get better. That he'd realize his mistake, that he was meant to live. But six months later, I walked to our favorite bridge and caught him there. I called his name, and he looked at me. He knew I was there. But he jumped off anyway. I watched him die. Then a few weeks later, I tried to do the same. First, I tried sleeping pills like he had, but my brother Cameron found me. Then I went to the bridge. I thought about jumping off. But I couldn't do it." He hangs his head, and I squeeze his hand again. The sadness on his face makes my own heart ache. The thought that Noah was in such a dark place tightens my chest. I don't want him ever to be in that mental place again.

He pulls his hands away to open his bottle of water and take a sip. "A few weeks before Tina had died, I'd caught my father kissing another woman during a party at our house. Though I didn't really understand—he said that they were just playing a game and not to tell my mom. I didn't, because I didn't want him to get mad at me. But I caught him a few more times. I told my mom what I'd seen. She ended up confronting my father about it, and he said that I just made it up since I didn't get the attention I wanted from trying to kill myself. She believed him. Or maybe she just wanted to. Our relationship had been strained before that, but at that point it broke."

My heart aches for him.

"After that I dropped out of school, and they sent me to live with my uncle. It's really difficult to talk about that time in my life. It's easier when I put it all in the back of my mind and don't think about it. Whenever I've spoken about it in the past, people always look at me differently. I didn't tell you because I didn't want it to change how you see me. If you looked at me like I was wounded, I don't think I could stand it." His eyes are on the table, not on me. But when he finally looks up again, I'm conscious of how I arrange my features.

"Noah, do you think that I don't understand the instinct to lock your past away? I struggle with that every single day. But we can't build a relationship with only parts of ourselves. You've seen my shadows; you know my past. How are we supposed to build anything together if you can't trust me with your past?" I *hate* that he lied to me, but I of all people understand why he did it. Isn't it easier to let someone see the walls you've built than what you're hiding behind them?

He folds his hands on the table and rests his head atop them. "I know," he finally says. "There's nothing I can do to make it up to you or to fix it. I've fucked things up with you, just like I do with everyone else."

"And what about Emma?" I ask. That announcement of their engagement is burned in my memory.

He winces again. "It's not what you think. Emma and I dated in high school. Then again when I went to college, after I'd moved out of my uncle's place. She told my mom that I'd bought her a ring and I was going to propose. I don't know if she was playing some type of game, but that was never the case. I didn't see things leading to marriage with her. My mom and I rarely spoke, so she didn't bother to talk to confirm it with me. After the announcement came out, Emma thought she could push me into proposing, since the world all thought it was true. But I broke things off with her." He glances toward the door. "I understand if you don't want me to stay. I can leave tomorrow."

Again, it feels like the fire inside Noah has dimmed, if not died out completely. Who is this man sitting in front of me? This isn't the Noah I know. He's been through a lot. We both have. But this isn't him. "When did you become such a defeatist?" I ask.

His eyes have pooled with tears when he looks at me. They're seconds away from spilling over. "I thought that—" His voice cracks. "After last night, I didn't think there was any hope."

When I really think about it, when I consider where my heart lies with Noah, I know that I can't close this book yet. I know with anyone else I'd use this as an easy out. But with Noah, I don't think I can do that. Not yet. "My head wants to be done with you. If the logical part of me was the only part with a say, I'd never have come back. But my heart doesn't want that. If you can drop the secretive bullshit—"

"I will," he interrupts me. "I'll be an open book. I'll tell you so much about me you'll wish I'd just shut up."

"Will you let me meet your family?"

He nearly flinches at that. "If that's what you really want." His voice has an edge to it. But I know he's not lying. It's not like he can get out of this.

"You only get one more chance. If you lie to me again . . ."

"I know. I swear to you, Claire." He takes a slow swig of his water. "Can I please kiss you?"

I can't help but smile, and I have to admit that sitting in the room with him like this without touching him isn't the easiest exercise. As soon as I nod, I half expect him to throw the table between us out of the way. Instead, he shoves up and closes the distance, pulling me into his arms. His chest crushes into mine, and my body molds into his. Noah's warmth bleeds into me, and I realize how much I've missed him.

His arms tighten around my waist, and I relish being in his grip again. Though I know he wants to kiss me, I bury my face into his shoulder, breathing in the scent of him. My heart aches with how much I missed him, how close I came to never being here with him again. My eyes prickle with emotion. I hate that despite the pain he's caused me, it feels like right here with him is exactly where I belong. Finally, when I feel settled, I look up to find him staring at me.

"What?" I ask.

"I've just missed you."

"I missed you too," I admit.

He plants a soft kiss on my forehead, and I tilt my head up, seeking his lips. The first kiss is soft, delicate, like he's afraid I may change my mind. I slip my hands under his shirt, seeking desperately the warmth of his bare skin. Something about my touch ignites him—his kisses shift from sweet to frenzied as if he's afraid he's imagined all this. He edges my shirt over my head, and my desire swells from my sex upward, until it reaches my head, making it swim. His tongue slides against mine, his mouth claiming me; our hands wander, and I edge him toward the bed. When the backs of my legs hit the mattress, I let myself fall, and Noah crawls over me.

His hands go to my pants, and he starts to unbutton them, and I notice he's shaking slightly, like this is our first time all over again. I take his hands in mine and stare up at him, hoping the look will settle his nerves. It's as if the weight of our time apart is still heavy in the air around us. But I'm desperate to shed it, to get back to where we were before all of this happened.

Noah's kisses trail from my lips down my neck and breasts, until he notches his thumbs beneath the waistband of my underwear and inches it off. Anticipation builds inside me, as I remember how skilled he's always been with his mouth. God, I missed this, him. His lips brush mine feather soft, and my sex throbs in response. Heat radiates from every place he kisses me, as if his lips are drawing a map on my flesh. I close my eyes as his fingers slide across my wetness, then inside. His tongue joins in, finding my sensitive nub. My fingers lace into his hair, and my eyes meet his. Emotion swims in his eyes, and my heart aches for him, all of him.

He works me expertly, like he knows exactly what makes me tick. Every movement builds a wave inside me, the strokes, the pressure, the feel of him against me, until finally it crashes down, shattering me, and I cry out.

Noah kisses his way back up my body, and my knees spread wider. My sex craves for him to enter. I don't just want him—I need him.

Slowly, he slides his head along my wet, sensitive folds until finally I buck, forcing him to slip inside. We groan in unison. It isn't until he starts pistoning inside me that I realize how much I've truly missed this, missed him.

I push Noah back, saying, "I want to ride you."

His eyes brighten. I don't have to say it twice. Within seconds he's on his back on the bed, his erection pointing toward the ceiling. My eyes crawl over him, taking in his length and his muscled body like it's the last time I'll ever see it. I straddle him, teasing him with my sex before I slide slowly down his cock, enjoying the feel of my body opening to him again. Once I take him to the hilt, I grind against him, until I feel the wave building again. Noah moans, his hands finding my breasts. His pleasure brings me to my own. I fall against the mattress, boneless and blissful.

"God, I missed you," he says as he kisses my hair.

I roll over and snuggle against him, my head resting on his shoulder. "I'd say I've missed you, too, but I don't want it to build up your ego more."

For a long moment we're silent, tangled together, panting as we recover. His chest heaves beneath my head, and I listen to the steady rhythm of his heart.

"How did things go back home?" I ask carefully. I don't want to pry into things I know he hates talking about, but at the same time, I want to know what happened and how he's feeling about his father's death.

"They could have been worse, but not great. My mother and father could not possibly be any more disappointed in me. My father made it clear right before he died that his stance hadn't softened on my career."

I raise a brow to that. "Why did he have a problem with your career?"

"Both my parents hate journalists. They think the media is filled with nothing but liars." There's an edge to his voice.

"And what exactly would your father prefer that you do?"

"Go into the family business. Coal, tobacco: that's where our family made the bulk of their fortune; now, though, he makes most of his cash on Wall Street trading this stock or another. Well, he *did*, I guess I should say." With my ear pressed to Noah's chest, I hear the echo of his voice through his body.

"And what does your mother do?"

"She sits around and hates anyone that isn't from money."

I grin at that. I guess technically I am from money, but I don't feel like it. "So she'll hate me then." But it strikes me that she'd like my mom.

"She already does." He laughs.

And somehow his words stoke something inside me, a challenge. Frustration ripples to the surface, and I can't help but be defensive. "She hates me? She doesn't even know me."

"She doesn't need to. She is very skilled in hating a wealth of people she's never met."

I prop myself up on my elbows to look at him. "Seriously, though, why does she think I'm worthy of hating?"

He sighs. "It's just going to make you angry." His fingers brush my hair again.

"Probably, but I still want to know," I say.

"Promise you won't take it out on me?" He tries to smile, but it falls flat.

"Yeah, yeah. Just tell me."

"She thinks that the only reason you're dating me is for the money," he says and looks at me as if waiting for a reaction.

Anger flares inside me, but I'm determined not to let it show. "And does she know that I'm fully capable of making my own money? Hell, I don't even take money from my own family. Why would I take it from yours?"

He kisses me softly, as if it'll diffuse my anger. And I hate that it works. My heart rate slows, but a heat of a different sort rises in its place.

"I know that. I tried to tell her as much, but there's no reasoning with her. Know how you feel about your mother?"

I nod. It's not that I hate my mother; it's that I want her to stay out of my life. For her to back off and stop trying to take control. A better daughter would cut her slack because of Rachel. But I'm not a better daughter. I want her to leave me alone.

"Well, that's how I feel about my mother."

I try to understand, but the difference is something I can't help but see. I never tried to keep him from meeting my family. I had no choice in the matter. But if the situation were reversed, what would I have done? Would I have had Noah meet them? I really don't know.

"I did see my youngest brother, Cameron, while I was there. I mean, I saw Lucas and Graham too."

"Oh?"

"I've been working with Cameron, my brother who's the cop, while gathering information about Tina's case," he says, glancing toward the files on the table.

"What have you found so far?" I ask, curious if I could help him any with it.

"Maryville PD just started trying to run the DNA they found on the new body against the familial database. They're hoping that they can figure out who this woman is."

"Are there not any pending missing person reports from around that time?" I ask.

"That's the thing—there are at least fifteen open missing person reports from that year."

My eyes go wide at that. Fifteen is a huge number, especially for a town the size of Maryville. That makes me wonder if there are more bodies that they haven't recovered yet.

"How about we go through it tomorrow? I'll see what I can help you find," I offer.

CHAPTER 16

I glance at the clock and see that it's nearly eight thirty. The ferry will be running shortly. If I catch the first one, I can make it back to Camden around the time Kenneth should be getting into the office. I climb from the bed, pulling on my clothes.

"Leaving already?" Noah asks as he rolls onto his side, propping his head on his hand.

I explain that I've got to get back to work. We've got to find out what's on that burner phone.

"Want me to go with you?" he offers, sitting up in the bed.

"No, you need to get back to your case. And if you go with me on the ferry, that'll eat up an hour of your day."

"Are you sure? I don't mind."

"No, really," I say, leaning over the bed to give him a quick kiss. Then I grab my shirt.

"Want me to come stay in your hotel tonight?"

"I don't know how long I'll be, but they gave me two keys," I say as I dig an extra out of my bag and hand it over. I explain to Noah where to find the hotel, then venture back out into Vinalhaven. It takes me a few minutes to reach the ferry, and once they pull up the gate, I walk on board.

After the twenty-minute trip across the choppy water, I find my car near the Rockport dock and then weave up Route 1, following the ribbon of road back toward Camden. Cold lashes me as I cut across the nearly empty parking lot toward the police station. After I throw open the front door, I trade the crisp air for the stuffy, overheated office. Blake and Clint are at their desks watching me shed my coat and drop it on my chair.

"Morning," Clint says, nodding to me.

"Morning. Is Kenneth in yet?"

"I'm not sure. I haven't been down that way."

I thank him and stride across the bull pen toward the dull hum. When I reach Kenneth's office, I find him hunched over the phone, which is still shielded inside the plastic bag. Latex gloves cover his hands, and I'm happy to see that he's followed protocol. Though it's already likely going to be difficult to get prints off the phone after it has been through so many hands.

"Hey, Detective," he says as he turns around.

"We get anywhere with that?" I ask as I motion toward the phone.

"Yes and no."

I try not to let his words knock the wind out of my sails, but we really need this phone to give us something. We have to track down the burner phone that's been texting the girls.

"Give me the bad news first."

"There are too many fingerprints on it to lift any good ones. Zane dusted it, and all of the prints are so overlapped even the new fingerprint algorithms aren't going to be any help with this."

At this point, because of where the phone was found and how many possible hands it passed through, a fingerprint would be tossed out anyway. We'd need proof that Trent purchased it, or we would need to have found this at his home.

"What else do we have?"

"This number texted Asha, Melanie, and Jessica. All the burner texts we found on their phones came from this number."

This is the break we've been needing. Excitement floods my veins. With this phone, we can finally get some answers. "Are there texts to other numbers? Ones other than those girls?"

"There are texts to a few other numbers, but it appears that they never responded."

"Were you able to find out who those numbers belong to?"

"One wasn't an active number, but the other two are Paige Wilde and Lucy Riggs," he says, squinting at the screen.

"Do you have a printout of those texts?"

He turns toward the printer, grabs a stack of pages, and hands it to me.

"Thank you for getting this to me so quickly. Can you also check the locations that phone has been at? We need to see if it was in the motels the girls were found at. I also need you to go through the call log to see if there's anything there."

"I'll get everything I can off of it."

"Thank you."

With the papers in hand, I walk back to my desk, grab my cell phone, and text Austin to meet me at the hospital. I let Zane and Clint know where I'm headed so they can update the sergeant. Then I grab lineup images of four random men, along with the headshot that the DA's office took of Trent. I need to check in at the hospital and find out if Paige and Lucy were both patients there and, if so, who they interacted with. If these girls saw Trent, they may be able to give me a positive ID.

As I reach my car, I get a text from Austin telling me that she'll meet me there soon. In twenty minutes, I pull into the visitor lot at the hospital. Snow spirals from the gray sky while I walk across the parking lot. The doors hiss open, and I find Nurse Jordan sitting at the desk. She glances up at me and sweeps her short black hair behind her ear.

"Hello, Detective. What can I help you with?" She shifts in her chair as I walk closer.

"There are two names I have, and I need to know if they were patients here."

She furrows her brows, lips pursed. I know that look. She doesn't want to answer me.

"You don't need to tell me anything about their treatment. I know you can't release that without their permission. I just need to know if they were here."

She looks at the computer to her right and rolls toward it, clicking the mouse. "If Vera asks, I didn't give you this information."

I nod. "We never spoke."

A tight smile quirks her lips as she clicks the mouse. "What are their names?"

I give her the names, and she begins typing. "They were both patients here. That's all I can confirm," she says, looking up at me again.

"Is there any way to determine if their records were accessed by anyone else on staff?"

"Not that I know of. Everyone is always sharing log-in information. I'm not sure how helpful that would be," she says with a shrug.

"Can you tell me if anything of interest happened to those two patients while they were here?"

Her eyes narrow. "I don't remember anything about either of them, so I'd say not likely."

"Did you see Trent Ibben interact with either of them?"

She raises a brow at that and leans in conspiratorially. "That guy who was fired for being a perv? Do you think he had something to do with what's going on around here?"

"I can't say anything about it. I just need to know if he was in either of their rooms that you saw."

"No, not that I ever saw."

"If you think of anything else, please give me a call," I say.

I walk back out to the parking lot just in time to see Austin's Fiat pull in beside my car. She climbs out, shoulders hunched against the cold.

"Did she give you anything?" she asks.

"We have confirmation that both women were patients here, but we need to check in with them to make sure they weren't hurt and to see if Trent approached them."

She nods. "Follow me. We'll stop at Lucy's first," she says, turning back to her car.

Austin climbs into her car, and I do the same, turning over the engine in my Mustang. I follow her up Route 1 back into Camden and through a small neighborhood until we come to a stop outside a Queen Anne Victorian house. The house towers four stories, with an elegant turret. We both climb out of our vehicles and walk up the shoveled pathway toward the house. I knock on the door, and the sound of foot-steps echoing on wood floors beyond warns me of someone's approach.

The door cracks open, revealing a short girl with long brown hair. She can't be older than fifteen, maybe sixteen at the most. She glances between Austin and me, confusion painted on her features.

"Lucy?" I ask.

"Yeah, I'm Lucy," she says hesitantly.

"Would you mind if we come in and speak with you for a couple minutes?" I ask as I flash her my badge.

She looks between us again, then back into her house, like she's considering grabbing one of her parents. Finally, she waves us inside, and we follow her into the dining room to the left of the front door.

"You're both cops?" she asks as we take a seat at the table.

I nod, then introduce myself and Austin. "I was hoping to talk to you about your stay in the hospital."

"Okay," she says, still looking confused.

I pull the lineup images from my jacket and arrange them on the table. "I'm going to show you five images, and I need you to tell me if you have seen any of these men before."

Lucy stands up, her dark hair shifting over her shoulders. Under the harsh lighting in the dining room, she looks remarkably pale. For a long time, she scrutinizes the pictures; then she points to Trent's. My heart leaps.

"You saw this man?" I ask.

"I saw him while I was in the hospital. He was really cute and seemed cool. He asked me for my number." Her cheeks go beet red, and she picks at her fingernails. "I know I shouldn't have given it to him."

"Did he call or text you?" I ask.

"Yes, he texted me to try to meet up with me. But when I didn't respond, he called. He wanted to take me to one of those ATV races." She crosses her arms tightly over her chest. "But I said no. I got a bad feeling about it."

"Did he ever try to get you to go anywhere else?" Austin asks.

She shakes her head. "No, after I told him I wasn't interested in going to the races, he never texted me again. He just ghosted me, which was . . . whatever."

"Did he say anything to you while you were in the hospital?"

"He told me that he was a doctor there and that I was really cute. That's it."

"Thank you for speaking with us today," I say to Lucy, then pass her one of my cards. As Austin and I walk out of Lucy's house, it's clear to me that we have a really solid suspect now. With the phone, Lucy's identification of Trent, the pictures on his phone, and the jewelry, we could start building a good case against him. Right now, it's still all too circumstantial to charge him with anything, but if we keep stacking this against him, his involvement will be difficult to deny.

I follow Austin across town to Paige's house. Her story is eerily similar to Lucy's, except that Trent didn't ask her about an ATV race; he skipped straight to the motel. Paige was so uncomfortable with it all that she blocked his number. After a second positive identification in the photo lineup, I know we're getting close.

CHAPTER 17

There's a dull roar of activity inside the station, a chorus of voices, ringing phones. I head straight back through the bull pen toward Sergeant Pelletier's office.

I find him sitting at his desk, a phone held between his shoulder and ear. His eyes meet mine, and he holds up a finger, then points at one of the chairs. I take a seat and try not to focus on his conversation.

"And how long will that take?" He pauses. "Well, see if it can be expedited and call me back." He finishes up his call before jotting something on a legal pad in front of him. His features are tense but nearly unreadable. I wish I could tell what lies beneath the surface, but there isn't even a hint.

"I spoke to the district attorney late last night. They've got Trent's case for child pornography and voyeurism on the docket. He's going to be tried in three months. She says that if we want to pursue murder charges, we need to get them evidence as soon as possible. The DA said they brought up the jewelry we have with Trent during interrogation, and he claims that he will take things home if they sit in the lost and found too long, and the hospital verified that story, though they couldn't verify every individual item."

"That's bullshit," I say before I can think better of it. My temper flares, and I clench my jaw against it. We know the items belonged to those girls, and Melanie was wearing the ring the days prior to her death, though her mother isn't certain that she was wearing it the day of her death.

"Trust me, I know. I don't believe a word of it." He sighs. "But it is what it is. If the DA needs more evidence, we'll have to get it."

"I know. In the meantime, we should institute some additional security for specific patients who fit the profile, after they've been released from the hospital." I've already mentioned it to Vera, but she didn't seem remotely interested.

"We have two officers in the hospital twenty-four seven, but it's not going to do much good if these patients are meeting up with their killer after they've been released."

That must be new. I hadn't heard about the officers. If I had known they could be spared, I would have recommended it sooner.

"Anything else?" I ask as I start to stand.

"No, just find out whatever you can."

I walk through the bull pen back toward Kenneth's office. He's had the burner phone long enough now that I'm hoping he knows *something*. I find him in his office engrossed in something on one of his three monitors. Though I try to decipher what it is exactly, his world is completely foreign to me.

"Hey, Kenneth," I say as I lean against one of the tables stacked high with computer equipment.

He turns around and offers me a nod. "Afternoon."

"I wanted to see if we'd gotten any further with Ibben's phone or the burner."

"There wasn't anything of use on his real phone, but I did find some interesting things on the burner," he says with a grin. He turns around and clicks open several programs on his computer. I step closer so I can make them out. "While looking at the burner phone, I found something odd. He took zero pictures on it. It's like he had planned to be able to ditch it at a moment's notice. It'd make sense for someone to keep the pictures they wanted on a phone they planned to keep around."

I cross my arms as I listen to him. He has a point. Since it seems that Trent really liked taking pictures of the women at the hospital, I can't imagine that he'd want to dump that phone and lose all the images.

"At first, it seemed the location data had been purged from the device. But I was able to pull up the Google account that links to the phone. While the Google account is clearly a throwaway, it was tracking every location this phone ended up at. I'm guessing the user had no idea that the account was tracking their every move."

I straighten at his words, my eyes narrowing on the screen. There's a long list of different coordinates and times. "Where can we place the phone?"

"The hospital, Bald Mountain Preserve, Camden Hills State Park, both motels the victims were found at, and near Trent's residence."

While it's still circumstantial unless we can tie him to this phone, this paints a very clear picture. Having it link back to Trent's home is going to be the biggest key in all of this. A defense attorney is going to have a hard time convincing a jury that Trent wasn't involved, given all these variables. But despite that, we need to prove it was Trent beyond a reasonable doubt. I consider the arguments that could be made. GPS signals can be wrong, and Trent does have neighbors. It *could* be argued that one of them owned the phone.

"That's not all," he says, spinning in his chair to face me.

I raise a brow to that. "Oh?"

"Before each homicide, or when I'd suspect the murders took place based on the timeline that we've seen, there was a call placed to another burner number," he says. He starts to crack his knuckles.

"Was he not working alone?" I ask. Was he calling someone else to the scene? Or was he communicating that he'd managed to do it? We know that Trent doesn't have a significant other. There's no one that he'd need to call and check in with at that time of night. Why else would he call anyone?

"I don't know," he says softly. "I'm just relaying what I've found."

"Is there anything else?"

He shakes his head. "That's what I've found so far."

"And we're sure that the number he was calling is a burner number?"

He grabs a sheet of paper and hands it over to me. "It was registered to a carrier about six months ago. It's a 917 number, which is a Manhattan or at least New York number."

"Does that mean the phone was purchased in Manhattan?" I ask.

He shakes his head. "No, when these devices are set up, you can pick any area code you'd like. They could be purchased anywhere; there's no way to know."

"Thanks, Kenneth."

I walk back to the bull pen with the new number in hand. There's a very real possibility that Trent wasn't working alone, and if that's the case, who was he working with?

CHAPTER 18

I lean back in my office chair at my borrowed desk. The desks around me are full, but the station is quiet, eerily so. My eyes ache from going over the case files again. Though I've looked through everything again, trying to find who our suspect two might be, nothing is sticking out to me. Not being able to connect these dots is killing this case, killing me. My phone rings, an unrecognized local number appearing on the screen. As I accept the call, I press the phone to my ear.

"Hello, Detective?" The voice of a young woman cuts through the static. "This is Tegan Hartley."

"Hi, Tegan," I say, clicking up the volume, hoping it'll help to hear her better.

"You had asked me to let you know next time there was a race planned. I got a call today that they'll need me out there tonight."

"Tonight? That's short notice," I say. But if we need to be out there tonight, I'll go. I need to find out if there are other women at the race who Trent approached, who has been sending out the messages about the meet ups, and if it's possible Trent brought our other suspect to any of these races.

"The shorter the turnaround time, the less likely it will be that we ever get shut down," she says, her voice fading in and out over the line.

I can see her point. Word travels fast in towns like this. The more time that goes by, the more chances everyone will hear about it. If they want to keep up the races, the only way they can do that is by keeping people like me from knowing about it.

"I can trust you with this, right, Detective?" Her voice comes clear through the static now. There's an edge to it. I know how much this must mean to her, what a risk she's taking.

"I'm not planning on shutting you down, if that's what you're getting at. And I'll make sure my partner knows why we're going out there," I say. And I mean every word. My goal isn't to break this up. If it's been going on this long, chances are it's not causing any major harm. And they'll just move it somewhere else anyway. Bringing people together like this helps build communities, helps keep them strong.

I get the coordinates of the meet up, promise again that I won't bust them, and end the call. Austin sits at her desk, typing away. I weave through the desks in the bull pen toward the coffeepot to grab a refill, and Austin follows me over.

"Do you have plans tonight?" I ask.

She raises a brow at that, her dark eyes filled with interest. "I'm not asking you on a date," I say with a smile. "Tegan called. The race is tonight. Can you come? It's at midnight." I don't know what Austin does outside the office, if she has a personal life, responsibilities. I don't like having to ask these things of a partner I'm not familiar with.

"Of course," she says. "I'm going to see this whole case through with you. If you need me there tonight, I'll be there."

"I need you to wear street clothes. While everything they're doing up there is not entirely legal, we're not there to bust them. We need to blend in. I don't want to spook anyone or tip anyone off to our presence. And I've given Tegan my word that we won't shut them down," I explain.

"I can do that," she says.

"And I appreciate if after this is all over, you don't go after Tegan or the others up there for the races. They aren't hurting anyone."

She shrugs like it hadn't even occurred to her. "That suits me just fine," she says.

———

At ten p.m., I start pulling on insulated leggings I plan to wear under jeans. Then I drag out a sweater, socks, and black leather boots. Noah eyes me as I get dressed, his eyebrow quirked as if he's absolutely loving the view.

"Do you think that'll be warm enough?" he asks.

"Says the guy who doesn't own a coat," I fire back. Noah has been in Maine for over six months and doesn't own anything heavier than a jacket. I'm always worried about him freezing to death. Maine isn't the kind of place that you can make it through without a coat for long. If we stay here through another winter, I'll have to buy him something warmer.

He smirks. "I have a coat."

"You have *jackets*. You don't have anything suited to this climate," I say as I shake my head at him.

"That's not true." He laughs low. "I have you."

"Oh, shut up," I say playfully. But the words make my heart swell and my cheeks flush. I missed him. I missed *us*. I just hope we can stay on steady ground, that he can remain honest with me.

"How long do you think you'll be out there?" he asks as I finish lacing up my boots.

"I have no idea how long these things usually go on for. But I'd say I should be back here by three a.m. at the latest. That is, unless we find someone we need to tail."

He nods. "I hope you find this guy."

201

"Thanks." I offer him a quick kiss and grab a backpack I've filled with a few things I might need, in the event we're in the woods longer than we expect. I've packed granola bars, water, extra flashlights, a map of the woods, a compass, a survival blanket, and a first aid kit, as well as the picture of Trent I intend to show around. Growing up in Maine taught me to be prepared. Though my parents were never the type, I grew up around plenty of other Mainers who knew the importance of being prepared in the wilderness.

On the way to Austin's to pick her up, I stop and grab us both some coffee. We're going to need something to keep us warm. We may be in early March, but the nights are still freezing. It's not anything we're not used to, but I have to be cognizant of it. Hypothermia can creep in fast. And it's not just myself I've got to look after; it's my partner too.

I turn down the street Austin lives on, in a nice, well-manicured trailer park. Each house has a decent-size lawn. Though most of the grass is covered by snow, I can still make out the paving stones marking where flower beds will bloom in the spring. Shoveled sidewalks line each roadway, spiderwebbing throughout the neighborhood. Austin lives in a single-wide with a fenced-in yard. I text her when I pull in behind her Fiat and notice several toys stuffed between her car and the side of the house, as well as a little car and a small bike. Does Austin have kids? She's never mentioned that. She doesn't have any pictures on her desk.

A few minutes after I send the text, she hops down the front steps. Austin has her dark hair pulled up on top of her head in a bun, and a flannel scarf is bundled around her neck. She's got on a pair of jeans and a puffy black coat. It's one of the few occasions I've seen Austin without her uniform, though I've tried to get her to stop wearing it several times. Her boots crunch on the snowy lawn before she climbs into my passenger side. I glance between her and the toys, then eye her carefully.

"Do you have a child?" I ask as I motion to the little bike.

She follows my gaze to the toys, and she stiffens slightly. The look on her face tells me that she never planned to bring it up. "Yes, I have a five-year-old, a daughter. Her name is Harper," she says.

"Why didn't you—" I start to ask, but she holds up a hand to stop me.

"Because if I talk about my daughter in that station, no one sees me as a cop. They see me as a mom. And that's the end of the story. You don't get two identities as a woman. 'Mother' overrides anything else."

I can see that. I know it would never change the way I saw her, but guys in a station . . . it's hard enough for them to take most female officers seriously as it is. The second a woman has a baby as an officer, all any of the guys ask is when she's going to quit to stay home with the baby.

"One of my friends is staying the night with her," she says, motioning toward the house. I take that as my signal to back out of the driveway.

As we drive, she tells me the story of how she got pregnant at sixteen and gave birth, then raised her daughter all alone. Everyone assumed Harper was Austin's sister, born shortly before her mother OD'd. Because of the nature of small towns, Austin made sure to keep her pregnancy under wraps. She wouldn't let herself fall into the stereotype of a teen mother. It made her determined to become something and someone else. And I understand it—well, as best as I can as someone on the outside looking in. I look at her life and wonder if it's something Rachel could have had. When my sister died, she was pregnant. A fact I would never readily reveal to anyone who didn't need to know. Noah understood this and left the details out of his article. But I can't help but wonder where Rachel would be. She'd have a fourteen-year-old by now. I can't imagine being the aunt to a kid that age. I don't know that she'd have been the best mother, but she would have tried harder than ours. An ache grows inside me, a longing for the life that could have—should have—been.

I pull off Route 1, my headlights illuminating the mist roiling across the highway. Darkness swallows the pine trees lining the road, coiling in front of us. In this light, the houses on either side are shrouded, soft shapes in the night. There are no streetlights. Nature grows up around us, houses becoming more scarce as we close in on the preserve.

We turn onto a dirt road and find several cars parked along a trail that curves up through the trees. I take it as our sign to get out and hoof it. My car wasn't made for four-wheel drive. It's not like we could make it far if I went off road. My stomach flutters with unease and excitement as I throw the car into park.

"There's no cell signal. We need to be careful to stay together," I say.

"I've spent a lot of time hiking up here. Chances are I'll be fine, but I'll make sure to stick close," she says as she grabs her bag and slings it over her shoulder.

"Good," I say before slamming my door. If one of us gets lost in these woods tonight, with the temperature in the teens, we may not survive.

A worn dirt path, rutted from ATVs or jeeps, stretches in front of us, cutting a gash between the trees. The pines tower above us, their iced tips catching the moonlight as they twist in the breeze. About a hundred yards ahead, figures walk up the mountain, their silhouettes outlined by moonlight. What sounds like miles in the distance, the low growl of an engine rumbles, stripping away the silence that cloaks the night. The fingertips of excitement crawl up my spine.

We trail behind the other patrons moving through the darkness, and I'm happy I don't have to worry about coordinates or instructions to turn at a boulder. I've always found landmarks difficult to follow. We're far enough behind the other attendees that they don't seem to notice us at all. Based on how many cars there were at the mouth of the trail, my guess is it'll be pretty easy to blend in. Hopefully no one recognizes Austin from her job.

"Have you ever hiked out here at night?" I ask. Strictly speaking, most of the hiking trails and preserves are off limits at night unless you're camping, but I know most people treat that as a suggestion rather than a rule.

She shakes her head. "I've thought about camping out here. But I don't think Harper would be up for it. Maybe in a year or two."

I try to imagine what it would be like to plan my entire life around a child. But I just can't picture it. Maybe I never will. After all, the world would have you believe that once a woman turns thirty, her ovaries turn to raisins.

"So what's the deal with you?" she asks, side-eyeing me as the trail ahead of us begins to climb. At the end, the sound of engines cuts through the night. Adrenaline buzzes in my blood as we approach. About a hundred yards ahead of us, an orange glow backlights the trees, illuminating nature and bodies alike. They've got a huge bonfire going.

"The deal with me?" I ask, glancing at her out of the corner of my eye.

"Are you married, involved, got seven kids hidden back on that island?"

A low laugh rolls out of me. "I'm seeing someone; that's it. No secret kids."

"Is it serious?" she asks.

I consider that, unsure how to answer, and finally settle on "I'm not sure yet."

We close the distance between us and the fire, and the scene begins to take shape. In front of the fire, beyond the flame, torches flicker, set up every twenty feet or so, outlining the makeshift track. Once we finally reach the ring of spectators, I see the track stretches to our left as well, cutting away into a path in the trees. Night crowds around the scene, a shifting, dark force that tickles the edges of the orange glow around us, as if desperate to press in farther.

A line of ATVs is set up in front of us in several rows of five, about fifteen vehicles in total. Fifty or so people circle the fire like fish swarming a lure. Several stragglers move north, following the path of the torches on foot. And I realize that there must be others stationed along the track to watch. It takes a long time for them to disappear, swallowed by the night, but I watch them the entire time.

To my right a familiar figure clad in leather pants and a motorcycle jacket is bathed in dancing light. Tegan glances at me and gives me a nod of recognition. But her stance and the look on her face make it clear I am to stay put. I have no intention of approaching her.

I keep my eyes peeled, watching everyone who has gathered. Tension is heavy in the air, thicker than the smoke coiling up from the bonfire. Several people with helmets obscuring their identities, clad in black jackets, approach the ATVs and straddle them. Not being able to see their faces makes me study them for a long time. I'll have to keep an eye on them when the race finishes. It takes a few minutes for everyone to find their rides. When they do, the night ignites into a chorus of roaring engines so loud it makes my teeth ache. The ground vibrates beneath my feet, and I clench my jaw as the noise rolls through me in waves.

A woman in a red plaid jacket steps in front of the rows of racers. I'm sure she's saying something, counting down, maybe, but it's too damn loud to hear anything. The engines surge, roaring louder; dust skitters as tires spin. The whole line explodes into movement, a cloud of dirt and rocks hurling backward. They rush past the woman, sending her hair whipping around her. They fade into the woods, twisting around a bend, taking the deafening sound with them. But my ears still ache, as if expecting it to return at any moment.

Instead of watching the race, I scan the crowd. Chances are I'm looking for a lone man watching the women a little too closely. As I look over the gathered crowd, they seem to shift as dancing light from the fires plays across them. There's no one here alone. Everyone seems to have come with a group. All the groups hover around the fire, moving together like they're in orbit around the warmth.

To my left, the engines roar again, creeping closer, and they whiz by, doing another lap. And I realize I have no idea how long one of these normally lasts. They circle again and again, until finally a woman who's nicknamed herself Moira the Destroyah comes in first.

With the race over, I take the opportunity to pull Trent's photo from my bag. I move through several of the groups, flashing the picture. In the first two no one has seen him. In the third group, a man with long dark hair and a thick black beard nods that he's seen him before.

"Can I talk to you for a minute?" I ask, signaling for him to join me away from the group.

He follows me. We stop a few feet away from his friends. His shoulders are hunched against the cold, his black jacket pulled up around his neck.

"I'm Jacob," he says, offering me his hand.

I introduce myself, and his eyes go wide. "I'm here investigating a crime."

"Oh," he says, glancing to everyone else.

"Not this—I'm not here to break up these meetings. This is unrelated to these meet ups. When is the last time you remember seeing this man?"

Jacob tips his head to the side as his brows come together. "A couple weeks ago. He was here hovering around Melanie. He seemed really interested in her."

"Did they leave here together?" I ask.

He shrugs. "I don't know. I didn't pay attention to that."

"Did you see him here with anyone else?" I ask, not wanting to lead him too much.

He shakes his head. "No, I only saw him."

"Thank you," I say, trying not to let my disappointment reach my words.

I finish up speaking with Jacob, then ask a few more people lingering around about Trent, but no one else has any information about him or someone he might have brought along. I edge over to Tegan, who is looking more relaxed than when I arrived. She eyes me as I approach. "Who manages the texts that go out for these gatherings?"

"Moira," she says, gesturing to the woman who won.

"You notice anyone here out of place?" I ask, keeping my voice low. "Or someone who was at the last two of these?"

She glances around the group, doing a slow turn. Then she offers me a shrug. "No one that stands out."

"Keep an eye out for me?" I ask. Austin hovers at my side. I turn to her, but before I can say anything, Moira saunters over. She flashes a toothy grin to Tegan, her teeth so white they look bleached.

"Did you see that shit?" Moira booms as she grins at Tegan. Tegan laughs, an authentic belly laugh. These two are clearly friends. "Who's this?" Moira asks when she finally notices Austin and me.

"This is Claire and Austin. They're friends of mine," she says.

Moira raises a brow at that. "Friends?" She scrutinizes us, as if trying to see if we pass a litmus test.

"You manage the texts that get everyone here?"

She nods. "Why? Who's asking?"

"I just want to know if you keep a list of names and numbers, so you can match up who is who," I say carefully. Moira seems a bit edgy, and I don't want her to think that I'm here to shut her down.

She crosses her arms as best as she can with the helmet dangling from her right hand. "Nope, it's all completely anonymous."

I pull out the picture of Trent. "Do you remember this man signing up for the texts?"

"No," she says a little too quickly. Her attention snaps back to Austin. "Do you two ride?" she asks, motioning toward the ATVs while looking between me and Austin. Clearly, she's not interested in answering any more of my questions.

I shake my head, but Austin takes a step forward. "No, but I've always wanted to."

Moira looks her up and down. And based on the pucker of her lips, I can't tell if she approves until she asks, "Well, isn't it about time?" She holds out her hand, and Austin takes it. I want to ask if it's a good idea, if she should, but she's swept away too quickly.

Moira climbs on her ATV and signals for Austin to climb on the back. She hops on without hesitation, slinging her arms around Moira's waist.

"Is that safe?" I ask Tegan.

"As safe as anything else."

She retrieves a pack of cigarettes from her pocket and lights one. The cherry glows in the low light, a thin flame compared to the pin-pricks of light all around us. The fire blazes and crackles, the heat of it lashing against me. My body seems to be at war, the cold nipping at my back while waves of fire heat my face.

The engine roars, and Moira charges into the darkness with Austin clinging to her back, hair flowing behind them. As they disappear, I search the spectators again. The small groups are dispersing, everyone headed in separate directions.

The sound of the engine growing again draws me back from my thoughts. Austin clings to Moira as they come around a curve in the trees. The ATV lurches as if it's hit something, maybe a hole in the dirt. My heart jumps into my throat, and time seems to slow as I watch Austin fly from the back. She hits the ground, and I swear somehow I can hear the hollow thud of her body slamming against the dirt over the roar of the engine. For what seems like a full minute but is probably seconds, everything stops. The ATV, the movements of everyone around me. It's as if the world is holding its collective breath.

Moira hops off the back of the ATV and shouts something, but her voice is drowned out by the engines still roaring all around us. She rushes to Austin, and then her eyes flash to me and Tegan. This time I read her lips.

"Help."

Austin doesn't move. She's on the ground about thirty yards from me. The bonfire crackles to my right and breaks the trance shock shrouded me in. Everyone runs to her at once. My mind flashes to every single corpse I've seen laid out before me. And she looks no different. Her pale skin glows orange from the fire. Her hair is matted in the back, and red seeps from her scalp. Blood. I know the risks of moving her, but I have to get her to the hospital. There's no cell service out here. She needs help and fast. My training kicks in, adrenaline organizing my scattered thoughts.

"Tegan, Moira, we need to get her on the ATV so we can move her to my car. I've got to take her to the hospital." The idea of taking her to *that* hospital makes my stomach turn. But there aren't any other options—where we are is too remote. I'm not even sure we can find her an urgent care facility at this time of night.

Tegan and Moira help me load Austin on the back, and we drive her slowly down the slope of the trail to my car. Cold wind lashes at me as we pull away from the bonfire. My stomach twists, and unease floods me. My skin is clammy from the horror welling inside me. I keep my hand on the side of her neck, feeling the subtle flutter of her heartbeat. She's alive—for now. Hot, thick blood oozes onto my hand, my arm, soaking through my shirt. I know that head wounds bleed—a lot. But still, seeing it like this makes a lump swell in my throat. When we get her close to my car, I throw open the back door, and we carefully lay her on the seat.

She groans, a low, pathetic sound, as we set her down. But I take this as a good thing. The dead don't groan. Tegan climbs into the passenger seat while I shove the key in the ignition. I flash her a look.

"You're going to need help getting her into the hospital," she says.

"Are you sure you're not just coming to be sure I don't squeal about your club?"

She rolls her eyes at me. "I don't care *that* much about it. I don't want anyone getting hurt." Tegan glances at the back seat as I throw the car in gear. "Or worse."

Dirt and rocks are spit out from my spinning tires when I pull out onto the trail that led us into the preserve. I haul ass back toward town. Once my phone has service again, I call Sergeant Pelletier and the hospital to let them know we're coming. Sergeant Pelletier has the same reservations about the hospital I do. But there's nowhere else to take her. All of the urgent care options are too far away or closed at this hour.

I fly down Route 1 and turn into the medical center fifteen minutes later. Every few minutes, Tegan has checked Austin's pulse and breathing to be sure she's still with us. I pull through the parking lot and under the emergency awning and honk the horn several times. I shut off the engine and open the back door just as several nurses emerge with a gurney.

"This is the officer?" the first nurse asks me, a tall woman with auburn hair, pale skin, and deep-brown eyes.

"Yes, this is Officer Harleson," I say. It occurs to me that after she's all checked in, I need to go to Austin's house to let her friend know what's going on. Austin will need someone to stay with her daughter while she's here.

They whisk her off. I pace the waiting room, a twenty-four-hour news channel blabbering in the background, but it does nothing to distract my racing mind. Twenty minutes later, Sergeant Pelletier arrives, and after I catch him up, I take a few minutes to call Noah.

"Hey," he says, his voice thick, groggy. Clearly, I woke him up. I glance at the time on my phone—nearly three thirty in the morning. I should have checked before I called.

"I'm in the hospital," I say, but before I can continue, he cuts me off.

"Shit, are you okay?" His voice is clear. He's wide awake now.

"It's not me. It's Austin." I explain to him what happened at the ATV race.

"Do they know if she'll be all right?"

"We don't know anything yet. They're still evaluating her. Having her in this hospital makes me so nervous."

"I know," he says; then the words seem to die on his lips. When he speaks again, his voice is quieter. "But this could be a good thing. It could draw someone out."

Though I can't deny that I've considered it, I'm not going to play games with her life. "Noah." My voice is sharper than I mean for it to be. "I'm not using her as bait."

"I didn't mean as bait. But if someone approaches her . . ." He trails off.

But I won't cling to what he said. I won't. I'm never going to knowingly put someone I'm working with in danger. Especially not my partner. However, I will make sure that Austin is on guard. Though Trent may not be able to get to her, if he was working with someone else, that person could still be looking for victims. We all need to keep our eyes open to see if anyone who shouldn't takes an interest in Austin.

"I don't know when I'll be back. So get some sleep," I say, wanting to derail this line of thinking before it really gets started.

We say our goodbyes and end the call. I return to the waiting room just as a doctor approaches Sergeant Pelletier. He's got on teal scrubs, a color much too cheery for the situation. It's a doctor I've never seen here before. The badge clipped to his pocket reads *Dr. Haresh*. His dark eyes are grim when I approach, and my stomach bottoms out. Anxiety settles inside me heavier than stones, and a cold sweat prickles my brow.

"You're here for Austin?" he confirms.

We both nod, hanging on his every word.

"She's going to be fine. She needed some stitches on the back of her head, and she has a minor concussion. Looks like her back hit the ground first, and her jacket hood popped up to cushion the impact of her skull. I'll release her to go home in twenty-four to forty-eight hours. She'll be sore for a few days, though."

I exhale sharply. "Are you sure?" I ask.

The doctor lets out a low laugh that makes it clear he's humoring me. "Yes, I assure you—she'll be fine."

After we finish up with the doctor, I pull Sergeant Pelletier to the side. "We need to make sure someone stays with her twenty-four seven."

"I was planning to. We've already got a couple of officers here on a rotation checking things out. I'll be sure someone stays outside her room at all times."

"Good," I say.

"She's going to be pissed when she finds out. She won't want resources wasted on her."

"It's not wasted," I say automatically. "She could be in danger."

He raises a brow. "I know that, and you know that. She, however, is going to think it's a crock of shit."

I shake my head but say nothing because I know I would do the exact same thing. "I've got to stop by her place," I say.

"For what?" he asks.

I don't know if Sergeant Pelletier knows about her daughter or not, so I try to keep it general. "I'm going to go check on something for her."

"Do that, and then get some sleep. It's almost four a.m."

Though I want to argue, I know better. He isn't the first sergeant to tell me to get some sleep. And if I'm honest, I am dragging ass. My eyes ache; my limbs are heavy. After I check on Harper, I really do need some sleep.

By the time I make it to Austin's trailer, dawn whispers along the horizon, turning the inky sky purple where it touches the horizon. Cold air still clings to the night, turning my breath into a cloud. My cheeks ache as a cold wind whips against them.

There are no lights on in the trailer, and I hate that I might wake Harper. But I really don't have much choice. I rap my knuckles against the door, starting soft, then growing louder when I don't hear any movement in the house. Finally, the door creaks open, and a bleary-eyed woman Austin's age peers out at me.

"Can I help you?" she asks, her words stretched with sleep.

"I'm Austin's partner," I start.

She looks past me as if searching for Austin. She takes a step back, and I swear all the blood drains from her face. It hits me what she must think, that I'm here to tell her Austin is dead. I look down, expecting that she's seen blood on my clothes, but they're too dark to show any stains.

"She's okay," I say in a rush.

She grasps her heart and takes a breath so deep I can hear it. "Come in," she says, opening the door a little wider. The front door leads straight into the living room. Inside, the walls are a pale yellow. Pictures of a little girl hang everywhere, a timeline of her aging from a newborn into a five-year-old. The pictures are accompanied by swirls and butterflies that have been painted along the walls. Against the left wall there's a plush blue sofa, and to the right is a TV in an entertainment center, packed from top to bottom with children's books.

The living room opens to a kitchen and small dining area. Beyond that, a hall stretches back to where I guess the bedrooms can be found. The woman motions toward the couch, and I take a seat.

"I'm Sam," she says. Sam has a wide face with small, close-set eyes. They're light blue, almost gray, which looks striking against her black hair. She's tall and lean, all arms and legs.

I introduce myself, though I get the feeling she already knows who I am.

"She's mentioned you." She perches on the edge of the sofa, teetering as if she plans to hop up any second. "What's happened?"

"There was an accident with an ATV. She hit her head. She needed stitches. But she'll be released from the hospital later today or tomorrow at the latest. There's no permanent damage," I say.

She listens intently the entire time I talk, nodding with nearly every word.

"Can you watch Harper until she's released?" I ask.

"Of course. I live two houses down. It's no trouble. I'm just so happy she's okay." She sniffles, and I know she's on the verge of breaking down. Her pale face is splotchy, her eyes glassy.

"We are too. Thank you," I say as I shove up from the couch. But as I do, the soft padding of footsteps catches my attention. A little girl with long brown hair steps from the darkness in the hall, rubbing her eyes with one hand, a little stuffed dinosaur in the other.

"Mommy?" she says, looking between Sam and me.

Sam hops up and closes the distance between her and Harper. She scoops the little girl up and pops Harper onto her hip. "Your mommy is busy at work. So it's going to be you and me for a couple days, kiddo. Doesn't that sound like fun?" She says it in a high voice, like she's so excited, all her earlier sadness hidden away.

"Yay!" Harper calls as the two of them spin in the hall.

"I'll get out of your hair," I say. I slide one of my business cards onto the kitchen counter, making sure Sam sees me do it. "If you need *anything*, just call me."

"I will, thank you," she says.

I climb back into my car, my limbs heavy as the adrenaline fades. I grip the steering wheel to try to keep my hands from shaking. The sun edges over the hills, turning the few scattered clouds pink and gold as I turn onto Route 1.

By the time I get back to the hotel in Camden, I'm so tired I can barely keep my eyes open. I fall into bed next to Noah, leaning against him. He stirs and presses his body against mine.

With his words in my mind and the echo of his heartbeat in my ear, I drift off into an easy sleep.

———

I wake up around six, light peeking through the edges of the blackout curtains. Noah is sitting up beside me in bed, his laptop open. His screen casts a blue glow across his face, highlighting the slope of his nose, his cheekbones, and the stubble flecking his jaw.

"What are you working on?" I prop myself up on my elbow and peer at his screen.

"Tina's case," he says, taking his eyes off the computer to look at me. His brows perk up, and the edge of his lip curls.

It sticks out to me that he calls it Tina's case, with no mention of other victims. To him, this is all Tina. It's as personal to him as Rachel's case was to me. It's clear when he talks about Tina that she meant the world to him.

"You should get some more sleep," he says.

I shake my head and draw up into a sitting position on the king-size bed next to him. Though I'm still a bit tired, I don't want to sleep anymore. I need something else to focus on so I don't think about Austin. After she gets out, we'll regroup and decide on our next move. But for now, I've got to do something. "Tell me about your case. Catch me up."

He straightens and shifts the laptop on his lap so I can see it more easily. "I've mapped out where all the bodies were dumped," he says, pointing it out to me.

"But they obviously weren't killed in the middle of that street," I say as I look over the map on his screen. Though the street looks barely bigger than an alley, it connects two major roads and is surrounded by businesses.

"Based on the trace evidence on the bodies, they guessed that the women were killed in a car or at least transported in a trunk. All had traces of chemicals or car grease, gasoline, oil, on their bodies. A few had tiny strips of latex gloves found on them, but no DNA."

"Latex gloves?" That tells me the suspect likely has been up to these crimes for a long time. Highly organized. And chances are those strips weren't left behind by accident. The killer wanted authorities to know he was being careful, that he wasn't going to leave evidence. "What was similar about these victims?" I ask.

"All single mothers. All had recently visited a hospital nearby. It seems a few had bad bouts of the flu. The cops assumed that all the victims were sex workers because of where they were dumped. Though based on looking at the records, that seems flimsy at best. They interviewed the other women that worked in the area; none recognized any of the victims except for one. And she hadn't been on the streets in years. There was nothing linking Tina to sex work. She had a good job."

It takes a long time for me to process what he said. Alarm bells go off in my mind, and my mouth goes bone dry. "The same hospital?" My voice breaks as I speak.

He nods.

"How far was the dumping ground from the hospital?"

"Less than ten minutes."

"How long after visiting the hospital did these women die?" My heart pounds, adrenaline humming in my blood.

"Within three weeks. Most within ten to fourteen days," he explains as he reads the details off the computer.

"Did these women have overlapping nurses or doctors?"

He shakes his head. "A few here and a few there. But for the most part, no. Some weren't even in the same parts of the hospital. So it could be a custodian, someone who would have a reason to be all over the hospital. Though the police looked into all the current staff at the hospital at the time, they were never able to find anyone that stuck out as a suspect. Apparently my father was considered a suspect in Tina's death for a short time, because they found evidence they'd been having an affair."

"Holy shit," I breathe. His father was having an affair with Tina?

"Yeah," he manages. "Though it's one other thing I'm sure my mother would never believe."

"I'm sorry," I say and squeeze his hand gently. "I know it'll take you a while to track it down, but could you check to see if any employees left the hospital after the killing stopped and moved to Maine?"

"You think . . . ," he starts but trails off.

"There are some elements that line up. It could be nothing. But it could also be something. It's worth checking it out."

"I'll look into it. It's going to take me a few days, and I'll have to see if I can get my brother to talk to their HR department."

"You think he'd do that?" I ask. Noah has made their issues clear, but I'm still trying to understand the dynamics.

"I'm sure he will if I really need it."

While Noah goes over the other details of the case, all I can focus on is how closely it aligns with mine.

CHAPTER 19

The next morning, I drive straight to the hospital. Though Austin has only been there a little over twenty-four hours, they're ready for her to leave, and so am I. I thought about visiting, but with the constant guard and her needing to rest, I decided to leave her to it. I pull up outside just as a nurse rolls Austin out in a wheelchair.

"This is so ridiculous," Austin mutters to the nurse in a tone that tells me it's not the first time she's said it. "I hit my head. I can walk just fine."

"Policies. There's nothing I can do about it, ma'am."

Austin shoves up from the wheelchair and strides toward my car, the nurse staring after her like she might say something else. But she seems to think better of it and turns, heading back to the hospital, pushing the chair.

"How're you doing?" I ask when she climbs into the car and buckles herself into the passenger seat.

"I'm fine. I'll be better when people stop acting like I'm a cracked egg. I want to go back to work."

"You sure? I'm certain that Sergeant Pelletier is going to try to send you home."

"Then he's going to get a piece of my mind," she says.

I can't help but smile at that. I'd do the exact same thing. "Do you want to swing by your place and see Harper before we head to the station?"

"She's at kindergarten. She won't be home. Sam texted me and let me know she dropped her off. Thank you for stopping by to tell her what was happening."

I had expected her to be annoyed with me. At least a little bit. But I'm sure she'd rather that I stop by and see Harper instead of one of the other guys from the station.

"I'll see her tonight," she says quietly enough I'm not sure if she's talking to me or to herself.

When we pull up to the station at ten, the parking lot is already filled. Usually it takes a bit for everyone to trickle in. I catch her up on what Noah is looking into for me.

She's quiet for a long moment.

"If we do connect someone between this hospital and the other in Tennessee, we would need to look at the victims close to that hospital."

"Why do you say that?" she asks.

"Whoever is doing this is highly organized. Careful. They're making sure not to leave DNA, fingerprints, and so far all the victims have come willingly."

"So when he was newer to this, there'd be more evidence left behind?" she asks.

"Most likely, yes. I would also guess that since our suspect isn't killing at home, there's a reason for that. Either they don't live alone, or they live too close to others who might realize what's going on."

"Like in apartments?"

"Yes, exactly like that. If he's too loud in an apartment, that's the end of it." Living in an apartment is what ended up getting Jeffrey Dahmer caught. Dahmer got so lazy near the end that his apartment was a wasteland of body parts. Hell, he had shrines of skulls and body parts in his fridge. The smell is what gave him away. If he'd had a place out of the way that no one had a reason to visit, who knows how long his murder spree would have lasted.

"We're looking for someone who can readily afford motels, someone who can easily lure these women without raising suspicion."

"Yes," I say. "And we're looking for someone who would have had a connection with Trent. So likely someone else who works at that hospital." Her words stoke thoughts already sparking in the back of my mind. "Austin. You were at that hospital. You need to be careful. Someone might approach you. It could be this guy."

A grin curves her lips, and she crosses her arms. Something passes over her features, and the look on her face unsettles me. She's excited.

"Austin, what are you thinking?" I ask when she doesn't say anything. But I have a terrible idea she's thinking the same thing Noah did.

"This could be perfect. I can lure this shitbag out into the open—"

"No," I say automatically. I know the desperation, the *need*, to solve the case. But I won't let her do this. I will not let another officer put herself in danger like that.

"I won't be in danger. It's not like I'm going to take a strange man to a motel. But if some guy approaches me, that would point us in a direction, right? And since all the victims so far went willingly . . ." She trails off.

"Willingly for now. The moment he can't get who he wants or needs back to a hotel, he'll drag someone back to one. A killer sticks to one MO for as long as it's comfortable. But if you push them, if you keep them from getting what they need, that will change. Believe me."

The look she gives me tells me that she doesn't believe me at all.

"Seriously, Austin, I need you to be careful. Stay aware of who is around you wherever you are. Trent may be locked up, but he may not have been doing this alone. We saw those outgoing calls on the burner phone around the times the victims were killed."

"Fine," she says, but the tone of her voice makes it sound like she isn't going to listen.

Inside the station, Austin walks straight to her desk, and I go to mine. I log in to the computer and begin to search for more details about the murders in Tennessee.

CHAPTER 20

Noah and I wake up early. I was stuck at the station late into the night, and by the time I got back to the hotel, he was already passed out. I didn't have the heart to wake him. Now, he stretches next to me on the hotel bed. And I can't help but find it hilarious that we're both paying for rentals but here we are, shacked up at a hotel across the water from them. It makes me question again if I want to keep my place in Vinalhaven or if I'm ready to move on. I still don't know.

Noah slides off the bed and strides into the bathroom. I roll over, propping my head on my hand. Within a few seconds he's back, leaning against the doorframe, a toothbrush sticking out of his mouth. He's shirtless, which always draws my eyes to those abs of his. I eye him a little too long, imagining him slipping back into bed with me, me running my hand along his chest. I bite my lip and push the thought away. I've got a case to focus on.

"So what'd you find yesterday?" I ask.

He holds his hand up, signaling for me to wait a minute. He disappears back into the bathroom. A second later he reappears, wiping the toothpaste residue from his lips. "I've got a long list of hospital employees. I got through about fifty of them yesterday. And I heard from my brother about the new victim they found. They matched her to a woman who went missing."

"Oh? Who was the victim?" I ask.

He walks over to his laptop and pops it open. "One sec, I've got to pull up her name." He types, his fingers clicking against the keyboard, then turns around. "Elizabeth McConnel."

"McConnel? The director of the hospital and the CEO both have the same last name." Is it possible that Elizabeth is a relative of Aidan's? Is this the missing link we've been looking for? "How many of those on the list moved to Maine?"

"So far, only a handful. Three were here temporarily. Only one worked at both hospitals. But she doesn't work there anymore. She retired about ten years ago and moved to Florida," he explains.

"Give me part of your list. I'll start at the end. You can keep working from the top, and we'll meet in the middle."

Noah hands over a list, and I'm thankful that he likes having a physical list in front of him. I'm the same way. I digitize things for my cases, but there's nothing like having paper, *real* notes, in front of me. That's why I still use a notepad, unlike some of the other officers, who have switched to tablets. Hiding behind a device makes it all feel much less personal.

I pop open my computer, plug in my mouse, and scan through the list of names. One toward the top of the page sticks out to me. Dr. Aidan McConnel. My heart pounds, the blood whooshing in my ears.

I pull my laptop closer and google his name. I find pages of results. Everything recent, on the first page, is from Maine. All stuff from the past few years. After I've gone through several pages, I alter my search to *Dr. Aidan McConnel + Tennessee*, and old results fill the page. One catches my eye.

Local Doctor's Wife Reported Missing

I click on the link as my heart pounds. The story from nearly sixteen years ago loads.

Dr. Aidan McConnel's wife, Elizabeth McConnel, was reported missing in the early hours of October 13. She'd gone out for an early-morning run, as per her usual routine, and has not been seen since. Despite several searches of the surrounding area, no hints to Elizabeth's whereabouts have been uncovered. At this time, Maryville police are asking that anyone with information please come forward.

We have reached out to Dr. McConnel for comment. We hope that he knows the whole town is praying for him and for Elizabeth's safe return.

I go back and look at the dates. Elizabeth's death was fifteen years ago, but Dr. McConnel moved shortly afterward. A few more minutes of digging reveal that he moved to Florida, where he remarried. Three years later, that wife died in an accident. She drowned in their pool.

"Noah," I say, my hand trembling.

"What's up?" he asks.

"I found something." My voice rises and my heart pounds, but I try to rein it in.

He looks up from his laptop at me.

"The director of the hospital in Camden is on this list." I quickly explain what else I've found about the two dead wives.

His eyes go wide at this news. Clearly, he wasn't expecting it. Maybe he didn't think we'd find any hits on this list. "Elizabeth was the victim that Cameron told me about. Those are the remains they found."

I pull up Aidan's bio to see where else he's worked. Tennessee, Florida, Savannah, Atlanta, and now Maine. "I need you to look around Halifax Hospital in Daytona Beach, Florida, between 2005 and 2008 to see if there were any serial killings there. I have to keep looking into this. There's got to be another stretch of time after this." My mind flashes to the deaths in Daytona that appeared on Roxie's search of the FBI database. Could those be related to this?

He nods. "On it."

It looks like Aidan was honest about one thing—he was in Georgia after living in Florida. It appears that after living in Daytona Beach, he moved to the Savannah area and lived there for two years, then moved to Atlanta. I'll have to call one of those precincts tomorrow to see if any of their homicide detectives remember anything. Or maybe Aidan was someone they looked at.

Noah and I go over everything again and again, until I feel like my thoughts are swirling in details about these cases. I may not know for sure yet, but in my mind, they're already linked.

Though it's early and I know I'll likely wake up Austin, I call her cell phone and warn her about what we've found. As soon as she assures me she'll call if she sees Aidan, I call Vera. All I have is a work number for her, and I know I can't leave the message I need to on her voice mail, so I tell her that there's an urgent matter I need to speak with her about. My next call is to Sergeant Pelletier to fill him in on what we've found. The phone rings several times before he picks up.

"Detective," he says, his words thick.

I fill him in on what I've found on Aidan and how I haven't been able to get through to Vera to warn her.

"I'll try to call the hospital and see if I can get her cell phone number," he says.

"We need to suggest that she go stay with a friend until we can investigate more. But it's looking like McConnel might be the one who was working with Trent."

"Good work, Detective. Let's catch up on this later in the morning."

After getting off the phone, I put in a breakfast order for the two of us from room service and go to get ready, and by the time I'm dressed, there's a knock at the door.

Noah pushes up from the bed to go to the bathroom, showing off his cut torso and muscled arms as he passes me. There are other things I'd like to stay shut up in this room doing with him, but none of that's going to happen until I solve this case. I dish out our plates of food, dive into mine, and pop open my laptop. The bathroom door creaks open behind me, and Noah approaches, kissing me on the top of the head as he grabs a plate and the coffee.

"Thanks for ordering this," he says and takes a bite of his bacon.

"It's the least I can do. You're helping me with this case," I say.

"I'm thinking that we're helping each other. It's looking more and more like we're after the same guy."

And I can't say that I disagree. With everything the research on Aidan has revealed so far, I'm getting concerned for Vera. Though I have worries about Austin, too, my hunch says his wife is more at risk, since he's never targeted a police officer before.

"What did you find out on Florida?" I ask.

He takes another bite of his food before speaking. "There was a rash of serial killings in 2005. Five women were killed. All had some kind of link to sex work, except for one. They were all strangled and dumped with their arms bound in wooded areas."

"Tina and the other victims in Tennessee weren't dumped in wooded areas, were they?" I ask, to be sure I remember correctly. It's so easy for the details of the cases to become jumbled.

He shakes his head. "Just the last victim, Elizabeth."

A few years ago, I would have thought it impossible for this to be the same serial killer. But if my case last year taught me anything, it's that sometimes killers will change MO if the circumstances don't fit their usual needs. While it's true that most serial killers do stick to their routines, something may have prevented this killer from strangling his victims again. Did he decide that dumping his victims in the city risked too much exposure? Did he turn to the woods because it was easier? Then again, maybe the killer just got bored.

If this was all the work of one guy, we're looking at twenty to thirty victims—possibly more. The thought makes my stomach sour. I can't blame law enforcement for not catching this guy. Sometimes law enforcement can be blamed, like with the miscarriage of justice I uncovered in Vinalhaven last year, but this is different. Taking off before he can become a suspect. If that's what's happened here, he is a detailed and focused killer.

I pull out my phone and dial Sergeant Pelletier. I fill him in on what I've found and ask him to put a car on Aidan's house. Just in case. We need someone watching him. It's the only way we can be sure that he doesn't kill again.

After Sergeant Pelletier assures me that he'll put someone on Aidan watch, I feel like I can finally breathe again.

Snow skitters across the street as I pull out of the hotel parking lot. I didn't bother to let my car heat up, so the cold remnants of the morning still cloud my breath. Pink light dusts the horizon, streaking the sky. Traffic is light, and I question whether I've forgotten a holiday.

The station is nearly empty when I pull up. I climb out of my Mustang, and tiny snowflakes tick against my leather jacket. My boots crunch in the layer of crisp snow that's frosted the parking lot. When I walk inside, the receptionist desk is empty. It's too early for her to be in yet. She normally shows around nine.

A couple of the guys from the night shift are still hunched at their desks like they're ready to knock off. I nod to each of them before I sling my jacket over the back of a chair. I make my way to the empty coffeepot. As I brew a fresh pot, I think about what I've got on my plate for the day. I have to call the precincts that would have dealt with any serial murders in Savannah and Atlanta. Though it's still early, I decide to put in a call to Savannah. If I can get ahold of someone before they're too busy, I have a better chance of getting some information out of them.

I search online for the number, grab the desk phone, and dial. Anxiety prickles in the pit of my stomach. The phone rings several times before someone picks up on the other end.

"Lieutenant Anderson." A woman's voice, deep and hoarse, cuts through the line.

"Hello, Lieutenant, this is Detective Calderwood of the Camden, Maine, police department. I think that a homicide suspect of ours lived in your neck of the woods for a while, and I wanted to see if you have any cold cases that fit the MO."

A chair squeaks in the background, and I can imagine her sitting up straighter. "Who is the suspect?" she asks.

"Dr. Aidan McConnel."

"A doctor? Angel of death MO?" she asks, her interest clearly piqued.

An angel of death is typically someone who works in a field where they care for others. Doctors, nurses, caregivers for the elderly. These killers justify their actions, their murders, because they believe that they are putting their victims out of their misery. They usually kill silently with medications, and because they're so rare, they're also difficult to track. Their body counts can reach the hundreds.

"There are actually two identified MOs for this suspect," I say.

"Really?"

"We've established strangling or suffocating and dumping victims either in the woods, in the middle of a city close to a hospital, or in a motel. This guy was in the vicinity when three murder sprees were taking place, so we're trying to determine if those murders can be traced back to him or not. It's a little too coincidental, if you ask me." I wouldn't normally volunteer this level of detail, but for a lieutenant, I've got to make a damn good case if I want any real information.

For a long moment, she's silent, and I'm afraid that I won't be able to get anything from her. But finally, she asks, "What locations?"

"Camden, Maine; Maryville, Tennessee; and Daytona Beach, Florida."

"What time period would Dr. McConnel have been here?" she asks, and I hear typing in the background.

"2008 to 2012, around then. It appears he moved to Atlanta in 2013."

"Serial-killing world tour." She lets out a dry, humorless laugh. And I can't deny that I had the same thought.

"With the vics we've identified so far, it appears all had sex not long before they died. In previous instances, Florida and Tennessee, he went after women who had a history or suspected history of sex work. All vics were dumped near a hospital, usually within a five-mile radius."

"Let me look into this. I'll see what I can find, and I'll give you a call back by the end of the day."

I pass her my contact information, thank her for her help, and end the call. After I hang up with Lieutenant Anderson, I call the Atlanta Police Department. The call goes about the same. I give a sergeant the information I have, and in return they promise to give me a call back.

By the time I'm done with the calls, the clock is close to eleven. I glance toward Austin's desk. She's still not there. I walk over to Sergeant Pelletier's office and catch him up on the calls I made.

He nods thoughtfully. "Thanks. Let me know what they say." He takes a sip from his coffee mug. "I've got Blake watching Dr. McConnel. The last update I've got is that he went into his house at eight p.m. He hasn't left there since."

If Blake is watching McConnel's house, am I overreacting about Austin not being in yet? I glance back over my shoulder. I'd rather have Sergeant Pelletier check in with Blake just to be sure. "Have you heard from Austin today? She's usually in by now." A bad feeling curls inside me, like a shark circling prey. She hasn't texted, called, or even sent me an email. Nothing.

He shakes his head. "She's still not here?"

"No, and I haven't heard a word from her today."

He grabs his desk phone and starts to dial. His brows furrow, creating a fissure between them.

"It's going straight to voice mail." He slams the receiver down, his cheeks draining of color.

My stomach shifts with unease, and my palms slick with sweat. My mind buzzes as thoughts, mostly horrible ones, linger there. "I'm going over there."

"I'll call Blake and make sure that McConnel is still there, but it doesn't hurt for you to go check things out. Call me as soon as you know anything," he shouts after me as I sweep out the door.

I weave between the bull pen desks, grab my leather jacket, and head out. Though the sky is still a blanket of gray, for now at least, the snow has stopped. Everything glitters, covered in ice, as I pull out of the parking lot. My heart pounds, as if urging me to drive faster, but my car isn't built for this weather. I've got to drive slowly. With every passing mile the silence seems to build. Every eventuality trickles through my mind. This isn't like her. Not at all.

It takes twenty minutes to reach Austin's trailer park. I pass a row of single-wides and turn into Austin's driveway. Her car is pulled under the carport, Harper's toys still strewed alongside. I scrutinize the house, searching for any signs that something might be wrong. But nothing is out of place. All looks right. But that doesn't settle the snake slithering through my guts.

As I shut my engine off, I say a silent prayer that she's okay. I throw open the car door, climb out, and slam it. Wind whips against me as I walk to the house, but my mind is so focused on what's inside that house that I can't feel it. It could be minus fifty, and I'm sure all I'd feel is the panic needling me. I climb the stairs, open the storm door, and knock. My heart nearly stops as I wait. I listen, trying to hear any signs of life inside the house, but there's nothing. Not so much as a footstep. No TV droning, no little girl babbling—it's as silent as the dead.

I knock again, this time harder. Hard enough that the side of my hand aches. But still, only quiet meets me. There's something wrong. Seriously wrong. I shift gears. I need to get inside the house. I try the handle, but it's locked. I lift up the welcome mat, searching for a spare key, but there's nothing.

"Dammit." I hop off the steps, eyeing the front flower bed, but there's nowhere for a key to be hidden. Sweeping along the exterior of the house, I make it to the back door and find it open a crack. Carefully, I pull out my service pistol from the holster and creep up the porch stairs, remaining as silent as possible. The back door leads me into a long hallway. In front of me is a laundry room; to my left, the kitchen and living room, which I've seen before.

From my vantage point, the rooms appear to be clear. Darkness swallows me as I step inside the hallway, turn right. One door down from the laundry room, I find a bathroom decorated in light blue, a cartoon snowman grinning from the shower curtain. The empty silence sets me on edge. The air is so thick with it I can taste it. The room beyond the bathroom is clearly Harper's. The walls are a soft yellow; cartoon dinosaur decals stick to them. I flip the light on, and that's when I see something pooled in the center of the room. Blood. The puddle is too large. Whether it came from Harper or Austin, it's enough to be fatal. My mind roars, but I shut the thoughts down. If I panic, it won't do any good. I have to focus, to find them. I grab my phone and call for backup.

I scan the room quickly, my heartbeat pounding in my ears, but there's no sign of Harper. With the light from the bedroom spilling into the hall, I can make out red droplets along the wood floor leading to the back room. My fingers tighten reflexively around the weapon in my hands as I creep forward. Halfway to the room, I glimpse a pale leg atop the bed.

My breath catches when I see her. She's splayed on the bed, naked, congealed blood pooled on her chest. A sob rises up inside me but gets caught in my throat. I can't let it escape. My eyes sting, burning from the emotion I'm desperate to contain. It's as if I'll be lost to anguish if the tears bottled there get out. I stay focused, because I have to—for them. Anger flares inside me until my vision darkens at the edges, my rage ready to boil over. This shouldn't have happened. He's never targeted a police officer before. He's always targeted young, vulnerable women. Austin shouldn't have fit his MO. I sweep the room to make sure it's clear, then call a bus and Sergeant Pelletier.

"She's dead," I manage to choke out while I try to keep my hands from shaking.

"Fuck," he breathes. I hate to do this. I hate passing along information like this.

"Sergeant, her daughter is missing. I'm going to search the house again, but we need to be ready to issue an Amber Alert," I say.

"Daughter? Do you mean her sister? Never mind. You can explain to me later. Go look for her—we're on our way."

Though the scene needs to be secured, finding Harper is of paramount importance. Preserving life will always come before evidence. The thought of finding that little girl is the only thing that keeps me going, that keeps me from breaking down. Adrenaline burns in my veins, my guts roiling as I start to search, considering where exactly a five-year-old might choose to hide. Because I can't allow myself to think that she's dead or that Aidan has her.

I check under Austin's bed first, then her closet and bathroom, but come up empty handed. When I walk back into Harper's room, I refuse to look at the blood on the floor. I check the closet first and find a wealth of toys but no Harper. She's not under the bed either. As I search the laundry room, sirens in the distance capture my attention. They're almost here. Back in the living room, I catch movement out of the corner of my eye. Something shifted behind the sofa. I put away my service weapon, snapping it back in place, and step closer.

"Harper, honey, is that you? It's Claire, your mom's friend from work. Do you remember me?"

She doesn't answer, but I see movement again, a shadow shifting along the wall. I take out my flashlight and peek behind the couch. Harper is huddled against the wall, her hands and the front of her nightgown stained red with blood. My stomach twists, and a wave of nausea punches me in the gut, but I fight against it.

"Harper, could you come out, please?" I can't imagine how terrified, how broken, this little girl must be. The sound of movement behind the couch causes me to step back and shut off the flashlight. When she crawls out, she stares up at me, her huge brown eyes like saucers. Her lower lip trembles, and tears well in her eyes. All at once she closes the distance between us and hugs me so tightly I'm not sure she'll ever let go. I scoop her up and prop her on my hip. Then I grab a blanket from the back of the couch and throw it around her. We'll have to take the nightgown for evidence, but for now, she'll have to stay in it.

"Harper, are you hurt?" I ask her as we step outside.

She shakes her head. "No, but Mommy is."

"I know. Do you hear the sirens? An ambulance is coming to get her now." I don't have the heart to tell her that the ambulance isn't going to do any good. The only person this little girl had in the whole world is now dead. She's all alone. My heart aches at the thought.

An ambulance and three patrol cars pull up in front of the house. Sergeant Pelletier climbs out of one of the squad cars and approaches.

"This is Harper," I say, motioning toward the little girl. Though I have a feeling Sergeant Pelletier already knows her name, just not that she's Austin's daughter instead of her sister.

"Hello, Harper," he says, looking at her.

She says nothing but doesn't shy away like other children might. Instead she stares him down, as if challenging him to say another word to her.

"Where is she?" he asks.

"Master bedroom. I haven't been able to secure the scene yet. I just found her," I say, motioning to the little girl.

"I've got it."

"I need someone to grab her a change of clothes, some of her things. We're going to have to call social services, or I can call the babysitter that watched her for Austin." I go down the list in my head, because it's easier to focus on what actions I need to take than it is to deal with the flood of emotions rising inside me.

He shakes his head. "I've already called. My wife and I are registered foster parents. We don't have anyone in our care at the moment; we can take her," he says. "Blake checked McConnel's house. He isn't there. Blake's now checking all the motels in the area to see if he showed up there."

I don't know what to say. It catches me completely off guard. But I prefer that to her being rushed off to a complete stranger. I process the information about Blake. Though he's already checked the house, I want to see it for myself. There may be some hint about where McConnel's gone. Or could he have gone back once he saw the squad car leave?

"I'll grab some of her things after the scene is secure. I'll have my wife meet us at the station."

Harper's eyes flash between me and Sergeant Pelletier. "I want to stay with you," she says to me.

I hoist her a little higher on my hip, and she clutches tighter to me. "I know. But I'm going to have to find who hurt your mommy."

"The man who hurt her," she says in a voice that's low, cold.

"Yes, the man who hurt her." Did Harper witness what happened? It's not like we could put a five-year-old on the stand during a trial. I fish my phone out of my pocket and google a picture of Aidan McConnel. "Do you know this man?"

She yanks the phone out of my hand and scrutinizes the image, her little nose wrinkling. She stares at it for so long I expect her to say no. But her lips purse, and finally she nods her head. "He hurt my mom."

"Thank you."

I carry Harper to my car, place her in the front seat, and turn on the heat. She pulls the blanket tight around her as she snuggles in. Footsteps crunch behind me, and I turn to find Sergeant Pelletier with a little purple backpack.

"I've put some of her things in there. There are also some juice boxes and snacks."

I take the bag from him. "Thank you."

After he disappears back into the house, I change Harper out of her bloody clothes, help her into clean ones, and stuff the evidence into a plastic bag. By the time she's changed and sucking on a juice box, the CSI team has arrived, and I hand off the bag to them.

When I head back to the car, Harper glances up at me, her eyes pleading. As if I can help sort this out for her. God, I wish I could. My heart is breaking for Harper.

———

A few hours later, I drive with her back to the station, stopping to get her lunch on the way. She gnaws on a chicken nugget while playing with her new toy, and if I didn't know what had transpired for her in the past two days, I'd never guess it. Children are resilient little things. When we pull into the station, the parking lot is swarming with media.

"Harper, I need you to sit tight in the car for a minute, okay? Please don't touch anything."

Though I know I probably shouldn't leave a five-year-old alone in a car, I need to make sure none of those reporters say anything in front of her that they shouldn't. There's a roar of voices as soon as I open the car door. Several reporters rush toward me, and I brace myself. News vans are lined all around the parking lot, their numbers displaying what stations they belong to.

"We have reason to believe that the Pen Bay Strangler killed an officer of the Camden Police Department. Can you comment on this?"

How the hell did this already leak to the media? Sure, they've been up my ass this entire case, but there's no way they could have known these details unless someone inside the station is talking to the press.

"I can't comment," I say, keeping my voice firm, steady.

A woman surges forward, shoving a microphone in my face. "Do you have any suspects yet? Any news on a pending arrest?"

"I need you all to back up. Get back to your vans. You need to be at least thirty feet from the station entrance so personnel can enter."

One of them glances at my car, and I move automatically, shielding Harper from view. Slowly, reluctantly, they move away from my vehicle. I walk to the other side, grab Harper, and get her into the building as quickly as I can. The last thing I need is her overhearing something about a dead cop and realizing they're talking about her mother. When I get inside, Sergeant Pelletier's wife, Tiera, is waiting. Tiera is older than I expected. I think she's probably got a few years on her husband. She's got a kind smile and long black hair flecked with silver, and her skin has a deep olive tone.

"Is that Harper?" she asks, peering at the bundle in my arms. Though I gave her new clothes that are plenty warm, Harper enjoys being cocooned in the blanket from her house—not that it surprises me.

Now that she's here and I've got to hand Harper over, something inside me shifts. I don't want to. If she stays in my arms, I can keep her safe. What if Sergeant Pelletier can't? This is the only piece of Austin left. What would she want?

Harper peers over the edge of the blanket to inspect Tiera. Curiosity sparkles in her dark eyes.

"Hi," Harper chirps at her.

"I'm Tiera," she says. "How old are you? Seven?" she asks with a smile.

There's no way she can think that Harper is really that old. But the little girl laughs, and I realize what Tiera is doing.

"No, I'm five," Harper says, her voice still lifted with amusement.

"Oh my gosh, really? You seem like such a big girl already."

Harper tries to squirm from my grasp. I set her down beside me, where she props her hands on her hips. "I am a big girl," she asserts, straightening to her full height.

"Oh, I know. I can tell," Tiera says. "I know you've had a hard day. Do you like cartoons?"

Her eyes light up. "Yep."

"Come with me, then. Let's go watch some until everyone gets back." She holds out her hand, and to my surprise, Harper runs over and takes it.

Tiera glances up at me. I close the distance between us and pass over the backpack with Harper's things. Tiera asks, "Are you going to be okay?"

I nod, though I have zero faith that I will be. Right now, it feels as if grief is pushing at me from all directions, threatening to suffocate me. While I still can, I escape to the bathroom. My cheeks are so hot they feel like they're on fire—until the tears fall across them. My hands shake, and my breaths come fast.

The room spins as emotion grips me. Reality slams into me. I lost a partner. A friend. A little girl lost her mother. If I had done more, if I had kept her safe, this wouldn't have happened. Rage swallows my grief. This could have all been avoided if we'd had her watched properly. How Aidan got past his tail to kill Austin is beyond me, but we could have done something if we'd just tried harder. I know it.

There's a knock on the bathroom door, forcing me to pull myself together. I can't wallow. I can't fall apart. Thanks to Harper, we have confirmation of who did this. We know who we're after. I need to find Aidan and haul in his ass before he hurts anyone else. He's hurt far too many people already.

I splash some water on my face. When I open the bathroom door, Sergeant Pelletier is waiting on the other side. Though he doesn't say anything, his cocked eyebrow says it all.

"I'll be fine," I lie.

"I need you to find McConnel. I called the hospital. He's not there," Sergeant Pelletier says.

"I'm going to sweep his house again. He could have gone back after Blake left," I say, urgency rushing my words.

"Take one of the guys with you."

"I will. Someone needs to try and call Vera," I say. He may be planning to kill his wife next. I explain the pattern we've identified so far. We need to try to find Vera and get her to the station. Sergeant Pelletier told her to stay with a friend for a few days, but I'd feel better if she were out of Aidan's reach. We need to get her away from Aidan without making it clear to him what's going on. If she learns what's happening and already knows about his crimes, she could warn him, allowing him a chance to escape. If she had no idea, she could try to confront him and put herself in danger. There's no real good scenario for how this could play out.

"We'll try to find her, and we'll get this guy, Claire."

I don't say anything, but the promise feels empty. Words so hollow I can hear the echo of them. We might get this guy, we might nail Aidan's ass to the wall—and then what? It doesn't bring Austin back. It doesn't repair all those lives he's already destroyed. It's as if all these women were connected by a web, by him, and he ripped it all out from under them, leaving only ruins and torn threads.

On my way through the bull pen, I grab Zane. He's easily the biggest guy on the squad. He's got to be six foot six, more than a foot taller than me. I hope he fits in my car. As we walk outside, I catch him up on the situation. Though I don't feel good about having another partner, I know how stupid it would be to corner Aidan alone. We know what he's capable of. I'm going to need backup for this. Based on how he left Austin's body, it's clear he's escalating. All the patterns we've seen before from him can no longer be trusted. And based on the other crime scenes, he may have a gun, a knife.

I throw the car in reverse and glance over my shoulder. Media still rings the parking lot, like a pack of vultures. I've got half a mind to back up a little too closely to them. But I decide against it. We don't need to be in the media for anything else. We've been in the spotlight enough already.

Zane helps me navigate through the streets of Camden to find the McConnels' house. We pass the small shops lined up downtown, the school, a large park. The farther we drive, the farther apart the houses become, and the larger they grow. We pull up in front of a pictur-esque white colonial with forest-green shutters. The lawn is covered in snow, and I note that the sidewalks and driveway haven't been shoveled. Usually in communities like this, if you've gone too long of a stretch without clearing the snow, you'll face a fine.

Zane pops open his door, and I follow suit. My boots sink in the snow as I step onto the lawn. A frigid wind blows past us, making the trees moan and ice break away from the branches. It skitters to the ground, clinking. I glance at the house, looking for any signs of life. I unholster my service weapon and creep toward the house, my heart pounding with every step. Adrenaline rushes into my blood, making my head swim.

"There aren't any cars here," Zane says, and I nod.

My phone buzzes. I grab it and swipe to accept the call. "Calderwood."

"We haven't been able to get through to Vera. She's not answering her phone," Sergeant Pelletier says, his words capped with static.

"We need to find her. Get a GPS trace on her phone." It can take a while to secure a warrant to compel a phone company to comply. We need to get a jump on it.

"I'm on it. Keep me updated on your movements," he says.

I end the call and reach the front door and try the handle, but I find it locked. Zane and I circle around the back of the house, listening intently for any signs of life, but there's nothing, nothing but the wind. I step up onto a deck that looks out over the forested yard and try the back door. Zane pushes me aside, fishing a lockpick kit from his pocket. He eyes me.

"You saw nothing. It was unlocked."

I hold my hands up. "Saw what?"

He slides one piece of metal into the lock, then another, and turns it slowly. After a click, he says, "We're in."

The back door opens into an immaculate kitchen, tall cabinets in a matte gunmetal gray, shimmering quartz countertops ticked with silver and teal blue. The backsplash is punched tin, in the style of old ceiling tiles.

From the kitchen I can see into the dining room, an austere, modern space filled with neutral-toned Swedish furniture with pops of blue and orange. We check an office and two guest bedrooms but come up empty. No sign of a struggle, no sign of life on the first floor at all. But more importantly, no sign of death.

My pulse thunders in my ears as I creep soundlessly up the cement stairs. On the second floor landing, I can see straight down the hall into a bedroom with an open door. The duvet, blankets, and pillows are strewn on the floor, which puts me on edge. The rest of the house is in perfect order. Vera doesn't strike me as the type that would leave an expensive duvet on the floor. I signal for Zane to check the other bedrooms while I continue down the hall. Once I slip past the doorframe, I see that it's not just the sheets, pillows, and blankets askew, but both of the nightstand lamps have been knocked over. Something definitely went down in this room.

From the bathroom, Zane calls to me. "Hey, Claire."

I walk into the large master bathroom and find him staring at the counter. A small plastic stick sits on the counter next to a pink-and-white box.

"Is that a pregnancy test?" he asks.

I glance at it, and sure enough it is. The digital readout says PREGNANT. I suck in a sharp breath. Is the baby Aidan's or Ian's? Did Aidan find out about the affair and force her to take a test? Vera has been a bitch through this entire investigation, but if she's pregnant, it's not just her well-being I need to be concerned about. There's an innocent life that doesn't deserve to be in the middle of this.

I text Sergeant Pelletier and warn him of the signs of a struggle, attaching pictures. If we can provide evidence of Vera being in danger, we may be more likely to get a warrant for a GPS ping or at least compel the phone service provider to lending their support.

An hour later, after we've secured the house, my phone buzzes.

"Calderwood," I say as the call connects.

"We've tracked Vera's phone. I'm going to send you the coordinates. We don't have a warrant for the house. Get out of there."

"Where are we headed?" I ask.

"Camden Hills State Park is the last place her phone pinged. We can't get a read on where she is at the moment. Her phone has been shut off. My guess is he took her up to the ski shelter up there," he says.

I relay this info to Zane, who nods. Clearly, he knows where this is. I'm not familiar with that park. I end the call with Sergeant Pelletier, and we climb back into my car.

"Head north on Route One, then turn left at the park, and we're going to follow the main drive all the way up," Zane says.

"You've been up there before?" I ask as I pull away from the house.

"When I was in high school. The place is usually empty. We'd go up there to drink, party. We had an arrangement with one of the rangers. He'd look the other way if he saw anything."

That doesn't surprise me. There's always some place like that. But how did Aidan find out about it? Any local, I wouldn't be surprised by. But Aidan has only been here a few years.

We drive up Route 1 past rows of houses built in the nineteen hundreds, small shops, bakers, butchers, and a small bookstore. Trees crowd around the road as we get closer to the park. The foliage parts, and a road appears on the left. I throw on my blinker and wait for a break in traffic. The road curves upward, carving a path through the forest, the evergreens rising on either side of us, blotting out the sky.

The ribbon of road spirals up the mountain. Frost clings to the branches, the needles. A gray sky casts a gauzy light on the road. The higher we climb, the more mist rolls across it, shrouding our path.

"It's coming up here soon," Zane says. And sure enough, the trees start to open up, revealing a cabin in the middle of a clearing. A BMW is pulled up alongside the cabin, one of the back doors of the car yawning open. The cabin is large—the size of an average three-bedroom house. It's got two windows on each side, but someone has tacked up blankets inside, blocking our view. On the side of the cabin facing us, a brick fireplace is inset in the wood. The walls are all weatherworn, splintered, a testament to the many winters they've withstood.

My phone vibrates in my pocket, and I grab it and see Sergeant Pelletier's name on the screen.

"Sergeant," I say.

"Blake just pulled up some information about Aidan. We have reason to believe that he owns several firearms."

That I knew. Even if I hadn't, most Mainers own at least one gun. Especially since he hunts, there's no way he wouldn't at least own a rifle.

"We're here now. We're checking out the situation, going to figure out the best way to proceed. There's a BMW here."

"I'm sending backup. Be careful."

It'll take them about fifteen minutes to get here, but that's time that Vera might not have. I signal to Zane that we should move in. With our weapons in hand, we creep toward the cabin. My heart feels like it's beating in my throat as I press my back into the rough wood wall. Though I try to listen for any signs of life inside, all I can hear is the echo of my own pulse. We skirt along the side, and I try peeking in one window, but the plaid blanket is pulled to the edge. I try the other, and through a slit in the second window covering, I see bunks pressed against wood-paneled walls, a wood stove, a small dining table.

In the right corner, a body is huddled on the floor, a pool of blood spreading around it. From here, I can't get a read on who the body might be. Vera? Aidan? A camper in the wrong place at the wrong time? From the sweep of the outside, it's clear that there's only one door, and that's on the other side.

I motion to Zane that we're moving in. We need to get to that door. I need to be sure he doesn't slip out. As we shift along the wall, I finally hear something inside, the muffled voice of a woman. My heart leaps. We approach the front door, and the voice becomes clearer.

"Please let us go. We'll leave. You'll never have to see me again," Vera says, her voice low, pleading.

My stomach twists as I listen to it. I've got no love for Vera as a person. She didn't care about a single one of the victims. But she doesn't deserve this. And the baby she's carrying doesn't deserve any of the fallout.

Heavy footfalls resound inside the cabin, and I guess that Aidan is pacing. Dirt and rocks skitter behind us, around the cabin. Our backup has finally arrived. I turn to Zane. "Go signal for them to be quiet and surround the cabin."

We've got to play this carefully. If Aidan realizes we've surrounded the cabin, he may snap and kill Vera, then himself. Or he may come out guns blazing, trying to kill any or all of us. The best way to do this would be to try to lure him out. But I doubt that it's possible. I want him alive, *need* him alive. There are things only he has answers to, his crimes. There may be many more that we don't know about.

Sergeant Pelletier glances around the corner, and I lock eyes with him. While several other officers approach him, I hang back, moving away from the structure so we can talk without being overheard. He lifts his hand up, signaling for the other officers to hold their positions.

"What's going on in there?"

"Vera is alive and talking. He's in there moving around. From that window." I motion toward the one on the left. "It looked like there was someone inside, injured, bleeding. I can't tell if they're still alive or not."

"Any idea who it is?" he asks.

I shake my head. "I can't tell if it's someone who was staying here or someone connected to this. There's no easy way to see them."

"What are you thinking?" he asks as his eyes move between me and the cabin.

"We need to throw in a smoke grenade and rush the place before he can hurt himself or Vera."

"How are we going to do that?" he asks.

I eye the cabin. We should be able to throw smoke grenades in each window. With four at once, the smoke will come at Aidan from all sides. That should be enough to distract him so that we can get inside. If he's unable to tell where anyone is, there's less of a chance that he can hurt them. We could use flash-bang grenades for this, but they can injure those inside a small building like the cabin, and I don't want Vera hurt. I break down my plan for Sergeant Pelletier. We're going to need everyone who goes in to have a mask. To be sure that someone can take Aidan down, we need to bust in the door right as the grenades are thrown in; otherwise, we'll have as hard of a time seeing in there as he will.

"Do we have masks for everyone?" I ask.

"I've got three in my car, but I think that's all that we'll have on scene," he says as he glances toward his patrol car.

"Are the other officers vested up?" I ask. We need to get in there sooner rather than later. Every minute that he's inside with Vera is another minute that we risk her life.

"I'll have Clint, Blake, and Zane get ready."

"You think I'm not going in there too?" I say, raising a brow. He said he only had three masks. I'm not letting them go in there without me.

"Look, they're built for this type of stuff. Aidan is a big guy. You're petite. It's safer this way."

I grit my teeth. "My size doesn't make me any less of a police officer. I went through the same training they did. I've taken down perps that outweighed me by at least one hundred and fifty pounds. I am going in there whether you like it or not. So pick the *two* other officers that you're sending in with me," I say, my words sharp as knives. I'm not sitting this one out. They called me in to hunt this guy, and that's exactly what I'm going to do. I will not stay on the sidelines while they finish this up for me.

"I'll have Clint and Zane get ready, then," he says, though the look he gives me tells me he's none too happy about it.

I nod to him and follow to get my mask. I know that it won't help too much with the visibility, but it will keep me from choking on the smoke or tearing up from it. Sergeant Pelletier waves Zane and Clint over, and we gather around the trunk of his car. While the guys put on their vests, I secure my mask and get the grenades ready. I speak to Blake and two of the other officers nearby, explaining that we'll do a countdown over the radios to signal when the windows should be broken.

"I don't like this," Sergeant Pelletier says once we start taking our positions.

"I've got my vest on," I say. "So does everyone else. We're as ready as we're going to be. We can get them both out of there alive; I know it."

For a long moment he's silent, and the only sound is the wind creaking through the trees. "It's time. Let's do it. But for the love of God, be careful."

"I will," I say.

I close the distance between me and the cabin just as sleet begins to fall. Tick, tick, tick against the windows, the walls, the officers surrounding the cabin. I clench my fists to keep my hands from shaking, but whether it's adrenaline or fear—or both—I'm not sure. I take my service pistol into my hand, clicking the safety off. The cabin has a fireplace, but there's no hint that they've lit it. No smoke spirals from the chimney. There's no crackling of logs inside.

Though it's freezing out, sweat prickles along my spine. My nerves are so on edge that my whole body feels tightly wound, like a spring. I glance to Zane and Clint, and they both walk over to flank me. Sergeant Pelletier works with the other officers, getting them all in position with their smoke grenades. A cold wind whips around us, making the trees crackle. Inside the cabin, footsteps echo against the floorboards. I hope that he isn't moving to the window.

I gesture to Sergeant Pelletier that we need to get moving. He nods to me, then disappears around the cabin. My pulse echoes in my ears as I wait for the signal. I reach forward, my hand resting on the door, though I don't dare to touch the knob yet. All around me, the radios crackle to life, signaling that it's time to move as they start the countdown. I grab the handle, shoving my shoulder against the door as glass shatters. The canisters hiss as they fly through the air and then thud on the wooden floors.

Something falls over, likely a chair, inside the cabin as I push inside. Through the dark smoke just beginning to sputter from the canisters, I catch a glimpse of Aidan standing near a table in the center of the room. Vera huddles in the far corner, thankfully out of his reach. I burst inside, Zane and Clint trailing me. Aidan whips his head around as the room begins to flood with smoke. He looks from me to his wife. I raise my gun, holding it even with his chest as I step closer. Only ten feet separate us. At this distance, I know I won't miss if I fire. But I don't want to kill him. We need to take him in alive.

He smirks at me as Clint comes into view on my left, his gun raised, and Zane appears on my right in a similar position. Zane moves farther to the side, placing himself between Vera and Aidan.

"Vera, are you hurt?" I ask without turning to look at her.

"No, I'm fine," she says, her voice trembling.

"Who's that by the window?" I ask.

"Ian. I was staying at his house after Sergeant Pelletier mentioned that I should stay somewhere else for a few days."

"You cheating bitch," Aidan spits.

"That's enough," I say to Aidan, nearly growling the words. Smoke filters up from the floors around us. I want to take Aidan in, but we need to get Vera out of here first. "Vera, get out of the cabin."

Behind Aidan on the table, there's a pistol. He's at least three feet from it, and I know that we could take him down before he grabbed it. But I can't risk Vera getting caught in the crossfire. The light steps behind me signal her progress. With every footfall, more and more smoke hisses around us. Aidan lets out a low cough and takes a step backward.

"Don't move, Aidan. We will shoot you," I warn. The mask is secured well to my face, but the smoke filling up the cabin is making his form a vague shape within the mist.

As Vera's footsteps inch closer to the door, I move toward Aidan. Adrenaline burns in my veins, begging me to take him down, to get him in custody.

"She's clear," someone yells outside. Aidan dives backward, taking his pistol in his hand. I hold mine steady, ready to fire.

"Drop it, Aidan," Zane and I say at the same time.

Aidan swings his pistol around, aiming it at me, and I know he's going to fire. Time seems to slow, stretching into infinity as his finger curls into position and he aims at me. I squeeze the trigger, firing off a shot toward his right arm. He shoots, the sound of the discharge cracking so loudly through the air that my ears ring. Pain cuts through my left shoulder, searing, as the bullet tears my flesh. I grit my teeth against the agony. But I can't stop. I won't. I close the distance between us and slam my body into his, knocking him off his feet. The gun clatters to the floor as he falls.

He strikes the ground so hard the impact reverberates through me, making my bullet wound ache. Aidan grunts at the impact, but the fight hasn't gone out of him yet. Zane and Clint barrel forward, their footsteps echoing on the floor. Aidan's fist flies forward, hitting me in the jaw. My mouth floods with the coppery tang of blood. I suck in a sharp breath. We're so close. We just need to get him cuffed. Wood groans and splinters beneath us as we struggle. Aidan knocks me to the side. I wheeze as all the air is forced from my lungs, and my vision dims when my head cracks against the floor. I roll away, and Clint slams his knee into Aidan's spine. Zane grabs both of Aidan's arms, yanking them back to cuff him.

Bodies swarm through the door—Sergeant Pelletier, Blake, and a mass of others I'm too dazed to recognize. Smoke clouds around me, and my head swims, making it difficult to focus on any one person in front of me. With every furious beat of my heart, my bullet wound aches and pulses. A body crouches next to me, and through the haze I'm able to make out Sergeant Pelletier. I hand my pistol over to him, and the edges of my vision start to fizzle from the rush of adrenaline.

"We need to get several buses up here," he says, and I'm not sure if he's talking to me or to some of the other officers. Sirens wail outside, making me wonder if he already called someone.

I glance toward Aidan, who's still unmoving on the floor, his hands secured behind him. But I pray that he's not dead. There are still too many unanswered questions. And that bastard doesn't deserve the release of death. I want him to rot in prison.

They force me into a patrol car with Zane, who rushes me off to the hospital, while a bus speeds up the slope to get the others. As the towering pine trees flicker past on either side of the car, they rise so high they blot out the sky. I let my eyes drift closed.

CHAPTER 21

My heart pounds as I bolt awake. For a long moment, my eyes scan the too-white walls, the equipment at my side, and it all clicks into place. The hospital, the shooting, Aidan. The few days here come rushing back to me all at once. Nurse Jordan shifts beside me, a clipboard in her hand as she takes my vitals.

"Well, your blood pressure and pulse are still normal. You need a few more days of rest, though," she says as she looks over my chart.

"I'm checking myself out," I say, then swing my legs off the bed. The room tilts, a sharp pain cutting through my shoulder. I grit my teeth against the pain and breathe steadily for a few moments before trying again. Since I'm stable, she won't be able to argue.

"You ripped all your stitches out last night. I need you to stay at least one more day. I want to be sure you don't end up with an infection." Her eyes are wide as I pull on a pair of pants Noah brought me and then a dark shirt. If my wounds start bleeding again, at least the shirt will camouflage it.

"I have to go. Thank you for your help," I say as I shove my feet into my shoes. My back aches with every movement. My body and the wounds are sore from last night.

"Where's Aidan?" I ask her.

She glances toward the door, then leans closer to me. "He's being held at the back of the hospital, with an armed guard." She sighs and looks me over. "If you're going to go, please at least promise that you'll come back tomorrow so I can check the wounds and make sure they're okay."

"I will if I can."

I grab my phone and call Sergeant Pelletier. It rings several times before he picks up. "How far did you guys get with McConnel?" I ask before he can even say hello.

"He's said a few general things, only about him kidnapping Mrs. McConnel and killing Dr. Munroe. He won't speak to anything else."

"I'm going to see what I can get out of him," I say as I pace the small hospital room.

"Claire, you really need to—"

"The hell I do. We need to get this guy nailed. I'll call you back when I've got something," I say, anger making my voice rise in volume.

"Claire, please—" he tries again, but I end the call. Then I phone Noah. He's got some files I want for my questioning with McConnel.

"Hey, I was just about to come see you," he says as soon as he answers the call. His voice brings a smile to my lips.

"Good, I'm ready to get out of here." I walk slowly down the hall toward the front door. "But there's something I have to do first. Can you bring your files? I need some of the information about the victims. They're holding Aidan here. I'm going to get a confession out of him."

"And there's no way I can talk you out of trying to do that while you're still recovering . . . ," he says, his words almost a question.

"Nope. Just bring me the files. I need to do this. How soon can you be here?" I ask, feeling antsy knowing that I'm in the same building as Aidan.

"Five minutes," he says.

I finish up the call with Noah and wait out front for him. The cool morning air blows against my face, and it feels amazing to be outside again. Only a few days in the hospital had me feeling completely claustrophobic. Footsteps click against the cement behind me. I turn and find the doors opening to let Vera out. She's got on a black pencil skirt and a flowy gray blouse the same color as her heels. She offers me a thin smile, but I just nod instead of returning it.

"Morning," she says as she squints against the sunlight. "I thought you were supposed to be here for a few more days."

"I was, but I have some things to attend to," I say simply, because I don't owe her more of an explanation than that.

She crosses her arms. "For what it's worth, thank you." Her words are stiff, as if she's not used to thanking people.

I force myself to swallow all the unkind words I have for this woman. She isn't thanking me because she cares about the patients. All she cares about is that I saved her own neck. But then I realize what she lost in all this, her husband and Dr. Munroe, so I nod to her. She strides back into the bowels of the hospital, disappearing. I can't imagine how uncomfortable it must be to work here with the man who tried to kill you being held in the back of the hospital.

Noah pulls up in my car in front of the hospital, slides out, and slings a messenger bag over his shoulder. I approach the car as he flips the bag open and hands me a folder. I glance at it, seeing some of the basics about the victims from Tennessee inside. This is exactly what I need.

"I've got to question him. Can you hang out here until I'm done?" I ask.

He nods. "I'll be waiting. Good luck."

I offer Noah a quick kiss before flinching at a pain in my shoulder, then walk back inside the hospital. Though I know he's probably itching to follow me and make sure I'm okay, right now, I'm glad he's keeping his distance. I need to get myself into interrogation mode, and I can't do that with him hanging around. There are two completely separate sides of myself, one that I show the people in law enforcement, and one that I am when I take off the badge.

I weave through the hospital, past open rooms and waiting rooms that are nearly empty. The hospital is eerily quiet as I walk through the halls. Aidan's in the back corner of the medical center, chained to a bed in a guarded room. I find Zane standing outside it, his arms crossed. He glances up at me as I approach, an eyebrow lifted.

"Why aren't you in your room?"

"I've come to interrogate my suspect," I say, pointing toward the folder in my hand.

He shakes his head, as if he expected this or at least was warned about it. "The sergeant told me if you wanted to get in the room, I've got to go in too."

"That's fine."

He moves out of the way, opening the door for me. As I walk inside, Aidan glances at me, the same cold, vacant look from our previous meeting hovering in his eyes. Tubes snake from his chest and arms toward poles on either side. His arms and legs are strapped to the bed. When I look at him, it's not just him I see; it's the ripples of what he's done, the people he's hurt, the lives he's destroyed. I know well that grief is a weight that will hang on your shoulders for the rest of your life. How much has he doomed others to carry?

I take a seat in the stiff chair beside his bed, and Zane hovers near the door, his arms crossed over his broad chest.

"Could I have some water?" he asks, eyeing a cup of water sitting on a tray next to his bed. Because of his position and his arms being strapped down, he can't reach it. I nudge the tray closer so he can sip from the straw.

"Just so you're aware, everything you say here today is being recorded. Anything you say can and will be used against you in a court of law," I explain as I turn on the recording app on my phone.

"I can have a lawyer, yeah, yeah. I know the spiel," he says, his voice so flippant I half expect him to roll his eyes.

"Are you asking for a lawyer?" I ask to verify. I don't want him to be able to argue in court that he mentioned a lawyer.

He shakes his head. "No, not yet."

I should breathe a sigh of relief, but I'm not wasting my time. "All right, Aidan, where were you the night of February twenty-first?"

"Where do you think I was?"

I'm not going to play these games with him. "Why don't you tell me where you were, and we'll see if it matches what I think."

He shifts on the bed, trying to sit up further, but his restraints don't allow for the movement. "And what if I told you I wasn't at home and I was really at a motel?" His eyes flicker in a way that sets me on edge.

"Then we'd need to have a discussion about why you were there," I say. Normally I'd just dive right in if a suspect said something like this to me. But I can tell by Aidan's demeanor that he's not going to give me the information I need—not yet.

He fidgets, staring at his lap. When he doesn't say anything else, I ask, "Where were you, Aidan?"

For a few moments, he's silent, so I press again. "Where were you the night of February twenty-fifth?"

Again, my question is met only with silence. I open the folder in front of me, glancing at the pictures on top.

"Aidan, have you ever been to Maryville, Tennessee?"

He finally looks back at me and raises an eyebrow. "I have," he says after a long moment, a glimmer in his eye.

Zane glances at the folder, and I can tell that he's got questions, but it's not like he can ask them with Aidan sitting right here. I pull out several of the pictures from the folder and place them on the table facing Aidan, next to his cup.

"Have you seen any of these women before?" I ask, tapping them.

He holds his hands out as if asking for the pictures. I pass him the first, and he appraises it before licking his lips. But he says nothing. The corner of his mouth quirks up as he glances at the images, if only slightly.

"Aidan, if there's anything to tell, now's the time."

He takes a long, slow sip of his water. "Did you know that my wife is cheating on me? That she got pregnant by another man?" Though he directs the question to me, it's clear it's not *really* a question. "It's been going on for six months. It's not the first time. She's done it a few times before. Every time she swears it means nothing, that it'll never happen again. But then there she goes . . . it doesn't matter what I offer, what I do for her; she always strays."

"And how did that make you feel?" I ask, and suddenly I'm reminded of the therapists I spoke to after Rachel died.

"Angry. Very angry," he says, his fists clenching.

"Angry enough that you had to do something about it?"

His jaw tightens, the muscles on the sides flexing. "Yes," he says so softly I almost miss it.

"How angry?" I ask.

"As angry as a man can get." He glances at the pictures again. "And my wife in Tennessee did the same thing to me. The cheating bitches got what they deserved."

Though I wait for him to continue, he falls silent. His eyes are far off, as if he's lost in thought. Finally, I decide that I'll need to say something to urge him on.

"Aidan, I can't help you if you don't tell me what happened."

"As if there's anything you can do to help me now." He lets out a low laugh that's as cold as the frigid winds outside.

"There may not be anything I can do, personally. But if you tell me what happened and why, the DA might take that into consideration during your trial." I don't specify how he can be helped, because at the end of the day, none of that is up to me. And honestly, I don't give a shit about helping him. I just want closure for the families he's destroyed. I hope they lock him up and he never sees the light of day again.

"I killed them all. Is that what you want to hear?" He practically hisses the words. The edges of his lips quirk with amusement.

"If that's what you did, then yes. I want to know who you killed and when."

He sighs and twists his hand so that the tubes snaking from his arm bulge against the tape strapping them in place. "I took my first life in 1998. My wife pushed me to my breaking point when she started cheating on me. I decided I was going to pick up a woman and do exactly what my wife had done. This woman was so beautiful but so much like my wife. I fucked her in the back of my car in Sandy Springs Park. But as she threw her head back, I looked at her long, slender neck. I don't remember how, but my fingers ended up around her throat. The next thing I knew, she was dead. I panicked—it wasn't what I meant to do. It just . . ." He stares off toward the wall for a minute, a glazed look in his eyes. "It just happened. I didn't know what to do, so I dumped her body in the woods. The way my heart raced as I drove away, I've never felt anything like that. That body, as far as I know, they never found her."

"What was her name?" I ask.

"I didn't ask her name. It didn't matter what it was. In my mind, she was Elizabeth. They all were. All ten of them in Maryville, Tennessee." The more he talks, the more his southern twang leaches into his words, as if he's usually far more careful with his speech than he's being right now.

"Did you know any of their names?"

He shakes his head. "No, their names didn't matter. After Maryville, once Elizabeth was out of the picture, I moved to Daytona Beach," he says, fiddling with the edge of his sheet.

"What year was that?" Zane asks.

McConnel looks at the ceiling, lost in thought. "2005, I think. The older you get, the more the years blur together."

"And how many women did you kill there?" I ask, trying not to rush my words. My heart pounds as I wait for him to respond. Now that he's opened up, I'm terrified that he'll stop.

"Six." A sly smile creeps across his lips, but his eyes remain distant. "But I think they only ever found five of them."

"And why did you start killing women there?"

His smile widens, flashing his sharp, white teeth. "Because there's no rush like it. At first, it was a way of punishing the women I was with. I *deserved* better than how they treated me. So they had to pay."

"You made them pay by killing other women?" I ask, the words bringing a sickness to the pit of my stomach. Knowing that evil like this exists in the abstract is one thing, but sitting just a foot away from it is like staring down the devil.

"Yes. All women are the same. You all have a sickness, a need to cheat. You're born whores, and you remain that way." His gaze traces over me, as if he's sizing me up.

"What year did you leave Florida?" I want to turn the questioning back to his crimes. He's going down the wrong path.

"In 2008 or 2009 I moved to Savannah. There I killed four women. After that, Atlanta, where I killed six more. And then, finally, here." He raises his hand as if to motion around, but the restraint holds it back.

"Was it just the five victims here?" I ask, my throat becoming raw as I count them off in my mind. Melanie, Asha, Jessica, Austin, and Ian.

"Yes," he says and then twists his hands in his restraints. His eyes lock on mine, and I realize that all the light has gone out of them. "I'm done talking," he says.

I shove up from the chair and glance at Zane. I have the closure I needed. I wanted to know without a doubt that he was responsible for the deaths in Tennessee. And now I know the full extent of exactly what he did. After he gets out of the hospital, we can lock him up. This bastard will never hurt anyone else again.

CHAPTER 22

The next day, after working on my paperwork for the case, I leave the police station. It feels like I've been inside most of the day. In reality, it's only been a few hours. My shoulder still throbs, like I suspect it will for a while. Though both Noah and Sergeant Pelletier think I need to be resting, I can't even think about that until everything is wrapped up. But there are still a few things I have to do before this is all finished. As I walk out to the parking lot, the spare key in my pocket pokes me in the top of my thigh.

If you kept it, maybe there's a reason.

I walk to the back of the parking lot and find my car. I slide in, the cold seats chilling my legs. As I slip my key into the ignition, I call Roxie.

"Hey, neighbor," she says, and I can hear the smile in her words.

"Neighbor? You got the job?" My voice is louder than I mean for it to be. I rein it in. "I can't believe you didn't call me."

She laughs. "You were a bit preoccupied."

"You know I'll always find time for you." This job can make it so hard to find a balance. In the back of my mind, I'm worried how Noah will feel when I have to choose my job over him. Though my work is important to me, I know I have to draw a line somewhere. But can I?

"I know. You don't have to do that. I know how it is. Don't feel guilty about doing good," she says as if reading my mind.

I turn down Route 1, pass a small downtown, and continue toward the hotel. The streets are lined with white wood-frame buildings, ornate churches that must be at least a hundred years old, and small, bustling shops.

"So tell me about the job."

"You're talking to the lead detective of the Bangor PD," she says with a laugh.

"Well, look at you," I say, the smile spreading so wide across my face that my cheeks ache. "Congratulations. You deserve it."

"I just want to dig in already. There's a stalking case with an author up here. I'm getting into it as soon as I get my stuff picked up."

"Gonna protect Stephen King now?" I ask.

She laughs as I pass through the shadow of towering oak trees. "You know I can't tell you that."

"Get me an autograph?" I joke.

"I'll see what I can do. How's your case coming?"

"We got our guy," I say. I wince as the sweat prickling on my shoulder seeps into my bullet wound, and I turn down the heat in my car. "Well, *guys*, actually. There ended up being two of them working together. I need to speak with Trent, our first suspect, so I can work out all the details for my report. But we've got them both in custody, so now it's just filling in all the blanks for the trial."

"Third time's a charm?"

"It was this time. Number three confessed," I explained.

"And what are you going to do now? You staying in that town? Moving somewhere more exciting?" she asks.

"I'm not sure yet. But I have decided to give Noah a key. I think you were right: I was looking for a reason to push him away. We've made our peace, though, and I'm hoping that he'll be honest with me from now on."

"Oh?" she asks, though she doesn't sound at all surprised. "Your first time settling down with someone. Those are some big steps, Calderwood."

"I'm actually going to give it to him when we get off the phone."

"Well then, get on with it. Call me later," she says.

"We better get dinner once you're settled," I say in an almost warning voice.

"Oh, we will. Don't you worry."

We finish up just as I turn into the hotel. The parking lot is just as empty as it was when we checked in, which isn't all that surprising in the off-season. My phone buzzes as I stroll across the parking lot. I glance at it, expecting the call to be from Roxie having forgotten to tell me something else, but it's Sergeant Pelletier.

"Sergeant," I say as soon as the call connects.

"Claire," he says, and his voice sounds off, like he was hoping he'd get my voice mail.

"Yes?" A bad feeling blooms inside me, and the back of my neck prickles.

"I just got a call from Vera. Unfortunately, Aidan—he killed himself."

I swallow hard. "He killed himself?" The words rasp out of me. How can that even be possible? He was shackled.

"It seems he got free while his guard was in the bathroom, made it to the drug-storage closet, and killed himself. He injected a lethal dose of morphine."

Rage builds inside me. I want to punch someone. My vision nearly goes red as I pace through the lobby toward the elevators.

"Claire, I'm sorry," he says.

"Yeah, me too." I end the call.

When I make it up to the hotel room, Noah is leaning back on the bed, his laptop on his lap. As the door snaps shut behind me, he looks over and grins. "How'd it go?" he asks.

"I was going to nail him to the fucking wall, but he killed himself. He took Austin, Tina, all those other women, and the prick killed himself so he wouldn't suffer for any of it." My words are sharp with anger, and I clench my fists against the rage building inside me. I should have killed him when I had the chance.

He pushes his laptop across the bed, crosses the room to me, and pulls me into a hug. His long dark hair tickles my cheek as he holds me. The stubble clinging to his chin brushes against my jaw.

"It's okay. You still got him," he says, stroking my hair. "Even if he doesn't go to prison, he's gone. He can't do this again to anyone else."

I know he's right, but I feel robbed. I want him punished. To suffer. And he just got away with it. He lived his life and escaped when it suited him.

Noah gives me a soft kiss on my cheek, and his eyes level on me.

"Are you going to be okay?"

I nod. I will be, because I have to be.

CHAPTER 23

It's taken me a few days to get approval from the DA and Sergeant Pelletier to question Trent. This is the last interview I need to do to finish out my case for Camden. The drive to Two Bridges Regional Jail takes about an hour. The whole way, as I carve through ribbons of road winding through evergreens and past pebbled beaches, I'm twitchy, uneasy. Questions I need to ask Trent pile up in my mind. I need to find out what his involvement was, what he knew, and when. I know it's likely we'll be charging him as an accessory, but I need to know just how deep this goes. With Aidan dead, we've got the media up our ass constantly about how no one has been charged for the murders.

I turn right down a stretch of road that curves behind trees so sharply it's as if the pavement has been swallowed by the forest. My car slows as I follow the turns, and then the trees fall away, revealing a sprawling parking lot and barbed wire–topped fences beyond. Guard towers rise every hundred feet or so, and even though the sky is shrouded in clouds, the shadows of armed guards moving inside are obvious. Though I know it's midafternoon, when the days are like this, it's as if I've been plucked out of time.

The wind is cold, thrashing relentlessly as I walk through the parking lot with my shoulders hunched. I approach the administrative building—meant for law enforcement and legal counsel—and flash my badge to the guard at the door. I know this all well enough that I left my service pistol back at the station, as it slows everything down.

"Afternoon, Detective," the guard, a man likely in his early twenties, says as he reviews my badge.

"They're expecting me," I say. He's writing my information on a clipboard.

"Head on in," he says, handing my badge back.

I walk through several doors, showing my identification each time. Though I didn't want a partner, admittedly now without Austin here, I feel a bit lost. A woman dressed in a brown uniform greets me and leads me down a hall to an interrogation room. We pass several other guards, dressed in identical uniforms to hers.

"We'll be watching through the mirror," the woman says. "If you need anything, just knock or signal for us. He'll be shackled to the table. So he won't pose a threat to you. You will be locked in, however, until you give us the signal that you're ready to leave."

"Thank you."

"Just give us a few minutes to get him down here," she says, opening the door for me.

I walk inside to find a room that's painted a light gray. It's barely a different shade than the concrete floors. In the middle of the room sits a long metal table with several different loops protruding from the top. Four chairs are situated around the table. At the back of the room, two small barred windows display the veiled sky outside. I glance over my right shoulder and find a one-way mirror that must be at least eight feet across.

I settle in one of the chairs at the table and fold my hands atop it as I wait. A few minutes later, the door slides open, and Trent is led in. His hands and feet are shackled, with a chain connecting them to another that circles his waist. Trent's hair is shaggier than the last time I saw him, and the orange jumpsuit makes him look deathly pale. He's got an angry-looking tattoo creeping up from the collar of his jumpsuit, but it's too obscured for me to tell what it is.

The guard shoves Trent down into a chair across from me before securing his shackles to the table and the floor. He grins wickedly at the guard, purring, "You know I like it rough."

The guard backs to the door, nods to me, and points to the mirror before leaving.

"Thanks for meeting with me today, Trent," I say, hoping the formalities might put him in a chatty mood. The last time I questioned him, he had nothing to say to me, and I'm hoping today goes differently.

"As if I had a choice," he scoffs.

"Either way. I need to talk to you about Dr. McConnel," I say.

He lifts his chin and looks down his nose at me. "And why is that?"

"Dr. McConnel told us about your involvement in the murders . . ." The lie comes out more smoothly than I expect. I doubt that Trent has heard about McConnel's death, and I have no plans to tell him about it.

The chains grate against the metal rings as he raises his hand, red flaring to his cheeks. "I had no involvement in the murders."

"That's not what McConnel told us. So why don't you tell me your side of the story."

He furrows his brows and looks down at the table, as if considering. His dark hair falls over his face. "Why should I tell you what happened?" he asks as he looks up at me through his curtain of hair.

I turn on the voice recorder on my phone. "I can't help you if you don't tell me what happened. But if you break it all down for me, the DA might cut you a plea deal. The DA informed me that you're acting as your own lawyer. Is that correct?"

He considers and nods. "I am."

"Because I want to make it clear that you can ask for a lawyer for this questioning if you'd prefer," I offer. I'm not going to take any chances that this interrogation could be thrown out by a defense team in the future. If I have it recorded that he was offered an attorney and declined, we are in the clear.

"I don't need one of those idiots to represent me. I've seen how that goes."

I sit back in my chair, trying to relax some of the tension I've been carrying in my shoulders.

"What do you want to know?" he asks as he adjusts the shackles on his wrists.

"How did it all start?" I ask.

"McConnel and I became friends at work. We talked about some of the women who worked there over beers. Then there was this one patient we'd both seen. She was so hot. We got to talking about her. McConnel told me about how he used to bring in women like crazy, but he'd gotten too old. The women he liked wouldn't go for him anymore." He stops, glancing toward his hands.

"That woman you spoke of, who was she?"

"Some stuck-up bitch named Lucy," he says. "She didn't give me the time of day. She flirted with me like crazy while she was in the hospital; she was dying for it." He lets out a low, humorless laugh. "But when the time came, she was just a cocktease."

"So you didn't kill her, then?"

He shakes his head. "I want this to be crystal clear." His words are as sharp as shards of glass. "I didn't kill any of them. When it all started, I didn't know that's what he was going to do. I brought the women to him because I thought he was going to have fun with them."

"By fun," I say, my voice rising, "you mean rape. You were luring them there for him to rape." The words bring up a sickness with them. Though I've seen pieces of shit like this before, and I know they exist, I have to compartmentalize that information away. Because how do you live out in the world every day knowing people like Trent and Aidan walk the streets?

"Yeah, I lured them in. I got to have a round with them first; that was our agreement. But we both had to be careful, no DNA, no fingerprints, no evidence. We both wore gloves and condoms. And made sure that we didn't leave any hair at the scene. After I was done, I'd call him. The girl would be tied up and ready for him. When he showed up, he'd knock on the door three times, he'd come in the room, and I'd leave. After that, I didn't know what he was going to do." Trent looks up at me, his features grim.

"Trent," I say as I lean against the table, my eyes leveled on him. "You really thought after he made you be so careful about DNA, leaving evidence, that he *wasn't* planning on killing them? They could have ID'd either of you. You had to have known."

"He said it would be our word against theirs. If there was no DNA, there was no case. Guys get off on rape allegations all the time." The words roll off his tongue so matter-of-factly I don't grasp their true meaning at first.

Rage rises inside me as I process what he said. But it's not anger at him specifically; it's anger at the whole goddamn system, because he's right. How often do men get off with a slap on the wrist after something as life altering as rape? It happens every day. I don't believe him that he didn't know deep down that these women would die, but I press on.

"When you left, they were alive?"

He nods.

"Was it your idea to tie the women to the bed, or was it his?" I ask, trying not to picture the girls in my mind as I say the words.

"His. These women were all game, though." He leans back in his chair, chains rattling. "I could have talked them into anything. I didn't make them do anything they didn't want to do."

"Do you not understand that what you did led to their deaths? They didn't ask to be killed, Trent." I lean my forearms against the edge of the table. His whole demeanor is making me want to leap across the table and strangle him with the chains.

"It wasn't me. It was Aidan. This was all him. I didn't want these women to die. I didn't know he was going to kill them. Stop trying to put this on me."

"Did it come as a shock to you when you found out that Melanie was dead?" I ask.

"At first, yes. Because I didn't know that's what he was planning to do. I thought it was just about fun. I panicked at first, because I didn't want to go to prison for murder. I didn't know that he was going to kill them, I swear. After Aidan told me that he'd spread ashes all over the scene, and we made sure to leave none of our own DNA behind, he said it looked like it might have been the perfect murder."

"If you didn't want to have anything to do with killing, why did you help him lure other victims to the motels?" I ask. That's been lingering in the back of my mind. If Trent wasn't a killer, how did Aidan talk him into continuing?

"At that point, he told me that if I didn't help him again, he'd turn me in and say that I did it all myself." He glances toward the door, his eyes darting between it and the one-way mirror. "Look, are we done here? If I don't get back, I'm not going to get my time outside."

"Just one more thing. Did Aidan mention to you after he killed Melanie that he planned to kill the other women you lured?"

He shakes his head. "No, he never told me that's what he was planning to do. But after he threatened me, I could put two and two together. I just didn't want to go to jail."

"And why did you meet up with them at the ATV races?" I ask. That's the one piece I haven't understood.

"All the girls from around Camden end up at those races at some point. I'd been to the races before I even met Aidan, hooked up with a few girls I'd met there. Whenever I saw a new girl at the hospital I liked the look of, I'd mention her to Aidan, and he'd go take a look at her and her chart. I'd flirt with them a bit, see if I could get their number. If I did, I'd start texting them on the burner to hook up with them. None of the girls wanted to meet up with me alone at first; they wanted to meet in a public place. So the races seemed like the natural place to do it. Dark enough that most people wouldn't remember seeing me, but still public enough that the girls felt like I was safe to be around. The perfect camouflage. Or at least that's what I thought." He gestures to me. "Obviously it wasn't, since you figured it out."

I nod and motion toward the one-way mirror. That's all I need from Trent. I grab my phone and shut off the voice recorder. With all this, I need to see what the DA thinks we can charge him with. While he didn't know Aidan's intentions with Melanie, he admitted to knowing with the other two victims. Homicide is unlikely, but manslaughter along with accessory may be on the table.

The guard comes back into the room, unshackles Trent from the table, and leads him away. I work my way back through the halls of the jail and climb into my car. I call Sergeant Pelletier and provide him the information that I got from Trent. When I get back to the station, I'll finish my report and send a copy of the interview to the DA. With that, I'll be able to put this case to bed.

CHAPTER 24

One week later, I stand in the parking lot, shrouded by the stretched shadow of an ornate church. In the weeks that I've been in Camden, I've driven by this church a thousand times and never given it a second glance, and now it's all I can see. Inside, the church is packed with people who've come for Austin's funeral. The sky above me is a clear, sparkling blue, one of the first blue-skied days we've had in months. All the spots around me are filled with cars, everyone else long since disappeared into the service. But I can't bring myself to take another step, to say goodbye to someone else. Maybe it's the past rippling through my mind, the ghost of what Rachel's funeral could have been.

"Are you sure you don't want to go in?" Noah asks, squeezing my hand. I'd almost forgotten he was here. I should have sent him inside. He stands to my left, wearing freshly ironed slacks, a button-up white shirt, and a black tie. Instead of a blazer, he's got on his black leather jacket, the one I always give him shit for wearing since he has yet to get a real coat.

"I just—" I start, but my voice cracks. I glance at him, and it breaks my heart, because all I can wonder is if or when I'm going to lose him too. Death follows me, and I'm trapped in a dance with it. A death spiral. Sometimes I wonder if I should even bother, if I should stretch myself beyond the bounds of my work. Is it worth it? But no matter how many times I ask myself, when I look into Noah's eyes, I know it is.

He loops his arm around my back, folding my leather coat tighter around me, steadying me with a touch I didn't realize I needed.

"Can we walk?" I ask, gesturing to the ancient graveyard beyond the church.

He nods and urges me forward. Though I try to walk, my limbs are leaden, like I haven't used them in years.

"One day you'll be okay," Noah says in a voice that's soft, even.

I glance at him. That's what I told him I said to Ryder Warren last year after his girlfriend died. He was the youngest member of a family of pariahs back in Vinalhaven, and everyone assumed that because he was the weird kid, he must have murdered his girlfriend. To comfort him, I said, "You're never going to be the same again. But one day, you'll be okay." Fresh tears paint my face as my boots squish against the wet earth.

The weather has finally warmed enough to melt off pockets of snow across the cemetery. White still clings around some of the ancient headstones and the mausoleums. The key is heavy in my pocket as I walk, poking me with each step, as if insisting I finally do something about it. I considered giving it to him a week ago, but something still held me back. I wanted to be sure. *Really* sure.

"There's something I wanted to talk to you about," I say, slowing to look at him. And suddenly, my guts are in knots. Why am I nervous?

An ancient oak tree twists up beside us, headstones littering the earth around it. They're so old many poke out of the earth off-center. Moss clings to the stones, and some of the names are nearly worn away.

"There's something I want to talk to you about too."

I swallow hard as my nerves prickle. What does he have to talk to me about? "You go first," I say, hoping a few minutes will help me gather my nerves.

"I just talked to my brother Cameron. He's moving to town," he says, his face impassive. Noah obviously has a lot of issues with his family, so I'm not sure how he feels about this.

"Oh?" I ask, hoping he'll give me more to go on.

"Yeah, he'll be here next month. Would you mind helping me find a place for him to rent?"

"Of course not." I offer him a smile. "How do you feel about this?" I ask, still unable to read him. I find it jarring. I can read most people so well.

"I think it'll be good. Maybe it'll give us a chance to get closer."

"He's the cop, right?" I ask.

He nods. "Yeah, he's been a beat cop for a few years now."

"If he hasn't found anything else around here, Sergeant Michaels told me they're looking for someone to replace Allen. He's moving to the mainland."

"I'll let him know about it," he says with a smile. "He was staying back in Tennessee until after my dad passed. He was actually thinking that he and I could get a place together."

"Oh" is all I can manage to say. Suddenly it's as if the key in my pocket weighs five pounds. Maybe I was right to wait. Maybe I shouldn't be giving him this key. If he's planning to move in with his brother, was I wrong about where I thought things were headed?

"What's wrong?" Noah asks, stooping to look me in the eyes.

I hesitate, then fish the key from my pocket and hold it out. Noah cups my hand, looking at it.

"What's that?" he asks when I don't explain.

"It's for you. I was going to ask you to move in with me," I say, my voice sounding far too fragile to my ears.

"You want me to move in with you?" he asks, his voice high with disbelief.

"I was hoping so."

When he's silent for a long moment, I add, "If you think it's too soon, I understand. You don't have to say yes." I feel much too vulnerable in his silence. My eyes drop to the ground, and my heart pounds so hard I'm sure he can hear it. When he says nothing, I tuck my hands in my pockets and sigh. Then, finally, he kisses me. The heat of his passion bleeds into me until my body quivers in response. I pull away from the kiss, catching my breath, and steady myself.

I stare out over the graves, the oak trees standing like sentinels over the dead. My heart twists at all the lives lost, the lives I've seen extinguished. But like those trees, I will always be here, watching over the dead.

"Of course I'll move in with you. Though if you ever want to, we can move back to my place in South Carolina."

I never thought I'd think the words, let alone say them aloud. "For now, I think my place is here."

He nods. "My place is wherever you are."

"You don't think your brother will be crushed?"

He kisses me again, soft and slow. "He'll just have to get over it."

ACKNOWLEDGMENTS

Thank you to the incredible editors who helped me with this book. Megha Parekh, thank you for helping me get *Next Girl to Die* and *Beneath the Ashes* out into the world. And Charlotte Herscher, thank you for helping me polish both of my stories to perfection. And of course, to the rest of the Thomas & Mercer team and everyone at Amazon Publishing, your work and support on this project are so very appreciated. Thank you for everything that you do.

Thank you to Laura Bradford.

To my critique partner, Elesha Teskey—without you, *none* of my books would be possible. Thank you for being there, listening, reading, and helping me make sense of every draft, no matter how bad it is.

Thank you to Stephen J. Nelson, MD, medical examiner for Polk County, Florida, for answering my questions about autopsies and investigations—your expertise was invaluable.

To Jodi Gallegos, thank you for answering my weird medical questions.

Thank you to Stephen Richey, founder of Kolibri Forensics and the host of the Skelecast podcast, for answering my forensics and investigation questions.

Thank you to Blaine Poirier (no relation, seriously!), my resident cell phone expert.

To my mom, kiss noise. Please rip out the sex scenes before you let anyone else in the family read this.

Thank you to everyone who read *Next Girl to Die* and is here for round two—cheers to you.

ABOUT THE AUTHOR

Dea Poirier was raised in Edmond, Oklahoma, where she found her passion in a creative writing course. She studied computer science and political science at the University of Central Oklahoma. Later she spent time living on both coasts and traveling the United States before finally putting down roots in central Florida. She now resides somewhere between Disney and the swamp with her son.